Offerings

A Love Story

Tina Williams

Bloomington, IN  Milton Keynes, UK

AuthorHouse™ *AuthorHouse*™ *UK Ltd.*
1663 Liberty Drive, Suite 200 *500 Avebury Boulevard*
Bloomington, IN 47403 *Central Milton Keynes, MK9 2BE*
www.authorhouse.com *www.authorhouse.co.uk*
Phone: 1-800-839-8640 *Phone: 08001974150*

© *2007 Tina Williams. All rights reserved.*

No part of this book may be reproduced, stored in a retrieval system, or transmitted by any means without the written permission of the author.

First published by AuthorHouse 9/6/2007

ISBN: 978-1-4259-8316-1 (sc)

Printed in the United States of America
Bloomington, Indiana

This book is printed on acid-free paper.

Chapter 1

Annie

Annie turned off the shower and stepped out into the tiny bathroom. The air conditioner had broken last week and she and her mother had decided to get through the rest of the summer without it. The entire house was still uncomfortably warm from yesterday's late-August heat and now the steam from the shower added to the humidity to make the room seem suffocating.

She looked at the clock. It was five-twenty-three. Seven minutes had passed since she had tucked the white plastic stick in the cupboard under the bathroom sink. She had wanted to put it in a place where her mother wouldn't see it if she should happen to get up to use the bathroom at this early hour. Seven minutes. She would have to hurry. The directions said at least two minutes and no more than ten. She quickly dried and put on the bra and underpants that she had brought into the bathroom with her.

She toyed with the thought of just leaving the stick in the cupboard. In her mind at that moment it seemed that the events of the future would be caused by the still-preventable opening of the cupboard door, rather than by the irreversible carelessness of nearly a month earlier. She pushed that fanciful thought aside and began to do what she knew she must. The nervousness that she had anticipated had not arrived. Rather, she opened the cupboard with a sense of certainty and a surprising lack of emotion. She picked the pregnancy test up from its place beside the tampons and behind her mother's hair dye and pretended not to see the results as she sat down on the fuzzy pink toilet seat cover.

She closed her eyes and opened them again and looked at the results as though she didn't already know what they were. There were two baby blue lines, making a plus sign. She took a deep breath in through her nostrils, released it, and waited for tears or anger or fear. Nothing came. Her mind wouldn't or couldn't take in the full meaning of what she was seeing. Instead, she had stupid thoughts about the lines themselves and what they meant. She stared at the blue "+' and thought of some of the times she had seen that same sign: in math problems, on yellow traffic signs warning of an intersection, after letter grades on school papers, in chemistry class to represent protons. And now she would add to that list. On a cheap white plastic stick to tell her she was going to have a baby.

She looked up at the clock again. It was five-thirty. She had twenty minutes to finish dressing and arrive at the restaurant. She wouldn't quite make it on time but Maggie and she covered for one another occasionally. She quickly parted, combed, and blew her long brown hair half-dry before pulling it back into the low pony tail that she always wore to work. While doing so, she avoided the eyes of the girl in the mirror, not wanting see any evidence of her condition. She once again reached in the cupboard and pulled out the small white paper bag that she had also hidden. On the bag in bright red letters was the logo from the out-of-town pharmacy where she had bought the test kit. Inside was the box that the kit had come in. She hurriedly put the wand and instructions back into the box and the box back into the bag and dashed to her room as she did every morning, in only her bra and panties, but this time carrying the white bag and feeling conspicuous doing so.

In her room, she finished dressing, putting on the clean white shirt and black slacks that she was required to wear to work. She quickly grabbed her name tag from its place on her dresser and white bag from where she had put it on her unmade bed. She went down the short hallway to the kitchen and grabbed her purse, taking her keys out of it and stuffing the bag into it, cringing at the sound that the waxy white paper made in the small stuffy house. She refused to go outside carrying the bag separately, even though at this early hour she knew that no one would see her with it, let alone care what was in it. She stepped out the front door and quietly closed it behind her, so as not to awaken her mother.

Outside, the sun was not quite visible but was lighting the sky. The early morning air was not fresh but felt good after the stuffiness of the house. It was obvious from the feel of the air that today would be another hot, sticky day. But by this time of year in northern Ohio, the heat and humidity was made more bearable by the promise of the coolness that would arrive with September.

She unlocked her small car and backed out onto the quiet side street. As she drove the short distance to the restaurant, she planned how to get rid of the little white bag without being noticed. This was an easy problem and it felt good to focus on it. She knew that she would have other things to think about soon. But for today, she gave herself the gift of not even listing those issues, let alone dealing with them. Today, only for today, she would throw away the white bag and ignore what she now could not deny to be true.

Chapter 2

Jack

As always, Jack woke up automatically with the first signs of daylight. He never used an alarm clock, although one sat on his headboard letting him know the exact time. But exact time wasn't usually important to him. Except for the occasional appointment with a doctor or a businessman, his days were pleasantly free from outside demands that caused him to worry about what time it was. Because he and his dad ran the farm together, they had to coordinate their schedules, but after working together for so many years they had the same patterns and showing up to do the same thing at the same time was natural and didn't require a clock for either of them.

On this day in August, he lay in bed a short while, planning out his day. Wheat harvest had been done for month, and it would be several weeks yet before the beans would be ripe. He had been working on the machinery and setting up a new computer program that they would use to track their yields. But today he didn't have much to do, a fact that didn't please him. He was looking forward to the rush of harvest and finding out how many bushels per acre of beans and corn they would get this year. It had been a good year overall, with a fair amount of rain, and they were expecting a good harvest.

But that was still a few weeks or more away. Today would be a good day to go to town for a cup of coffee to make the time pass more quickly and find out who had bought or sold equipment, grain, or land. He enjoyed the company of the old farmers, many of them long ago retired, who sat and gossiped the morning away. He had another reason for going, but he didn't acknowledge it.

Later, he could drop in down the road at his parents' house to see if his mom needed any help with the tomatoes. She felt it her duty to supply the world, or at least her corner of it, with fresh produce and Jack felt it his duty to help her. Every year she promised everyone that she would plant less but every spring she planted just as much "just in case some don't come up".

He supposed that he could do some cleaning in the house, too. It was hard to stay in to get that done this time of year, though, when the sun was so bright. It seemed unnatural to stay indoors, even though by noon the air-conditioning would be an inviting contrast to the August heat.

Having tossed these ideas around in his head, he got out of bed and went to the bathroom to get ready for the day. He noticed in the mirror that his hairline was continuing its retreat toward the back of his head. He smiled weakly at his reflection, noticing for the first time the wrinkles around his eyes when he did so, and gently pointed out to the man in the mirror that he wasn't getting any younger. He was beginning to wonder if perhaps his ship left several years ago and he hadn't been on it.

He had turned thirty-one just a few weeks ago. For the last ten years, his birthday had been marked by the absence of phone calls and cards rather than their presence, which suited Jack just fine.

He pushed the thoughts to the back of his mind as he dressed, putting on clean blue jeans, which he wore year-round regardless of the temperature, and a t-shirt. Since he wasn't anticipating working around farm machinery today, he put on his tennis shoes rather than his work boots.

He went to the kitchen and stood at the window above the sink, which faced east. By this time, the sunrise was its most colorful. As he did every morning, he spent a moment looking at the sunrise, saying a prayer of thanks and offering himself to God once again. And each day, he was sure of two things. The first was that God was listening. The second was that God was utterly, exasperatingly silent.

Just then the phone rang. At this early hour he knew it must be his mom or dad. He answered good-naturedly, "Jack Schroeder, at your service."

"Good morning, Jack." He was a little surprised to hear his mom's voice. He was expecting his dad to be calling, asking him to buy a part that they needed in town or to come down to give him a hand on any number of the small tasks that could be done around the farm.

"Well, good morning, Mom."

"Are you busy this morning?" There was an unusual hint of tension, perhaps worry, in her voice.

"I think my boss is giving me the day off," he joked. "Why?"

"Kate and John just dropped Christopher off. Her labor started in the middle of the night. It looks like I'm going to be a grandma again today."

He felt the now-familiar mixture of joy, excitement, and, perhaps, jealousy. He had felt this combination of emotions with the arrival of each niece and nephew. The new baby would be the eighth.

"Is everything going okay so far?" As a single man, Jack had been spared the details, but he knew that Christopher's birth had been long and difficult for Kate and hoped things would be easier for her the second time around.

"So far, so good, but it'll probably be a while yet. I'd like to go to daily Mass this morning to pray for a healthy baby and then sit at the hospital. I was wondering if you could baby-sit this morning."

"Sure, I'd love to," he answered. He babysat a lot for all of his nieces and nephews and enjoyed the company almost as much as he enjoyed the peacefulness that followed their departure. "What's Dad doing?" he asked, not to avoid babysitting but just out of curiosity.

"He's going with me." Her voice was now smug and happy. Just a few years ago Frank wouldn't have wanted to "waste" the day in such a way. He would have thought of something that needed done. He was, indeed, with each year and with the birth of each grandchild, becoming more sentimental.

"I was just going to go to town for a cup of coffee. Do you think Christopher would like to go along?" The question had no need for an answer. Christopher tagged along with both him and "Grandpa" regularly and loved sitting with the farmers at the diner.

"He's ready whenever you are."

"I'll be over in a few minutes."

Jack hung up the phone and took a minute to think of his sister and wondered how she was doing at this moment. He thought of her husband, John, and imagined for just a moment what he was experiencing and what it was like to see your own child being born. He said another quick prayer, this one for his sister, her husband, and their new baby.

He took his wallet and cell phone from their customary place on the counter and stuck them in his pockets. Two caps hung beside the door, both from seed corn dealers. He grabbed the newer and cleaner one and stuck it on his head. He left the empty house and drove his pick-up truck the half mile down to the home place, leaving the radio off and letting the silence surround him.

Moments later, four-year-old Christopher sat buckled in beside him on the front seat of the pick-up. He was skinny kid with straight red hair that had just been wet down and combed by his grandma. He was dressed in green shorts that were printed with a jungle scene and a matching green t-shirt with a yellow parrot printed on the front, the kind of outfit he wouldn't be caught dead in in a couple of years. He talked Jack's ear off during the 15-minute drive to town, explaining to Jack that a baby was going to come out of his mom's tummy, his voice so full of animation that Jack could tell that he thought that this must be as new and surprising to his Uncle Jack as it was to him. He was very excited about the idea of being a brother for the first time and talked about what babies are like and all the things that he could do to help, repeating the things that his mother had been telling him for the past months.

Jack pulled into the diner that was located at the edge of town, on the old highway. Since the bypass was built several years ago, the diner had lost a lot of business from the travelers and truckers but the town itself provided enough customers to keep things going. Although it was badly in need of some up-dating, it was clean and well-run with simple but good food, and, more importantly to those that came in, cheap prices. This made it a favorite among the old farmers.

Jack recognized most of the vehicles in the parking lot, not that there were many. Like his, most were large late-model pick-ups. One could easily separate out those owned by the retirees by the lack of dust and scratches. Although there wasn't a big crowd, it looked like the regulars were all there, which he had expected at this time of morning during this break after the wheat harvest and before the soybean harvest.

He glanced to the side lot where the employees parked and saw, as always, the little white car that Annie drove and, as always, he anticipated the smile that would greet him when he walked through the door.

Chapter 3

Annie

Annie liked the day shift at the diner. The early mornings had a sleepy feel that gradually built up to the hectic lunch hour and then wound down again by the time she left. In the mornings, most of the customers were farmers that sat at the counter that spanned the front of the dining area. They talked slow, drank slow, and were slow to leave. The tables that took up the rest of the space were slow to fill, most of them remaining empty until the noon hour. The salad bar that separated the counter from the dining area sat dark and silent each day until midmorning after the farmers trickled out the door and before the lunch crowd rushed in.

Annie had just poured coffee for the only table that was occupied and was on her way to return the half-full pot to its place on the burner when Jack walked in with Christopher. She gave them the same hearty welcome and sincere smile that she gave all of the regular farmers when they arrived. She stopped to talk with them on their way to the counter to sit with the other farmers. "Good morning, Jack." She stopped and squatted down to talk to Christopher face to face. "Good morning, how are you, Christopher? Couldn't you get Grandpa out of bed this morning?"

Christopher grinned and giggled, enjoying the joke about his grandpa who, as far as Christopher knew, never went to bed and certainly never slept late. But he was too shy to reply.

Jack answered for him, "He wanted to come with me instead this morning because I promised to let him drink as much coffee as he wants. Do you think you have enough?"

"I'll go start another pot right now." She went behind the counter and busied herself with a new pot of coffee that would soon be needed.

At the counter, Ralph, a retired widower, moved one stool over to give Jack and Christopher two adjacent stools. As he did so, he looked the boy up and down, and said, "Why, are those your legs or did you come riding in on a chicken?" The other old men laughed but Jack and Christopher ignored the comment as they took their seats on the stools.

Christopher's head was barely above the counter but Annie could see enough of his face to know that he was delighted as always to be sitting among the grownups. She walked over with two thick white coffee mugs and put them in front of Jack and Christopher. "Here you go, boys. Christopher, I made yours nice and strong, just like you like it."

Christopher, too short to see what the mug contained, looked a little worried, but he picked it up carefully, took it off the counter and lowered it into his lap. He peeked into the cup, saw the orange juice and grinned. "Yep, just like I like it."

Annie grinned back, giving him a wink. "Would you like something to eat with your coffee? It's a long time until lunch."

"Toast with peanut butter, please."

"Coming right up." She wrote the order on a piece of paper and handed it to Maggie in the kitchen. Then she warmed the row of coffee cups that sat waiting along the counter, taking in the conversation.

From two bar stools over, Al, a retired bachelor farmer, leaned forward and asked Jack, "Any news over your way, Jack?"

Knowing that Al was more interested in corn than babies, Jack replied, "The test plot for that new seed corn we were trying out seems to be about a week ahead of the others and the ears are completely filled out."

"Is that right?" This was Al's standard reply to just about anything, from weddings to election results to news of an unexpected death. "Do you think it's worth the price they're asking for the seed?"

"I don't know. You'll have to ask me again after harvest, but I'd say no. It's a pretty penny that they're wanting for it right now."

As Annie was putting the small plate with a piece of toast in front of Christopher, he leaned over to Jack and she heard him whisper, "I have to go potty."

"Well, okay, then, let's go."

Annie watched them walk toward the restroom in the front corner opposite of the entrance, Christopher naturally putting his small hand into Jack's larger one. The scene tugged at her heart and she reminded herself that tomorrow was when she was going to think about things like fathers and children. She let out a sigh that none of the old men noticed and turned her attention to calculating the check for the people at the table.

After they returned from the restroom, Christopher started chewing the middle out of his toast. A good friend of Jack's father, Vince, who sat halfway down the counter, spoke to the young boy, "So, Christopher, are you a brother yet?"

Christopher had obviously been waiting for the subject to come up and answered almost before the question was finished. "My mom's at the hospital right now!" This statement carried with it all the excitement and pride that his little voice could contain.

"Well, isn't that something? You'll have to take good care of that baby, you hear?" Vince replied.

"Yes, sir," Christopher was very serious this time, taking the task very seriously.

Now Ralph spoke to Jack, gesturing towards the boy, "You know, Jack, if you got one of your own, you wouldn't have to borrow someone else's."

The old farmers, especially Ralph, were always questioning Jack about why he didn't get married. Annie knew by now that Jack would be quick with a comeback. She wondered if it bothered him, though. She also wondered, like the rest of them, why he had remained single for so long. "Why would I want to do that when it's cheaper and easier just to borrow someone else's?" He paused for effect. "I think some wise old man told me that once." The farmers at the counter all laughed and looked down at George, who, indeed, was wise, old, and always borrowing something.

Annie tried to hide her grin. After more than a year of listening to the daily banter that went on among them, she knew as well as any of them when points had been scored in the game of words that they played with one another.

But Ralph continued, "You know, babies are awfully fun to make, Jack."

This time it was Vince that provided the comeback, defending Jack as he often did. "You must have a pretty good memory to remember back that far, Ralph."

Ralph wasn't so easily deterred. "You need to find yourself a pretty young girl and give it try." He gestured toward Annie, "Like Annie here."

Annie wasn't going to let this continue without her input. "Why, Ralph, don't you know that Jack's too young for me? I like my men old and bald and grumpy. That's why I took this job in the first place, so I could spend my day around such attractive men."

They all chuckled and laughed to be called attractive. It was a label that for most of them hadn't fit in a traditional sense for several decades.

Ralph stood up, leaving a dollar to cover the 80-cent coffee and the 20-cent tip that was the standard. "Well, darling, anytime you want a date, just let me know. I still got my matchstick. No one's tried to strike it for quite a while, but you never know; with a little patience we might be able to get it lit."

Annie smiled, not offended or surprised by his off-color comments. She took it for what it was: good-natured, harmless flirting from a good-natured, harmless old man. She replied, "I'll let you know," with an amused grin.

After Ralph left, the conversation resumed its normal flow, touching on the familiar topics of long-range forecasts, machinery parts, and grain prices, all of which were still being discussed at length by the old farmers long after Annie had taken away Jack and Christopher's dishes and wiped clean the counter where they had sat.

Chapter 4

Jack

After they left the diner, Jack took Christopher back to his grandparents' house. He knew that the arrival of a new baby in the family wouldn't slow the ripening of the tomatoes in this heat, and he thought he might as well pick them for his mother. He and Christopher found two empty bushel baskets in the outbuilding next to the garden. He gave one to Christopher to carry. After a few simple instructions, they went to work. Christopher enjoyed throwing all the "yucky" ones as far as he could, which wasn't far at all, into the adjacent field of soybeans. They worked until almost lunch then Jack carried the filled baskets up to the house and set them by the back door.

Jack looked down at Christopher and said, "So what are you going to make me for lunch?"

Christopher thought about this carefully before asking, "Got any bologna?"

"Let's go to my house and check."

When they walked into his house, they were happy to feel the coolness of the air-conditioning and after a check of his refrigerator and cupboards, they decided on a ham sandwich, some chips, and apple slices, dipped in peanut butter, of course. After washing their hands in the kitchen sink, Christopher put the sandwiches together while Jack did the other simple preparations for the meal.

When they sat down to eat, they made the sign of the cross, bowed their heads and said the customary Catholic prayer before meals. Christopher mumbled through parts of it but hit all the key words. Jack noticed how carefully and precisely he made the sign of the cross and said very clearly the words which went with it. "In the name of the Father and of the Son and of the Holy Spirit. Amen." It was obvious that his mom and dad had been working with him on this.

Christopher ate well and then went to the bathroom to wash the peanut butter from his fingers which was very necessary because he had run out of apple slices and had used his fingers to scoop up the last of the peanut butter on his plate. Jack was clearing the dishes and contemplating the possibilities for the afternoon when the phone rang.

It was his mom calling from the hospital, letting him know that the baby had been born. Kimberly Marie and her mom were both fine and ready for a visit by Christopher if Jack would bring him. She and Jack's dad were both hungry and were going to go out for a sandwich but would stop back at the hospital to see Christopher with his sister before they went home for the day.

Jack agreed to take Christopher to the hospital, having expected that he would, but not knowing when. He told Christopher the good news when he walked back into the kitchen with clean but dripping hands. They had both gotten dirty and sweaty in the garden, so Jack dug out a clean outfit from Christopher's backpack that Kate had given to Jack's mother and that Jack had thrown in the truck that morning. They both changed clothes, washed their faces and combed their hair. Once again, Jack stood looking at his reflection as he had this morning. This time with Christopher beside him, comically standing on his tiptoes and giving little jumps so he could see himself in the mirror. Jack laughed out loud but at the same time Ralph's words rung in his head "If you got one of your own, you wouldn't have to borrow someone else's."

They drove to town again. During the morning, Christopher had calmed down but now the anticipation of seeing his new sister had him talking non-stop once again. His exuberance was overwhelming and by the time they got to the hospital, Jack was more than ready to be there.

Jack walked up to the reception desk, carrying Christopher's backpack by the top handle. They were greeted by a former classmate of Jack's. "Hi, Jack. I bet you're here to see your sister. Let's see… Is she in room 16 or 18? Let me check the computer." She tapped on a few keys and then looked up. "That's what I thought. Room 16. Right down that hallway to your right." She looked over her desk at Christopher. "Is this little guy the big brother?"

"He sure is."

"Okay, he's welcome to go back, too, then. Congratulations!"

Jack and Christopher walked a few steps away from the desk, and then Jack stopped and squatted in front of Christopher so that they were eye-to-eye. "Okay, now remember, you need to be quiet in the hospital and be nice to your mommy. She's probably tired. She's had a big day." He looked back with big eyes and nodded his head.

The door to room 16 was open. Kate, who shared Jack's light brown hair and wide smile, was sitting in the vinyl-upholstered chair next to the bed holding the baby that was wrapped tightly in blankets, only her puffy round face visible to the world. His brother-in-law John sat on the edge of the bed, leaning over to look at his baby. Their faces displayed the wonder and joy they felt. Both were oblivious to his presence. Jack knocked timidly, feeling very much like an intruder.

Upon hearing the knock, John sprang into action, grabbing the camera from the hospital table. Kate greeted Christopher, "Hey, Christopher, do you want to see your sister?" Christopher stood still. After all of the anticipation, he was unsure of this new situation.

Jack nudged him. "Go ahead. She won't bite. She doesn't have any teeth yet."

Christopher walked over to his mother and new sister and looked uncertainly at the baby. "What do you think?" his mother asked.

The baby was wide awake. She opened her mouth wide in what appeared to be a yawn. One tiny pink fist made its way out of the blanket. "She's pretty cool."

John snapped several pictures of Kate with Christopher and the baby. Jack was called into duty to photograph all four of them. Then Kate got up, Christopher sat down, and the baby was placed on his arms, which he held straight out, more as if to receive a giant present than to hold a baby. More pictures were taken as Kate stood guard; ready to snatch the baby up at the first sign of trouble. The baby squirmed and made noises and Christopher was quick to let his mom take the infant back into her arms.

She handed the baby to Jack next. He took her carefully. He was used to babies by now but one this new still made him nervous. He looked down at the baby resting in the crook of his arm and marveled at the beauty of his new niece. 'Thank you, God, for the blessing of this baby,' he thought silently.

"How about a picture of Kimberly with her godfather?" John suggested. Jack looked up from his study of the infant's face to see Kate and John both grinning at him. They had not yet discussed it with him, so he was surprised and responded, "Why, sure." It was both consent for the picture and acceptance of the honor that they were bestowing on him.

The picture was snapped and Jack asked, "So who will be godmother?"

"We thought Elizabeth." Elizabeth was the youngest of Jack's four sisters and the only one who was not yet married. She was a sophomore at the state university about an hour and a half away. She had started fall classes a week earlier and she had been disappointed that the baby had not been born before she moved back into the dormitory.

"Have you called the sisters yet?"

"No, I'll do that this afternoon. I'm sure Mom's told them by now that today was the day, but hopefully I can call them with the details before she does. John is going to take Christopher home for a while and I'll do it then."

"Don't you need to rest?" His sisters, the three of them that were mothers, amazed him at their resilience after childbirth. If Kate weren't dressed in a robe and in a hospital room, one would never guess that she had just given birth. She looked like she was ready right now to go home and take charge of the household again.

"I'll rest while I talk on the phone. Don't worry, big brother, I'll take a little nap, too."

"Okay. I'm going to go so that you can do that." He handed the baby, now sleeping, back to his mother, giving Kate a kiss on the cheek. He addressed both parents, "Looks like you two have another fabulous kid. Congratulations."

"She must take after her uncle, then."

"Let's hope not, poor kid."

He shook hands with his brother-in-law, congratulated him again, and offered his help with Christopher any time that it was needed.

He walked back down the hall, meeting his mom and dad at the hospital entryway, on their way back from their lunch. He talked with them just a minute, got in his pick-up and headed out of town. The country road that led back to his house stretched out before him, like the coming afternoon and evening, long and empty.

Chapter 5

Annie

The one day grace period that Annie had given herself ended. It was time now to do something and she knew that her first course of action should be to inform the father of the baby that she carried, a baby that seemed more imaginary than real. Annie tried to call him on his cell phone but kept getting a message that the number wasn't in service. Since she didn't have his number at college, she waited until Saturday, hoping but doubting that he had come home for the weekend already.

She waited until her mother left to run some errands late Saturday morning. She had to look up the number in the phone book, because she had rarely called his house. Keaton, Lyle and Beverly. She had seen them at football games and around town here and there, but she didn't really know them. Mr. Keaton ran the local shoe store. He was clean-cut and handsome for a man his age. Mrs. Keaton was slightly overweight but always well-dressed and never seen without her hair done up and make-up on.

"Grandma and Grandpa Keaton," she said the words out loud, hoping they might have a ring to them. They didn't. The idea of a plus sign on a plastic tube making her a mother was ridiculous and the idea that it would also make these strangers grandparents was even more ridiculous.

She dialed the number. It rang three times, during which Annie pictured Beverly on the set of Happy Days, washing dishes, drying her hands on an apron, and walking quickly through a tidy, tastefully-decorated kitchen to the phone. She finally answered. "Hello, this is the Keaton residence." The combination of the woman's cheerfulness and her formal manner of answering the phone made Annie feel tongue-tied.

"Hello, may I speak with Eric, please?" The effort of masking her nervousness made her break out into a sweat.

"He's not here. May I take a message?" The cheerfulness had been replaced by an unmistakable coldness.

"No, there's no message. Thank you." She hung up quickly and stared at the phone. Damn. She should have asked if he was home this weekend or what his number at college was. She braced herself and hit the redial button.

The phone only rang once this time. "Hello, Keaton residence." Her voice was cautious this time.

"Hello. I'm sorry to bother you again, Mrs. Keaton, but I was wondering if you could tell me if Eric is home this weekend." The words spilled out too quickly, revealing the urgency of her question.

There was a long pause. "Are you the girl he was running around with this summer?"

The question caught her off-guard. In a small town, news traveled quickly and it had been known to reach even the mothers of those involved with surprising quickness and accuracy. But she hadn't expected to be asked about it. "Yes, I suppose so."

"You ought to know that he and Jenny are back together. I think I can speak for him by telling you that he'd rather not be bothered." Her voice left no room for discussion of the matter.

"Oh. Okay. Well, thank you for letting me know."

There was silence on both sides, neither one knowing how to end the conversation. Annie finally added, "Have a good day." She rolled her eyes at the stupidity of her own utterance.

The mother responded, "Thank you. And you too." Her voice was now apologetic, almost kind.

Annie hung up. Eric had been dating Jenny for four years. When she had decided to spend the summer studying in Washington D.C., he had been angry and broke up with her. But Annie had known all along that the breakup was temporary. She and everyone else in town knew that they would get married and have a great life together. So where did she fit in? She didn't. And the baby? The baby didn't either.

Although she hadn't really accomplished anything by the phone call, she was at a standstill until she decided her next step. She now changed her focus. The other task she had given herself for the day was to tell her mother the news. She dreaded this. Not because her mother would be angry or disappointed or judgmental; she wouldn't be any of those things. Cindy was more a friend than a mother to Annie.

In fact, in many ways, Annie was the mother. Annie had supported her mother through three divorces and various other crises. She had listened to her mother's problems from the time she was quite young and had learned to pitch in when her mom was too tired or depressed or stressed out to keep the house clean or the bills paid. But, in spite of sometimes less than ideal circumstances, her mom had never neglected to make her feel loved or to be sure they had a safe home in which to live.

Ultimately, they had a close, loving relationship, but it made Annie sometimes wish for traditional parents. In high school, her friends' complaints about the rules their parents imposed upon them made her envious. And right now she found herself wishing for a mom who would do what a mom was supposed to do when faced with a daughter's pregnancy: yell at her for having done something so stupid and then cry because she had thought she had raised her better than that.

As if conjured up by Annie's thoughts of her, the back door opened and her mother came in with two plastic bags of groceries in one hand. "Hey, honey, I got some salad mix and a can of ravioli for lunch, what do you think?"

"Sure, Mom." She got up and helped her mother put away the things that she had bought at the store.

Her mom was slim and attractive, with bleached blond hair that she wore in a bob. She was wearing short jean shorts and a pale green sleeveless shirt. Both were tight but not too tight, just nicely flattering. She had had Annie when she was a teenager, so she was not yet forty and she looked younger than that. One would guess she was closer to thirty. They were often mistaken for friends rather than mother and daughter.

As they ate, she and her mother chatted comfortably about details of her mother's morning errands and shared information that was practical for the week to come: how much money was in the checkbook, their schedules for the upcoming week, what the weather was going to do. They also talked about how their jobs were going. Her mother was a receptionist at one of the two dentist offices in town, a job she had gotten two years ago, after her last divorce. She talked about how the hygienist and the dentist had had an argument recently. Annie talked about how busy they had been lately at the diner and how the heat always made people want to go out to eat rather than cook at home.

After lunch, when they were carrying their plates to the dishwasher, Annie took a deep breath and said in a strong, matter-of-fact voice, "Mom, I'm pregnant."

There was the slightest pause in her mom's steps before she resumed her motions. "Are you sure?" She put her plate in the dishwasher.

"I took a pregnancy test." Annie put hers in also.

"How far along are you?" She returned to the table and picked up the salad dressing and returned it to the fridge.

"Only about a month, I think." Annie picked up the two glasses that sat on the table and stuck them in the dishwasher.

As she had predicted, there were no harsh words or tears. Instead, her mom walked over to her and hugged her and said, "Why, Annie, that's wonderful! You'll be a great mom. Don't you worry about a thing."

They sat back down together. There was no need to ask who the father was. The romance between Annie and Eric had been encouraged by her mother and he had spent some time at the house during the summer. Eric was popular, athletic, and from a well-respected family in town so Cindy was delighted that her daughter had attracted his attention. When Annie told her that he had gone back to his girlfriend, she glossed over it by assuring Annie that once she told him about the baby everything would be fine.

"I don't know, Mom. I think they make a great couple. Maybe I shouldn't mess things up."

As usual, her mother didn't help her with the decision, not that this decision was anyone else's to make. "Well, whatever you decide is fine, honey. You know that you and the baby are welcome here if things don't work out with Eric."

"Maybe I should give it away," Annie said and thought that such words were intended for old furniture and extra clothes, not babies.

"Don't be silly," her mother protested. Her tone made it clear that it wasn't to be discussed. So Annie remained silent, but with her thoughts only she argued that it wouldn't be silly to entrust a child to someone who could better care for him or her than she could.

With nothing else to be done or said for now, she and her mom worked together on some household chores that afternoon, just like it were any other afternoon. Her mom had a date for supper that night with a man who had been in for a root canal a week ago. After she left, Annie poured herself a bowl of cereal for supper and sat in front of the TV while she ate it, unaware of what she was watching.

She still needed to talk to Eric. She would call a friend who was likely to know Eric's number and set up a meeting with him. She couldn't be sure that he wanted nothing to do with this baby until she heard it from him. She pictured his face, handsome but arrogant, and wondered if *she* wanted anything to do with *him*.

Chapter 6

Jack

Impatient for harvest to arrive, Jack scheduled full days for himself as September began. He made final plans for harvest and evaluated the soybeans each day as they continued to dry and grow more brittle, hanging in their pods, waiting for the combine. But bean watching was not a time-consuming task. To occupy the rest of his time, he made lists of things that needed done around his house, inside and out, and worked on both crossing off the things at the top of the list and on adding more chores to the bottom of the list. He visited his new niece and took Christopher for the afternoon several times, giving his sister the opportunity for a welcome nap. He also helped his mother with the crazy amount of produce that flowed in a steady stream from her garden to her kitchen and then down to the basement, having been stewed or diced or pickled before being packed into canning jars.

He also went to the diner every weekday morning during that time, which was not his usual custom. He had long ago noticed that the old men basically repeated the same tired conversations over and over again and he had found that once or twice a week was to his liking. That allowed him to enjoy the colorful characters that sat on their stools and to listen for the few new bits of information that speckled their endless chatter.

But regardless of the knowledge that everyday visits were tiresome, he found himself heading to the diner every morning during those weeks. He knew that sitting there sipping coffee wasted time and shortened his day considerably. But until harvest, that was the goal.

It was during these few weeks of daily visits that Jack noticed that Annie gradually stopped smiling. This was a noticeable change. Over the course of the one full year since she had graduated from high school and started working the weekday morning shift at the diner, she had developed a real style with the old farmers and even the grouchiest of them couldn't help but respond favorably to her genuine gladness to see them walk through the door.

Because she continued to make good coffee and continuously warm it for them, nothing was said about her change in spirits although everyone must have noticed. She still worked efficiently and did all she had always done, but without the enthusiasm that had always been so refreshing to a group of old men that loved to complain about, among other things, "kids today".

By Maggie's gentle teasing earlier in the summer, Jack knew that she had been seeing someone and he guessed that a breakup was the cause of the change in her. But when she began looking tired and pale, he started to wonder if it might be something more.

The days passed by, and as he carried on conversations with the other farmers about how the beans were testing and when they might test ready for harvest, he was aware of her every move, trying to figure out what the problem was but never daring to ask her.

It was the coffee that finally made Jack realize what was behind the change in her. Every time she poured a cup, she turned her head to the side to avoid the smell of it. He had been around his sisters enough to recognize the signs of pregnancy when he saw them, and he knew that it was often a strong smell that would make them queasy. Once he knew, or thought he did, he looked for changes in Annie's figure that might confirm what he suspected but he knew that those wouldn't come until later.

Jack had always counted on Annie to do the welcoming and initiate the little bit of small talk which they would occasionally share. He found himself doing this now, trying to cheer her up or, perhaps, draw a small bit of information out of her. But he was unsuccessful on both counts. Polite responses were all that he received in return for his efforts. He could tell that she was focused on fighting the waves of nausea that came with each freshly poured cup of coffee and that this battle left little energy for conversation.

On the last day before harvest, Jack walked into the diner, hung his hat on the rack, and sat down with four other farmers, who immediately asked how much rain was in his gauge that morning. It had rained just a little overnight and after they gave the fields one more day to dry out, the beans would be ready.

Jack knew that for the next few months, his coffee would be fixed by his mother and handed to him in a green metal thermos that was older than he was. As much as he was looking forward to the activity of harvest, he realized that he had become pleasantly accustomed to coming to town for his coffee each day during these past few weeks and he would miss the company of the men he was sitting with. He also wondered if Annie would be showing by the time things slowed back down and he was able to return. 'That's none of your business.' He silently scolded himself.

"Where you going to start?" Vince asked as Jack turned over the coffee mug that sat, like most of the others, turned upside down on the counter in front of each stool waiting for customers to claim them.

"Well, we were going to do the old Miller place first, but with the rain last night, I think it'll be kind of soft. My guess is that Dad'll want to start over by my place." He noticed out of the corner of his eye that Annie looked particularly pale this morning as she poured his coffee and refilled Vince's cup, emptying out the pot. "What about you?"

Vince was starting to answer when Annie put the coffee pot down quickly on the counter and rushed to the bathroom.

Jack sat for a short time while Vince talked about his fields. He listened intently to what was said to him, but it wasn't Vince's voice that he heard. After years of silence, he heard God speaking to him.

When he thought about it later, he couldn't recall debating whether or not to do what he did. If he had, he might have stayed where he was. But he didn't. He got up from his barstool and, as though he were watching someone else do it, he walked toward the restroom. On his way past, he grabbed a package of two saltine crackers from a basket on the end of the empty salad bar.

He walked into the women's restroom without hesitating. Inside he noticed that one of the doors of the ugly metal mauve stalls was still swinging slightly. She was bent over the sink directly across from the door with her back to him, splashing water on her face. Because of the running water, she didn't hear the door open and he watched her undetected for a moment. He could see in the mirror that her face was pale and her eyes were watery and red. It seemed awkward and a little too personal to stand there and watch her wash her face, but there didn't seem to be any appropriate words to announce his presence. Finally, she turned the water off and straightened. She looked in the mirror and was surprised to see his reflection behind her own. Through the mirror, their eyes met and held, while water dripped off of her chin and onto her white cotton shirt.

Jack looked away first. He walked up to her and held out the cracker package as she turned to grab a paper towel from the ancient dispenser that hung on the wall beside the sink.

"Here."

She glanced at the crackers, then pulled out a brown folded towel and dried her face. "I'm not hungry," she said in a tired voice, on the verge of tears because she had finally lost the battle to control the nausea that had been increasing steadily for the past few weeks.

"I know you're not hungry." He paused awkwardly. The next words came painstakingly slow. "It's just that...well...my sisters...always eat these when...they're...well...uh...not hungry."

She looked up and met his eyes once again, this time face to face. Her expression held both the comprehension of the meaning behind his words and the confirmation of his suspicions. She took the crackers that he was still holding out and said quietly, "Thanks."

He left the restroom and walked across the front of the diner, past the counter where his full cup of coffee sat, to the door that he had walked in just a few moments ago, automatically grabbing his hat on the way out.

The men at the counter sat in front of their lukewarm coffee and waited for a refill. After Jack's departure, Vince turned to Ralph and asked, "Now what do you think all that's about?"

Ralph responded, "Beats me." He stood up and peered into the kitchen through the service window. "Hey Maggie, you think you could come make us some more coffee?"

Chapter 7

Annie

The restaurant where they had agreed to meet was just off the outer belt of Columbus where Eric attended school. Annie sat in her car and took a deep breath. She willed herself to relax in this moment between fighting the traffic and facing Eric, but the sound of the cars whizzing past on the highway made it difficult to slow her thoughts. She tried to collect herself, to prepare for what lie ahead. She vowed not to get emotional, something that was increasingly hard to avoid lately. "Just do what you need to do," she repeated to herself several times.

It was sunny and pleasant on this Saturday afternoon, but the late September air was chilly, so she had worn a jacket. It was not yet time for supper, so there were only a few cars in the lot. His wasn't one of them, but she was a few minutes early and hadn't expected him to be here yet. She had suggested the time and the place when she called his dorm number, having finally obtained it through a mutual friend. She wanted to meet somewhere where no one would know them and at a time when there would not be a large number of people to listen to their conversation. And she didn't want to be alone with him. That's what had gotten her into this mess.

It was no longer than a few minutes before his car pulled into the space next to hers. They both got out and met at the sidewalk in front of their cars. They greeted each other politely, neither one smiling. She hadn't told him why they needed to meet but she was sure that, although he probably wasn't certain, he at least suspected.

They walked in and the hostess showed them to a table in the center of the restaurant. "Could we sit over there instead?" Annie pointed to a booth in the corner. The hostess agreed and they walked over and sat down. She handed them their menus and assured them that their waitress would be right with them before she left them alone.

They didn't speak, hiding behind the large menus, pretending that choosing what to have for supper was extremely important. The waitress came over and took their drink orders. After she walked away, Annie put her menu down on the table. He did the same. Annie looked at him. Because he sat facing the main area of the restaurant, he easily avoided her gaze; looking off in the direction that the waitress had just gone. She could tell he was scared and it gave her confidence. She had already gone through what he was in the middle of: the wondering and the waiting to be certain.

"So how's college? Are your classes this year as hard as you thought they'd be?"

He finally looked at her. "No. They're okay." He met her eyes. "Look, Jenny and I are back together."

"I know. Your mom told me." She knew that this would shake him even more. He had worked so hard to keep the fact that he was seeing someone else a secret from his family. Although she wasn't necessarily trying to make him nervous, he was and a part of her was enjoying it. He was usually so relaxed and confident that it was a pleasant change.

"When'd you talk with my mom?" Yes, he was definitely nervous.

"I called the house a few weeks ago, asking for you."

"Do you think she knows?"

"Knows what?" Yes, she was enjoying this moment.

"Knows that I was seeing you," he responded, annoyed that she was making him state the obvious.

"Definitely. She asked if I was the girl you were running around with this summer."

"Shit."

"Does Jenny know?" Annie asked him, feeling sorry for the woman that would end up marrying the person that sat across from her.

"No and I don't plan on telling her."

"I'm pretty sure someone will. You know how people are. I'm surprised no one has yet." Their conversation was interrupted as the waitress put their drinks in front of them and took their order. A hamburger and fries for him, noodle soup for her.

He resumed only after the waitress was a safe distance away. "Yeah, someone told her that they saw us together but no one knows how far we let things go." His voice was a low whisper now.

"They will soon." She willed the words to be nothing more than a casual reply in their conversation.

His mouth tightened and his eyes bore into hers with an intensity that scared her. There was no trace of his earlier nervousness. She looked away, unwrapped her straw and stuck it in her soda. He was the one that said the words and she was glad that she didn't have to. "You're pregnant."

She nodded and made herself look back up at him. The words hung in the silence until he spoke again.

"I'll give you money to see a doctor."

"I don't need money for a doctor. I have insurance."

"Does insurance cover that kind of thing?"

Then she realized what he meant. She felt the hurt and anger rising up inside her and begin to fill her eyes. She closed them, hoping to hide her tears from him but knowing that he had already seen them. She was quiet, gathering control of her emotions.

"An abortion?" She said the word out loud. She hadn't raised her voice but she hadn't whispered the word either. It sounded ugly and harsh in the quiet restaurant. His eyes darted to the other tables where some other customers sat. Although they probably hadn't heard what she said, she knew he was embarrassed and was glad.

Her question needed no affirmation from him so she didn't wait for one. Her reply was simple and determined. "I won't."

He leaned forward, angry at her. "What do you want me to do? I'm not rearranging my whole life just because of one lousy night." She didn't bother to argue that it hadn't been just one night and that he hadn't thought it was lousy at the time. She wondered what she had ever found appealing about him.

"I'm not asking you to rearrange your life. I'm just telling you. I thought you might like to know." The angry tone of her words now matched that of his.

"No, I wouldn't like to know."

They both wanted to walk out and go home but knew they couldn't yet. They sat in angry silence, the time dragging on, until their food came and provided a welcome distraction. The smell of his greasy meal made her slightly nauseous, and it seemed completely appropriate. She looked at him and the plate of food in front of him and thought how appealing both would have been just a few months ago.

Although her taste buds hadn't been working well for the past month, the bland warmth of the soup was comforting. As she ate, it settled her stomach and calmed her nerves so that she was able to finish what she had come for.

When she finally spoke it was rationally and with a renewed sense of purpose. "I have a lot of decisions to make and I need to know where you stand," she began. She spoke very quietly now, more to lower the level of tension between them than because she was worried someone might hear. Her words were slow and deliberate. "You'd like me to have an abortion and I won't. But what if I gave the baby up for adoption? Would you sign the papers and give up all rights?"

He swallowed a French fry before answering. "Gladly."

"What if I keep the baby? You'd be responsible for child support."

He thought about it before answering, chewing and swallowing a bite of his hamburger. "Look, I don't want this kid ruining my life. But I know I have responsibilities so I'll do whatever I legally need to do but not one thing more."

"Would you want visitation rights or…anything?" She wasn't exactly sure of all the possibilities that existed.

He dipped a fry in ketchup and looked up at her. "What do you think?" His voice dripped with sarcasm like the acidy red sauce dripping from his French fry.

At that moment, any remaining thread of emotional connection was severed. She knew that he would not be a help to her or to the baby but that also meant that he wouldn't interfere. She felt free and it felt good.

She stood up and put on her jacket, leaving the last few bites of her soup in the bowl. She smiled to herself as she took the two little packages of saltine crackers that she hadn't used and stuck them in the pocket of her jacket. She had discovered that they were, indeed, quite helpful to have around.

She looked down at him where he still sat. Her words were those of a person in charge concluding a business meeting. "Okay, then, I think that I know everything I need to know in order to make some informed decisions. I'll let you know what I decide."

She walked out, completely forgetting to leave any money for the food. She laughed out loud when she thought of it on the way home. "Well, I hope he can at least take care of that."

Chapter 8

Jack

Jack had the image of Annie stuck in his mind and he couldn't stop thinking about her. He had been thinking about her smile when he had overfilled the bin on the combine and spilled soybeans out into the field. He had been imagining what she would look like a few months from now when she was swollen with the child that he knew she was carrying, when he had pulled the combine out of a field and left a whole section undone. He had went home one night with the image of her and a faceless man conceiving that baby only to be radioed by his father a half hour later asking where the hell he was and why hadn't he come to pick him up like he was supposed to.

And now he had made another mistake. "Looks like I ran into that stake on the south side of the field." He said into the two-way radio that he and his father, Frank, used to communicate when they were working in the fields. Jack's father couldn't believe what he was hearing as Jack went on. "I busted up a few of the spokes on the header."

"Goddammit, Jack, how many times have you driven around that stake? You knew it was there! What the hell were you thinking?" Frank loved farming but his temper flared easily this time of year and it had been a frustrating harvest so far. He had come to depend on Jack. He was normally so reliable. More importantly, he knew how Frank wanted things done and shared the same opinions as his dad so that little time needed to be spent explaining details or debating the next step.

Jack had no acceptable excuse for the mistake, so there was silence on his end of the radio, but Frank didn't wait long for a response. He didn't wait long on anything in the fall. Before more than a few seconds passed, he sighed impatiently and said, "Let me get the rest of these beans in the grain bin and I'll be right over."

Frank and Jack inspected the header. The damage wasn't serious, but they would need a part from town. It was early Saturday evening and, although the implement dealerships kept long hours during harvest, they were already closed. They would have to quit for the night and wouldn't be able to get the part until Monday morning.

Tomorrow would be a day of rest anyway, as it was every week, even during planting and harvest. There were, at times, exceptions to this, but the exceptions were rare and even then the work would have to wait until after church services and Frank and Jack would always take time out for Sunday supper, when the sisters and their families would all come over and visit, like they did every week.

On this particular Sunday, the new baby, Kimberly, was getting baptized. This meant that Elizabeth was home from college. Although Jack was kicking himself for having been so careless, he was glad he was going to have the chance to visit with her a little tonight. In fact, he had accidentally run over that stake because he had been busy rehearsing his side of the conversation that he hoped to have with her about Annie instead of paying attention to farming.

He went home and showered. As he had expected, it wasn't long before Elizabeth walked in through the door that separated the house from the garage. She had walked the half mile from her parents' house on the cool, pleasant evening. As always, she didn't knock but rather announced her presence after she had already stepped into the kitchen. "Hey, big brother, anybody home?" He came out from the hallway in his bare feet, wearing a clean pair of jeans and pulling on a clean t-shirt. He gave her a hug.

He was close with all four of his sisters, but he was probably closest with Elizabeth. He had moved out of his parents' house and into this house that had once belonged to his grandparents five years ago, when she was fifteen. Whenever she had wanted "space" during her teen years, she had come over and made herself at home. He had missed her last year when she went away to college, had been glad to have her around again last summer, and had missed her all over again in mid-August when she left again.

She opened the refrigerator and pulled out a Cherry Coke from the carton that he had bought in anticipation of her visit this weekend. "My favorite, how'd you know," she joked. He had supplied quite a few Cherry Cokes for her over the years.

She sat down at the beat-up wood table that had been handed down from their parents, pulled the tab, and took a drink. He got his own and joined her. "Boy, is Dad pissed off about the header," she said.

"Yeah. I don't know what I was thinking." That was a lie. He knew exactly what he had been thinking. He took a swig, then said, "So, I really hate to change the subject, but how's college?"

She always had a lot to say and always said it in an entertaining way. She described classmates and professors in detail, focusing on their idiosyncrasies and doing impersonations at times. Jack laughed through much of it, enjoying her company. After a while, she stopped and said, "So how about you? What have you been doing besides torturing Dad?"

He told about how their new farm software was working and about Kimberly and the other nieces and nephews. She had only been gone a little over a month, so it didn't take long to report what she had missed.

And then he asked what he had been waiting to ask her for the past few weeks, trying to sound casual. "Annie Norton was in your grade, wasn't she?"

Elizabeth was surprised at the question but immediately knew the connection. "Yeah. Is she still waitressing at the diner?"

"Yeah."

"I heard she was seeing Eric Keaton this summer." Jack recognized the name from the shoe store as well as from the football games that he had attended. He knew that he had been in Elizabeth's class and knew that he was a good athlete. She continued, "I don't think they're together anymore, though. He's back with Jennifer Woodward. They've been seeing each other forever. Everybody knew they'd get back together." She went on, "They'll get married and live in a perfect house with two perfect kids and a perfect dog. Yuck. They make me sick." Jack wasn't surprised at her reaction. She had a dislike for anything too normal.

"Do you know her very well?"

"Who, Annie?"

"Yeah."

"She wasn't one of my best friends but I had some classes with her. She's nice – and smart. I had senior English with her and she blew the teacher away with some of the stuff she'd say. I'm surprised she didn't go to college. Her mom works at the dentist office uptown. I don't know about her dad; I don't think he's around." She studied her brother's face.

He avoided her eyes. It was hard to notice under his deep tan, but she knew him well and noticed that he was blushing.

"Jack, are you interested in her?" Her voice was kind and teased him gently, trying to coax him into telling her all.

He had known that asking Elizabeth about Annie would inevitably lead to this question. In spite of his rehearsals in the combine, he hadn't come up with a better response than "Maybe."

"Jack, that's great!" Her excitement was out of proportion with the tight-lipped response that he had given her. "Are you going to ask her out?"

"I'm thinking about it." He'd been thinking about little else. "Do you think she'd go out with me?" The words came out of his mouth but they were the words of a teenager. He hated the way they sounded. They implied class rings and meeting in the hallway between classes and hoping it would last until prom.

"Probably. She went out with Eric, and you're so much better than he is. Even if you are older. And balder. And less handsome."

"Thanks for the encouragement."

"You're welcome. What are sisters for?"

"I thought they were for helping to pick out an outfit for attending a baptism." He was pleased with himself for effectively changing the subject that had become uncomfortable. They went through the small living room and back to his bedroom so that she could give her opinion on which tie she liked better; he only owned two. Jack noticed that she glanced around the sparse room and at the twin bed that he had slept in since childhood. He wondered if he was imagining the trace of pity that seemed to cloud her usually happy face.

After she had given her advice, they went back out into the living room and talked a little more. Then she got up and said, "Well, I better go. The old folks are probably wondering where I am." He walked with her to the door. She turned to look at him. "In case we don't get to talk alone tomorrow, good luck on the Annie thing."

He didn't want to ask the question but he couldn't let her leave without asking it. "Do you think I'm too old for her?"

She looked at him very seriously and he could tell she had already thought of it and knew it was a problem. "Honestly?"

"Honestly."

"No, but she might think so."

"Would you go out with a 31-year-old man?"

"Not without imagining who they've been sleeping with and why, if they're worth having, no one else has snatched them up."

He looked down at his feet and let out a breath. He looked back up at her and could tell she was sorry for saying it. But it was what he already knew and he appreciated her openness rather than resenting her bluntness.

"I didn't say I wouldn't go out with someone your age," she insisted. "I just mean I would be cautious, that's all."

He gave her another hug. "Thanks, sis."

He watched from the window as she disappeared into the darkness of the deserted country road, her stride full of the energy and confidence that defined her. The house was quieter than ever. He was tired and decided to take this opportunity to catch up on the sleep he had been deprived of for the past few weeks. But as he lay in bed, his attempt to sleep proved futile. He thought about what Elizabeth had told him. So Eric Keaton was the father. And he probably had no intention of marrying her. In spite of his weariness, he lay awake a long time, thinking and praying.

Chapter 9

Annie

When Annie returned from meeting with Eric, the house was empty and her mother had left a note on the counter telling her that the budding relationship with Mr. Root Canal was continuing and that she wouldn't be back until later. This allowed Annie some time alone to sort through the mess that was her life.

She went to her room and pulled her high school yearbook from the shelf. She leafed through the pages and let her eyes find Eric. She saw him wearing a suit and tie, smiling out at her from his senior picture. His teeth were too white and even. She turned the page and saw him in his football uniform. He was the second one from the left in the front row. Another turn of the page and she saw him with his arm around Jenny. The words "Cutest Couple" were written under that picture. She turned back to his senior picture.

She let memories of high school flow freely into her mind. Eric had been in some classes with her. That wasn't much of a coincidence. It was a small school and all the students had classes with one another.

In their senior year, she and Eric had sat next to one another in Physics for a good part of the year and had talked before class, developing what could perhaps be called a friendship. She remembered looking forward to the few minutes before class began and how her heart had raced during those short conversations. His lop-sided smile used to make her knees go weak. He would lean over his desk towards her when he spoke to her, invading her space in a way that was both uncomfortable and intoxicating. Sometimes when he talked he would reach out and touch her arm, a touch that would cause her whole body to tingle.

As she sat there on her bed remembering this, she realized that remembering was all she was doing. Her knees weren't weak; they were quite strong. And the thought of him might be nauseating but it wasn't intoxicating. Whatever he used to do to her, he didn't do it anymore and she was glad.

Although she was crazy about him back then, she had known that he had a girlfriend and she also knew that he used the same smile, the same look, and the same touch, with many of the other girls in the class. She suspected that many probably reacted the same way. "He was a flirt and you fell for it," she scolded herself out loud.

But she knew that that wasn't the truth behind why she had given herself to him last summer. There had been a whole year between graduation and when they started seeing each other. In that year she had grown wiser and more mature, although the baby that she carried was proof that she had a ways to go yet. But she wasn't dumb and never had been. She had known in high school what he was and she definitely knew last summer what he was, a self-centered charmer. Her body may have fallen for it but her brain didn't. No, this pregnancy wasn't a simple result of letting a boy use his charms to get into her pants.

"Then why'd I do it?" She spoke the question out loud and lay back on the bed, analyzing her actions of the previous summer more deeply than she had before. All the reasons swirled around in the air above her and she couldn't pinpoint one. Sexual attraction, yes. But also loneliness and boredom. Curiosity. A desire to show her somewhat promiscuous mother that she could have sex too. A need for life to be more than work and home. A yearning to feel like she was good enough for him.

"Love?" she asked herself whether or not that should be tossed into the air to join all the other reasons. "Definitely not," she answered herself.

She drifted off to sleep, exhausted. Hours later, she crawled under the covers and noted that her mom still wasn't home.

The next day, she and her mother sat down for Saturday lunch together. This week the menu was Ramen noodles and carrot sticks. Annie asked, "Mom, do you regret not marrying my dad?"

Cindy was annoyed by the question. During her junior high years Annie had often asked about her father and said bratty things like "I bet my father would have let me do it," or "Not even my own father cares about me."

Cindy made it clear that she didn't appreciate the question. "Annie, we've been through this before. It wasn't a choice. He was already married." She had shared the fact that he was a married man with Annie during those adolescent years, seemingly unashamed of it.

Annie dropped the subject. She already knew everything that she was ever going to know, which wasn't much. None of the three husbands that her mother had married had been her real father, although each of the three had been decent men who tried to be a good substitute. She had never known who her father was or anything about him because her mother had stubbornly refused to answer her questions about him. Annie had always had an empty place, only knowing half of who she was biologically. It seemed to her that even if her father chose not to be present, that she should at least be able to know his name and that he should at least have been man enough to accept some type of responsibility for her. Her mother should have insisted on it.

Of course, it was her current situation that brought all of these feelings to the surface. She thought of little else that weekend. In the end she decided that the damage had been done. It was too late to choose a decent father for her child. The years had taught her well that all she could do now was to make the best of what was and not wish for what wasn't.

Chapter 10

Jack

Sunday morning was the one morning each week that Jack lay in bed past dawn. On Sunday, his early morning prayers at the kitchen window were replaced by Mass. The thoughts of the night before had not been resolved in his mind, but in spite of that he had fallen into a deep, peaceful sleep. By the time he awoke, the sun was up and he felt rested.

He looked at his clock and was surprised to find that it was 8:30. He couldn't remember the last time he had slept so late. Mass was at 9:30 and he was supposed to be there at nine o'clock to get some instructions on his part in the baptismal ceremony. He quickly got ready, putting on the tie that his sister had suggested, and rushing out the door for the short drive to church.

St. Mary's Catholic Church was the focal point of a small village just two miles from his house. In the village, there a was also a bar that, in addition to the usual beverages that one would expect, sold bread, milk, eggs, and pizza, saving the handful of residents a trip into the bigger town now and then. The boarded-up building where Jack had attended elementary school sat on Main Street, just down from the church. The public school district had been bussing all of the kids into town for at least fifteen years now. Across from the school was the post office that his uncle ran. The school kids had always looked forward to their turn to cross the street and collect the mail for the school. And there were some houses, the best of which were modest and the worst of which were trashy. On the edge of town, past the houses, was the cemetery.

He pulled his pick-up into the gravel lot of the church at nine o'clock sharp on this crisp early October day. It was clear and the air had a bite to it. The first frost was probably less than a week away and the leaves were starting to turn.

His parents and Elizabeth were standing inside the entrance of the church. Kate and John had not yet arrived with the baby. Jack had enough nieces and nephews to know that this was to be expected. With young babies, there was always a last minute minor emergency involving something coming unexpectedly out of one end or the other of the innocent-looking creatures.

Elizabeth couldn't resist the drama of disguised inquiry in front of Jack's mother. They both knew that she would have been thrilled by her son's interest in a young woman and this fact made it very important to Jack that she not know anything about it. "Good morning, Jack. Did you have any sweet dreams last night?"

"Good morning, Elizabeth. I can tell you're wide awake and ready to roll this morning." He scowled at her and wondered why he had trusted such a high-spirited person with such delicate information.

Kate and John arrived and unloaded the kids. Baby Kimberly was wrapped in a ruffled pink and white baby blanket that had been crocheted by Jack's mom. John held Christopher by the hand. He was dressed up, wearing last year's tan pants that stopped at his ankles. His long-sleeved button-down shirt fit him well and Jack remembered it from last year when he used to swim in it. Kate seemed surprisingly trim and her skirt and blouse were flattering and modest, her hair was in place, and she wore just a hint of make-up and perfume. She looked slightly stressed but very happy as they walked into church together.

"Sorry we're late. Kimberly decided to fill her diaper right as we were about to leave." Jack had guessed correctly.

Just then, Fr. Bill came rushing in, having just said Mass at another small parish. "So, this is the lucky lady that's going to be baptized today." He peeked into the opening of the blanket from which Kimberly peered back.

They went to the front of the church and each person in the family, including Christopher, genuflected in reverence as they approached the altar. The sun was shining in the stained glass windows and lights weren't yet on, giving the church a yellowish glow. A few elderly people were kneeling in the pews praying the rosary and few more were coming in, but the church was still almost empty. Father led them to the baptismal font beside the altar, where he quickly walked them through the steps of the ceremony in preparation for the real thing that would take place in front of the congregation in a few minutes.

They had all agreed to skip the customary rehearsal because all the participants had been through this before. This was Jack's third god-child. Each of his other two sisters had also chosen him for the godfather of one of their children. Although this was Elizabeth's first godchild, she had witnessed many baptisms and felt comfortable with the ceremony. After the brief rehearsal, Christopher and his grandparents sat down in the front pew and Kate, John, Elizabeth, Jack, and, of course, Kimberly returned to the back of the church where they would remain and walk up with the priest during the opening hymn.

As they were waiting for Father to put on his vestment in preparation for Mass, Kate reminded them, "Jack, you have the first reading and Elizabeth, you have the second."

"Right," they both responded. Between the business of the harvest and the absentmindedness that had plagued him lately, Jack had forgotten to look his reading over, but he read in front of the church regularly and he didn't consider his lack of preparation a problem.

Mass began with Father's announcement that it was the 27th Sunday of Ordinary Time and that today the church would celebrate a baptism. Kate and John responded "Kimberly Marie" to Father's question "And what name do you give your child?" They walked up to the front and took their places with Christopher, Frank, and Meg, who by now had been joined by the other two sisters, Mary and Sarah, and their families, filling up the first two pews.

When it was time for the first reading, Jack approached the lectionary, found the first reading, and began in a loud, clear voice. "A reading from the Book of Genesis." He heard the amplified voice that didn't sound like his own proclaiming that "it is not good for the man to be alone" and ending with "the two of them become one body." The words resounded in him and he returned to his pew.

He was attentive for the rest of Mass. He listened to the Gospel. He promised to help raise Kimberly in the Christian faith and watched her eyes widen in fear and surprise when water was poured over her forehead. He lit her baptismal candle from the Easter candle in the front of the church. He watched the bread and wine become the Body and Blood. He received Christ in the Eucharist.

After Mass, the family went to Kate's house for Sunday dinner, breaking from the tradition of supper at his mom's house. The sisters shared stories about their husbands and kids, the brothers-in-law watched football, and children huddled around their new cousin, giggling at the funny faces that she made and the rude noises that came from her.

When Jack returned home late in the afternoon, he was at last free to open his well-worn Bible that sat on the end table by his recliner. He found the passage that he had read out loud in church that morning and reread it. It was as though the ancient words had been written for this precise moment, to encourage and strengthen him for what he now knew he was about to do.

Chapter 11

Annie

Annie pulled into the parking lot of the diner on Monday morning at 5:50 wondering how she would ever find the energy to stay on her feet until two-thirty when she got off work. She was nauseous as usual and her pants and blouse were uncomfortably tight. The truck that she saw parked in front added to her misery. It meant that someone would be at the door as soon as she turned on the lights, expecting the coffee to be ready. She parked under the lone security light, got out of the car, grabbed her purse, and closed the door.

"Good morning." The words coming from nearby startled her, but she immediately recognized Jack and wasn't frightened. She should have recognized his truck.

"Jack. Good grief. You're early this morning." It was the first time that they had seen each other since harvest began, since he had given her the saltines. The knowledge of her pregnancy floated in the air between them. "We don't open for another ten minutes, you know.

Give me time to get the coffee on." As she talked, she walked quickly to the back door that opened into the kitchen. He followed her.

"I was hoping maybe you'd let me in a few minutes early."

She turned the key, unlocking the door. She looked up at his face, fuzzy in the darkness. She had been ready to tell him he'd need to wait but changed her mind. "Alright, go around to the front door and I'll be right up to let you in."

Annie made her way through the restaurant, flipping on lights on the way to the front door. She unlocked it and pulled it open for him. He entered with a "Thanks."

She immediately busied herself starting a pot of coffee, the same as she did each morning. She felt his eyes on her and waited for him to take a seat at the counter but he didn't.

"Would you like to go on a walk with me?" He said the words to her back as she put the coffee filter into the top of the coffee maker. She put the pot on the burner and flipped the toggle switch. She turned to him.

"What?"

"Would you like to go on a walk with me?" The question was so unexpected that she couldn't muster a response. Noting her confusion, he explained. "Not now. I mean sometime, maybe sometime when you get off work or in the evening."

Still unable to respond to him, she walked back into the kitchen where Maggie had arrived and was setting out eggs and turning on the griddle. "Doesn't he know how to tell time?" the older woman asked.

"I guess not," she replied. She grabbed a carton of cream from the walk-in refrigerator and walked back out into the dining room, letting her body push open the swinging doors that separated the kitchen from the dining room. Maybe he would be gone. He wasn't.

She pulled a tray of miniature white ceramic pitchers out from under the counter and sat the tray in front of where he stood. She busied herself pouring the creamer into the pitchers. She wished he would sit down instead of standing there, watching her. She finished filling the pitchers and put the carton down heavily on the counter and looked at him.

"You know I'm, well…I'm…" She remembered how he had had trouble saying the word to her in the restroom. This time it was she that was having trouble saying it. She gave up and began setting the pitchers along the counter, talking to him as she did. "A walk? Why do you want to go on a walk?"

"I wanted to talk about the possibility of us getting married."

She finally stopped the flow of activity that she had carried on since her arrival at the diner. She looked at him but he wasn't in focus. She tried to replay his words in her mind but they were garbled and she wasn't sure if she had heard them correctly. She watched as he walked around the counter and approached her. He gently took the pitcher of cream that she had forgotten that she held and put it on the countertop.

"I just want to talk about it. Maybe we'll decide that it's a crazy idea. But maybe we'll decide it could work." He grabbed several napkins from a metal dispenser, and squatted to wipe up the cream at her feet that she hadn't known that she had spilled. She took two steps backward to give him room as well as to distance herself from him.

He stood up and looked into her eyes. "How about 4:00 Wednesday at Stepping Stones Park?" He had obviously thought this through. She didn't know what to say so she just stood there, saying nothing.

Jack put the soaked napkins on the counter and awkwardly waited. When she didn't answer, he said, "Well, I'll be there. If I don't see you then, I'll be back in for coffee after harvest, just like always." He walked to the door, grabbed his cap from the rack, and turned back to her, "Four o'clock Wednesday, Stepping Stones," he repeated. And he walked out the door.

    She stared at the door as if it would give her the answer to the question that she should have articulated before he left. All day as she served coffee and plates of eggs and, later, sandwiches and hash browns, she wondered what had made him suggest such a thing. By the time two-thirty arrived and she walked back out to her car, she had decided that the only way to find out was to be at Stepping Stones Park at four o'clock on Wednesday.

Chapter 12

Jack

Monday, Tuesday, and Wednesday were long, tortuous days for Jack, days when his thoughts went back and forth like the combine in which he sat. At one end of the field, he remembered Annie's reaction, or lack of it, when he had blurted out his idea. He kicked himself for ever having been stupid enough to think that she would take such a thing seriously. By the time he reached the other end of the field, he was thinking about how sure he was that God had broken His long silence and that he was doing what he was finally being called to do. And then he turned, and the combine and his thoughts went the other direction, back to where they had just come from.

On Wednesday, he told his dad that he would need to take off in the afternoon for a while. He knew that such a statement in the middle of harvest would be met with prying questions, and he was right. He answered as vaguely as possible which greatly annoyed his father.

Mid-afternoon he went home, showered, and put on his newest pair of jeans and a button-down plaid shirt. He was fairly certain that it didn't really matter what he wore because Annie wasn't going to be there to see what he was wearing, anyway. He grabbed his cleaner cap and headed out the door, muttering "I can't believe I'm doing this."

Stepping Stones Park was on the edge of town, nestled in a quiet neighborhood. It was a low area that sat beside the river that ran through town. The river was shallow where it ran through the park and, when there hadn't been much rain, one could step from one side of the river to the other on the large flat stones after which the park was named. The city had recently constructed a cement walk path that made a long oval that encompassed a flat grassy area. One side of the path ran along the south bank of the river and the other ran along a narrow, wooded area that separated the park from the backyards of the neighborhood which sloped upward to higher ground.

Jack had been to the park with his nephews and niece a few times and had chosen it because it was quiet. Not many people came here and it made a good place for a private conversation.

He arrived a few minutes early and his stomach turned somersaults when he saw her car parked in the small lot. He had rehearsed, but for a performance that he was pretty sure would be cancelled for lack of an audience. He felt unprepared and scared, but mixed in with both emotions was the feeling that this was the right thing to be doing. Right, but not easy.

Chapter 13

Annie

Between Monday morning and Wednesday afternoon, Annie thought of little other than the strange encounter with Jack on Monday and the upcoming second encounter with Jack planned for Wednesday.

She had spent the past month and a half trying to look at her options objectively and now she did the same with this new possibility. Jack's proposal, if one could call it a proposal, was surprisingly interesting and, to her astonishment, she found herself thinking that it might actually be the answer that she had been looking for.

So on Wednesday, after the lunch hour had died down at the diner and she had completed her usual routine of preparing things for the supper crowd, she went home, washed the grease of the diner away, and dressed for a walk in the park. Her mother was still at work and she was thankful not to have to explain where she was going. The jeans that she pulled on, her loosest pair, were only slightly tight around the waist. She chose a warm sweater so that she wouldn't need a jacket.

She looked in the mirror and smiled. The new and welcome fullness of her breasts pushed the material of the sweater out, forming two nicely rounded mounds. She pulled most of her hair back into a barrette, but left the hair at the nape of her neck loose. She looked seriously at the girl with the womanly figure and briefly tried to grasp the magnitude of what she was about to do. Unable to do so, she grabbed her purse and hopped in her car, wanting to get there before Jack.

Annie intentionally arrived ten minutes early. She knew that her response to Jack on Monday had been anything but reassuring and she didn't want him to think she wasn't coming. In fact, given her response, or rather lack of it, she wondered whether or not he himself would be here. He wasn't yet.

She got out of the car and walked to a picnic table that sat at one end of the oval, near the parking lot, and waited. The air was crisp and clear. She heard the sound of the river gurgling as it flowed over the rocks a few yards away. The trees weren't yet in the full color of fall, but a few trees were ahead of the rest, showing off in brilliant reds and yellows.

In spite of the beautiful weather, the park was nearly deserted. A middle-aged man walked his dog in shorts, loafers, and white socks that reached to his knees. Two young women power-walked in trendy sweat suits. Even though the women were at a distance, Annie could tell from the way their heads moved that they were talking as fast as they were walking. It was the perfect place to have a private conversation. She knew this was not a coincidence but rather a result of Jack's planning and she wasn't surprised. She knew from eavesdropping on countless conversations at the diner that, as a rule, he thought things through carefully.

He pulled in and parked right in front of where she sat. His blue truck was covered with the dust from the fields. But when he stepped out, she noticed that he and his clothes were immaculately clean. She had been so absorbed with the issue to be discussed that hadn't thought until now that this meeting would be interrupting a very busy day of harvesting.

He walked up to her and smiled hesitantly. "You're here."

She stood and smiled back. "I thought maybe you'd changed your mind."

He looked at her with his deep brown eyes and said only, "No." The word was strong and determined.

"This isn't a yes, just a maybe." She needed to make it clear immediately.

"I know. I'm just glad it's even that." They automatically began walking along the path that curved toward the river, keeping time with each other with a slow pace, each one not wanting to go too fast for the other, either with their steps or with their words.

"I've been thinking a lot." She turned to him and asked, "Do you mind if I tell you what I've been thinking?"

"I'd love to hear it." He said earnestly. She guessed that he was relieved not to have to have the burden of carrying the conversation.

They had followed the path past the curve and were now along the river. There was bench facing the river with its back to the path. He gestured to the bench with his ever-present cap, which he held in his hand. "Do you want to sit down?"

They sat. Someone could have easily squeezed into the space that remained between them on the bench. They both looked at the moving clear water and her words began to flow.

"When I found out I was pregnant, I starting thinking about my choices. I guess the first choice anyone in my situation makes is whether to let the baby grow or, well, not let the baby grow." She didn't move her gaze from the water but she could see from the corner of her eye that his head had turned suddenly towards her. She went on quickly. "That was easy. I knew I couldn't have an abortion." He looked forward again and seemed to relax a little.

She took a deep breath and the words tumbled out as she exhaled. "So the next choice is whether to give the baby up for adoption or to keep it." She paused. "I'm still thinking about that. It's such a hard choice. I think adoption's the best thing for the baby, but then I try to imagine what it would be like to have this baby and then go home and pretend nothing happened. I don't know if I can do that." She turned to him, talking to his profile. "What do you think?"

He leaned forward, his elbows resting on his knees. He looked down at his green cap and turned it slowly in his hands. "Well, I think adoption makes good sense." He paused, still looking down. "You didn't say if you want to be a mom."

She didn't hesitate. "I do." The enthusiasm in her voice betrayed her desire for the baby. She had shared with only a few people the fact that she was pregnant and she had not told anyone until now that she actually wanted this baby, barely even acknowledging that fact herself.

Her voice was once again matter-of-fact as she continued after those two words. "It's not a question of wanting the baby. I want the baby, but I want what's best for the baby and maybe that's not me." Tears silently spilled out of her eyes before she even knew they were there. She let them fall, not wanting to draw attention to them by wiping them away, hoping he wouldn't notice them. She continued. "So if I keep the baby, and I'm not sure I will, there are usually two choices there, too. Either I raise the baby with the father or alone."

He turned his head to look at her. She stared straight ahead not wanting him to see the tears and sadness in her eyes. "Did you talk to him about it yet?"

She bowed her head. She was ashamed on Eric's behalf. "Remember the first choice I made, what I decided I couldn't do?" A fresh supply of tears ran down her cheeks but her voice remained miraculously steady. She dabbed at her nose with the back of her hand. He reached into the back pocket of his jeans and pulled out a clean and neatly folded thin blue cotton handkerchief and offered it to her. She was grateful that he didn't comment on the tears or try to comfort her.

"He thinks that would be a good idea, huh? To just get rid of it?" He saved her from having to say the rest. She was grateful for that, too.

She nodded, and then continued. "He doesn't want any part of this baby. So he made that choice for me. I'm not raising the baby with its daddy. That's out. Then I was down to two choices. Either adoption or raise the baby by myself. I don't like either one. If I give the baby up for adoption, I don't have my baby. If I raise the baby by myself, the baby doesn't have a father. So that's why I'm here."

He clarified again, "So you can have the baby and the baby can have a daddy." For the first time since they had sat down on the bench and she had begun to speak, they looked at one another. The usually quick-witted brightness of his eyes was softened by his compassion for her. She looked away and he once again looked down at his cap. They sat for a long moment, thinking about that simple summary.

She breathed the fresh air deep into her, into the space created by the words that she had released. She was satisfied that she had made it clear why she had accepted his invitation but now she needed to know why he had extended it in the first place. "So that's why I'm interested. But I don't understand why you're interested. Why would you want to marry me?" It was the question that had been plaguing her for two days.

He started slowly and then picked up speed. "Well, I know you have a great sense of humor. You're dependable and hardworking," He grinned over at her, teasing her. "You make great coffee." He had to think a minute. "You're kind to old men. That'll come in handy." She chuckled, appreciating his sense of humor about the age difference between them. "And you're beautiful." His voice was serious again. "And you have a smile that makes me want to smile too." She had still been smiling from his comment about old men but now immediately stopped. For the first time that afternoon, she felt very uncomfortable.

She added one more thing to his list. "And you know I slept with someone that I shouldn't have and I'm carrying his child."

She could see the affection for her being replaced by sadness before he turned and stared ahead at the trees on the opposite bank. She knew the words that he said were only a small part of what he was thinking. "I can deal with it. We all have things we need to be forgiven for." Pain flickered briefly across his face and vanished so quickly that Annie wondered if she had imagined it. "And it's not like you were unfaithful to me." She could tell he was sorting it out as he spoke. "No, I think I don't have the right to either hold it against you or to forgive you for it. I think that's between you and God."

They sat in silence. Finally she stood up and started walking. He did the same. This time their pace was brisker, moving them quickly forward. Both looked ahead at where they were going, with their minds and words, as well as their eyes.

"Do you think it could work, Jack?" His name sounded too intimate as she said it and she cringed. She didn't know that he was marveling at how wonderful his name sounded when she spoke it.

"I think it could."

"I don't want to get divorced."

He teased her again, "I think we have to get married first."

"You know what I mean. I don't want to get married if it's not going to work. My mom's been divorced three times."

"So you're an expert on what not to do. That'll come in handy. And I'm an expert on what *to* do. My parents have a great marriage."

"But don't you think we should make sure we agree on some basic things before we jump into this?" Maybe if she and Jack thought things through they could be more successful than her mother had been.

"That's probably a good idea," he agreed.

They reached the end of the oval, where they had started. The sun was low in the sky and the air was cool. The other two cars had gone and the parking lot was empty except for his truck and her car.

"So now what?" The question was hers.

"Do you want to go out to eat?" That wasn't the type of answer that she had in mind.

She was exhausted and needed to be alone. She also sensed the same in him and guessed that he had suggested it because he felt like he should. "My mom's home by now. She's probably wondering where I am. And I'm tired."

"I should get back home, too. My dad was, well, perplexed, as to why I had to go to town when we were in the middle of things."

She smiled. She knew Frank and knew that there were probably better words than "perplexed" to describe his reaction.

"I know you're busy with the harvest. Why don't we just think things through for a little while and you can call me when you want to get together to talk again?"

"Okay. But I won't wait long. If we're going to do this, I want it to be soon." His reasons didn't need to be explained.

"Yeah, me too."

They both stood there at the edge of the parking lot for a moment, not knowing how to part ways. She spoke first.

"Well, okay, then, give me a call whenever you can."

"Okay, I will. Soon."

And so they went to their vehicles and got in. Annie followed his truck out of the neighborhood and watched it turn away from her. She wondered what he was thinking as he drove off.

A few hours later, when she took off her jeans before bed that night, in her pocket she found the handkerchief that he had handed to her as they sat on the bench. She sat on the bed and held it, feeling the softness of its worn cotton and the slight dampness that remained from the tears that she had shed. She was happy to have evidence that she hadn't dreamed the entire afternoon. She wondered when he might call and she wished that they had arranged a specific time for that call.

Chapter 14

Jack

The sunshine lasted the rest of the week and through the weekend. They had agreed that they would both think about what they were considering, but Jack was uncertain of how long to give this consideration. He was already convinced that this was what he wanted but how long should he give her to become convinced too? The answer that he came up with was when it rained. When it rained them out of the fields, then he would call her. That was probably what she was expecting anyway; she knew how farmers operated. Besides, taking time off on another sunny day would reveal his impatience to her as well as draw a lot more questions from his mom and dad, questions that he didn't want to answer yet. He was surprised at how easy it was to wait. The earlier restlessness had vanished and instead he enjoyed the time of reflection.

Even as he waited patiently, Jack looked forward to the next step in this strange courtship. He found himself listening more attentively than usual to the weather reports on the radio as he sat in the combine or hauled corn back and forth to town in the old grain truck. He wished for rain, although he knew by now that wishing for rain, or sun, was futile. He was wise enough to know that God would give either one as he saw fit and that He would provide for all of their needs. It seemed to Jack that God often used the weather to build character and patience in those who depended on it for their livelihood; testing their trust in Him. He didn't question God's judgment when it came to the weather. But there were other things that God did that he still questioned, not matter how much he told himself not to.

Although Jack would have liked rain, the weather was perfect harvest weather. The days were clear and bright and the sun made the brown brittle cornstalks glow. The nights were cold and the first frost came on schedule. The cloudless night sky allowed the huge low harvest moon to illuminate the fields. And it wasn't just the weather that was cooperating. The yields were good and the prices were decent. They had had no breakdowns besides the few problems caused by Jack's earlier carelessness. Overall, it was the kind of harvest that they hoped for each year.

And, in spite of Jack's preoccupation with his personal life and the hurried pace of harvest, he took time to marvel in the glory that surrounded him. He praised God for His abundance as he did each year as he maneuvered the combine back and forth along the rows or watched the grain go up the auger into the round metal bins. Jack was glad that farming was not a profession in which you could be tricked into believing that success and profit were a result only of your own skill and hard work. While skill and hard work were certainly necessary, God's blessing was essential. He wondered, as he often did, if there was such a thing as an atheist farmer. He had never met one.

As agreed, he also thought about what important topics should be discussed before he and Annie were ready to declare themselves ready for marriage. Since last Sunday when he had stood at the lectern and heard God's word in his own amplified voice, he felt certain about what God was asking him to do. Now that Annie seemed willing, he could think of very little that would convince him that it wouldn't work. He had been drawn to Annie since he had met her and over the past year he had come to know her as an honest and kind person. Those things seemed to him to be a solid start. He knew from watching his parents that it was commitment rather than lack of differences that made a marriage last, so he wasn't worried about disagreeing with her about a few things.

But one thing did worry him, and that was the issue of religion. It was the one and only issue that he decided that he needed to talk to Annie about. He didn't think she went to church. She had never mentioned anything about church. On the contrary, she had talked about how hard it was to get up on Monday after sleeping in on the weekends. If she did go to church, he was almost positive she wasn't Catholic.

Jack hadn't necessarily planned on marrying, but in times when he had imagined that he might, he had assumed that it would be to someone that his mother might call "a nice Catholic girl." So he had never thought that the problems that existed in interfaith marriages would apply to him. And now, as he thought about what was involved, he was challenged to clarify in his mind the importance of his faith and passing on that faith to his children.

He had always treasured the Catholic faith and all that it meant, from the beautiful sacrament of sharing the Eucharist to the simple routine of making the sign of the cross before and after prayers to the firm stand the Church took on social issues. It was essential to him that any child that he would call his own would be brought up with the same traditions, learning the love of God through his family first but also through the Church. Yes, Annie would have to agree that the child would be baptized into the Church and be a practicing member of the faith. He prayed that she would agree to this condition and didn't know what he would do if she didn't.

But what about Annie? Did he have the right to impose his faith on her too? Should he demand that she join the Church? That was more difficult than raising a child to be Catholic. He found himself wondering how adults become Catholic. Of course, he knew there was a process of classes and initiation into the Church. But what about the deeper beliefs that make them want to join? How does that happen? He could only conclude that it was a gift of the Spirit that wasn't his to give. So he ultimately decided that if she didn't want to join, he had no right to demand it of her as long as she was supportive of his faith and the passing of that faith to their child.

During those sunny days when he watched the sky for rain clouds and offered prayers of thanksgiving and thought about sharing his faith with the child and, hopefully, his wife, he also thought about forgiveness. He found himself thinking of the past, of what he had done that had demanded his acceptance of the forgiveness that God offered, and hoped that Annie could find the same forgiveness.

And he thought about what Annie had done. It wasn't just his mother that thought that he should marry "a nice Catholic girl". He had always thought that it was important, too. Although it was never said, the word "nice", when said in a certain tone, implied virgin. Whenever Mom had tried to play matchmaker for him, she had always said "You should ask her out. She's a nice girl."

Jack knew that even more than ten years ago when he was in school, more and more girls, and of course, guys, didn't live up to the old-fashioned ideal of waiting for marriage. He also knew it was much worse these days. His parents had always encouraged his four sisters to be "nice" girls. He also knew that all of his sisters had struggled to live up to the standards of their parents and of the Church, with varying degrees of success.

But, like he had told Annie in the park, it was between her and God. He had meant it when he told her that he could deal with what she had done. No one, himself included, was perfect, and he didn't expect that of her. The only important question was if he could love the child as his own. He knew in his heart that the answer to that was yes.

On Tuesday morning, six days after their walk in the park, Jack woke up, as usual, just as the sky was beginning to hint at dawn. By the weakness of the light he could tell that the sun didn't want to get up any more than he did. He had been up until 2:00 a.m. finishing a field of corn but needed to get up. He wanted to be in line at the grain elevator in town with another load of corn when they opened to avoid waiting for hours later in the day. He dressed, stopping only briefly at the kitchen window for a quick prayer, and went to his parents' house. He accepted his thermos of coffee from his mom, who was still in her nightgown, and drove the grain truck to town under cloudy skies. He was pleased to be third in line at the elevator, which would open in half an hour.

He sat in the cab of the truck that was littered with field dirt and grain tickets. He turned the motor of the old truck off while he waited, so the chill of the morning air slowly crept in. He poured his coffee into the little cup that went with the thermos. He thought about everything and he was happy. He had waited for ten long years not understanding what it was that God wanted from him or for him and now he understood. He felt the change in his life that was about to occur as surely as he felt the coffee warming him. He knew it was coming just like he knew the rain was finally rolling in from the west.

Chapter 15

Annie

Annie was also watching the forecast during that time, hoping for rain. She knew the farmers well enough to know that "when you get a chance", really meant, "when it rains". Even though he had said "soon", she didn't worry or wonder as the week ended and the next week began and the sun continued to shine and phone refused to ring. She knew that he would call her as promised and she also knew that his intentions wouldn't change.

Thoughts about a potential marriage to Jack rolled around in her mind. The time after she got home from work and before her mother arrived home was the best time of the day for serious thinking. And on Thursday, just one day after her meeting with Jack, she arrived home to her quiet house, changed her clothes, and readied herself to write a list of things to discuss with him. She dug through her desk drawer for a tablet of colored paper she had received as a gift the Christmas before and had never used. There were pages of different colors and she flipped through the colors. She avoided either pink or blue; those colors were too full of

Offerings

significance these days. She carefully tore out a lime green page from the middle. She chose a pen from the cluttered kitchen drawer and sat on the sofa cross-legged. She touched her pen to the paper and sat in stillness, unable to start.

She had thought that making a list of things to talk about with Jack would be easy. There were so many things that she had seen her mother argue with her husbands about. But as she sat down and tried to really list what she and Jack needed to agree on, it was difficult. Money? What about money? They both had to spend it wisely, of course. What was there to discuss? She put in on the list anyway. Children? How many? What about discipline? That definitely goes on the list. She put the words "number" and "discipline" as subtopics under "children". But then she stopped. What else was there really? The things that her mom and stepfathers argued about were little things like doing the dishes and leaving the cap off the toothpaste and a hundred other little things. She couldn't put little things like that on the list. She looked up at the clock. An hour had passed and she had written four words.

She gave up and hid the list in her room before going back to the sofa and picking up the phone to call the doctor for her first prenatal visit, something she decided it was time to stop putting off. To her dismay, they had an opening for the next afternoon.

On Friday afternoon, Annie showed up to her appointment with the one and only ob-gyn in town. He was very young for a doctor, probably not much over thirty. He had come to town a few years ago, taking over the practice of the retiring ob-gyn. She had seen him a year ago, at her mother's insistence, for her first female examination. He had been very kind, talking to her in an unhurried way, about whether or not she was sexually active, birth control options if she should choose to become so, and the necessary breast exams and office visits she would need in order to check for cancer.

She walked into the waiting room with mixed emotions. While she certainly didn't want to be poked and prodded, she did want the confirmation from him that everything seemed to be fine. And she knew that she would find in him a comforting demeanor both now and as the pregnancy progressed. She signed in and sat down on a vinyl chair that squeaked loudly in the quiet room. There was only a middle-aged woman waiting, reading a trashy-looking paperback novel that seemed to Annie not to be the best choice of reading material in the gynecologist's office. Annie picked up a Parents magazine from a small table and turned the pages without reading it.

A very pregnant woman walked in holding the hand of a small blond girl, who in turn was holding the hand of a half-dressed plastic doll that hung from her grasp. The mother signed in and sat down slowly. The girl had a Kool-aid mustache and kept asking her Mom questions about where they were going next and what time it was and why some chairs were blue and some were orange. The mom answered her in a patient and low voice. Annie continued turning pages and wondered when the woman's baby was due, if she knew the sex, and if it was kicking right now.

She was called back. When told, she stepped on the scale, went in the bathroom and peed in a cup, and held out her arm for a blood pressure check. The nurse left her alone to put on the flimsy paper gown. Sitting on the edge of the examination table waiting for the doctor, she was suddenly afraid. What if the baby wasn't fine? What if there was a problem? More than anything she was afraid that he would tell her that she wasn't pregnant after all, that it was a virus, not a baby, which was causing her to be nauseous and tired.

The doctor knocked softly and then entered the room, breaking the spell of her fear with his presence. He was an overweight man with glasses. His voice was as soft as the rest of him. "Well, well, let's see here." He looked at the notes in a folder and asked her about the date of her last period and how she was feeling. Did she have an appetite? Were her breasts tender? How was her energy level? Was there a chance of sexually transmitted disease? Did she smoke or drink?

He leaned her back, called in the nurse, and began the physical examination. An urge to protect her baby overwhelmed her. Although she knew that his actions must be safe, she had to fight the urge to stop him from touching her. She wanted to protect the tiny being that she was now so constantly aware of carrying within her and his hands felt invasive and threatening.

When he was done he pulled off his gloves and took her arm, helping her to sit back up. He told her to get dressed and he would be back so that they could talk. She dressed and having her clothes on made her feel more protected. She sat in a chair near his rolling stool and waited just a moment before he knocked again and came in. He looked at her chart and then looked directly at her. "Well, well, everything seems to be just fine. Your symptoms and the size of your uterus match the date you've given for your last period. I think we can expect a baby about April 24th."

"April 24th," she repeated, relieved to hear a due date rather than the confirmation of the fears that she experienced a few moments earlier.

"Now, I see on your chart that you don't list any serious medical conditions. What about on the father's side?"

"I don't know about my father's side."

He smiled. "No, I mean the baby's father's side."

"Oh. I don't know."

"Do you plan on having the baby without him?"

"Yes."

"Do you think you could get a general medical background from him?"

"Maybe."

"Are you aware of all options available to you?"

"You mean abortion and adoption?"

"Yes."

"Right now I'm planning on keeping the baby, but I'm not real sure yet. Abortion's out but I'm still thinking about adoption." But she was thinking about it less and less.

His look was full of concern. "I know it's too late to lecture you about making sure to have a good father for your baby. But you and your baby need support. Even if you do decide to give the baby up for adoption, you'll still need support during the pregnancy. Having a baby isn't an easy thing. You have to take good care of yourself both physically and emotionally. Do you have someone to help you?"

"My mom." Of course, she wasn't about to tell him about some guy at the diner that had suddenly proposed. And it was true that her mother would be there to help her.

"And do you live with your mom?"

"Yes."

"That's good."

He wrote her a prescription for prenatal vitamins and ordered a routine blood test. He explained that she should see him about every six weeks until the end when he would want to see her more often.

She cried all the way home from the doctor's office. The tears were tears of relief that the visit was over. They were also tears of joy that she and the baby were fine. And they were also tears of sorrow that she had done this all wrong and that the baby's real father wasn't there to share it.

When she got home, she was surprised to find her mom already there. She was cooking supper, which was a rare event. Since there were just the two of them, they often ate something out of a can or, if finances allowed, went out to eat. But her mother was a good cook when she wanted to be and Annie found the smell of the sauce simmering on the stove to be appealing. She hadn't enjoyed the smell of food for what seemed like a very long time. It turned out that her mom had taken off work early to be home to greet her after her appointment and wanted to know what the doctor had said. Annie shared her due date and the fact that everything was fine.

After supper, they turned on the TV and Annie found her mind wondering back to what the doctor had said about getting the medical information from the father. She would need to do that. Then what? Would Jack need to legally adopt the baby? Did they need Eric's permission for that? She pulled the lime green paper from her drawer and at the bottom of her short list she wrote "Father". She frowned. What she needed to talk to Jack about was Eric and with each passing day he seemed less and less like the father of this baby. She crossed out "Father" and wrote next to it, "Eric".

Chapter 16

Jack

After Jack had unloaded his corn from the truck, the rain began to fall in big drops onto his windshield and the sky told him that the rain would continue for a while. He had heard the predictions on the radio yesterday, but he had stubbornly refused to contact Annie until he actually saw the rain falling. As he pulled away from the elevator and flipped on the windshield wipers, he decided that he would stop in for a cup of coffee and talk to her in person.

    He pulled the grain truck into the parking lot and parked it across several parking places that sat away from the diner, knowing that they would not be used this time of day. As he stepped down out of the truck, his mouth was suddenly dry from nervousness and he was aware of what he was wearing. He usually wouldn't have given a thought to his dusty canvas jacket, worn jeans, and work boots but now they seemed inadequate as he dashed through the rain from the truck to the diner door.

He hung his rain-speckled cap and jacket on the rack by the door and walked over to the counter. He was pleased to see that only Ralph and one other man that he didn't know sat at the counter. Annie wasn't in sight. "'Morning Ralph."

"'Morning Jack. Haven't seen you around for a while."

"Why, no. Dad's been cracking the whip, you know. Won't even let me stop for a cup of coffee unless it's raining." It was running joke among the group that Frank was the slave driver and Jack was the lazy servant. Such comments were often made by others and by Frank and Jack themselves. Everyone knew that it wasn't truly the case and if it had been, everyone would have been wise enough not to say a thing.

Annie came through the swinging doors from the kitchen, laughing, her head turned, sharing a joke with Maggie who stood just inside the kitchen. She looked like she was feeling well this morning. She turned to the counter and stopped for just a moment before greeting Jack in her customary warm manner.

"Well, look what the cat drug in. Good morning, Jack." The smile that he had watched disappear during September had returned.

"Good morning, Annie." His stomach was doing somersaults. "Got any coffee left?"

"I think I can scrape a little out of the bottom for you." Her eyes smiled at him, telling him that she was glad he was there. He was relieved. He had worried that the six days that he had waited for this rain might have been longer than she had in mind. But she didn't seem to be irritated with him in any way. He turned over his cup and she poured coffee into it and scooted a pitcher of cream over to him, knowing that he used it. He thought about the last time he had been in here and how she had let the cream run unto the floor. He could see her standing there with her mouth open and the empty pitcher still in her hand as clearly as if he were looking at a snapshot.

"You awake Jack?" Ralph's voice was as irritating as his very presence, which was keeping him from saying what he needed to say to Annie. "I asked what you made on the Turner field that looked so good in late summer."

"Oh, about 40."

"Not bad."

"We hoped for a little more but, no, it's not bad."

Annie was standing a few feet away, filling salt shakers on a tray the same way she had filled the pitchers, taking advantage of the light crowd to catch up on some work. He was hesitant to interrupt her. He blamed his jitteriness on the extra coffee this morning as he attempted to call her over to him. "Hey Annie." She looked up and put down the salt container to give him her attention.

"You need a refill?" She stayed where she was.

"Yes." She got the pot from the burner and walked over to him. She and he were both surprised to find that his cup was still full. She smiled and added a small amount to the cup without saying a word, filling it to the brim.

"Are you doing anything for supper tonight?" His words sounded more casual than they felt.

"I certainly hope so. Did you have something in mind?" How was it possible that she could be the cause of the inner chaos that he felt but yet at the same time be so reassuring?

Jack was very aware of Ralph listening to every word as he responded. "Would you like to have dinner at my house? I thought you might like to see where I live." Jack saw Annie glance at Ralph's face and he could tell that she wanted to laugh at the old man's reaction to this exchange. Her amusement put him at ease and any discomfort that he felt at speaking in front of Ralph changed to enjoyment.

"I'd love to," she replied. "Are you cooking?"

"I guess I am. It wouldn't be very nice to invite someone to dinner and ask them to bring the dinner, now would it?"

"What time did you have in mind?"

"Can I pick you up about five?"

"I can drive out." He knew she didn't know where "out" was, but appreciated the offer.

"I know, but it's a ways out and I don't mind. I'll need to come back to town to pick up a bucket of chicken anyway," he joked.

"It's a good thing I'm not coming over for the food then." He knew this flirtatious comment was solely for Ralph's benefit and played along.

"Maybe you can come over for dinner and we'll just skip the dinner." He resisted the urge to turn so that he could see Ralph's reaction to *that*.

She agreed to be picked up and gave him directions to her house. Jack left the customary dollar on the counter, leaving half his coffee in his cup. He patted Ralph on the shoulder and said "Well, see ya Ralph."

"See ya Jack. Now, don't do anything I wouldn't do." While this was a pretty standard method of saying farewell, Ralph's tone held the implication that he thought that Jack was probably about to do something that Ralph wouldn't do. Or, probably more accurately, would love to do if only he could.

He grabbed his hat and jacket and put them on against the cold rain that had gotten heavier since he had walked in. As he drove back home, his thoughts raced as fast as the windshield wipers. He chuckled to himself about Ralph and admired once again Annie's good-natured teasing of the man. Then he started thinking about the evening ahead and debating what to cook and what to wear and what to say. He tried to picture Annie and himself sitting at his table and having dinner together and it seemed too outrageous to even imagine. Besides a few unimportant times that his sisters had set him up with someone, he had never really dated. He hadn't expected it to be both so frightening and so thrilling.

Chapter 17

Annie

After work, Annie showered and changed, putting on a darkly flowered skirt not because it seemed appropriate but rather because all but the one pair of jeans were uncomfortably tight now, and that pair was in the laundry. She pulled on a brown sweater that helped to make the skirt seem more serious. She didn't know if she should treat this as a date or a business meeting. She decided it was probably more of the latter.

She left a note for her mom, who wouldn't be home from work until after five. The note said she was going over to a friend's house for dinner. Not a lie at all, but she knew her mom would ask for details when she got home, wanting to know who the friend was and what they ate and did. She would ask these things not because she was nosy or worried but because she and Annie tended to share their lives with one another in an easy and open way. She realized that she didn't want to share any news of Jack with her, at least not yet.

He pulled in at five o'clock promptly. He walked up to the door, a courtesy that Eric had never shown her. She wasn't accustomed to the climb up into the pick-up and felt clumsy and awkward as he held the door, waiting to close it until she had carefully gathered the folds of her skirt inside. As they drove out of town, she noticed from the safety of her side of the cab that, although the outside of the truck was still filthy in spite of the rain, the inside seemed to be recently cleaned. Her feet made two wet spots on the immaculate floor mat and there was a smell of some type of powdery air-freshener.

As they traveled out into the country, she saw the typical white two-story farm houses that dotted the flat land. Each sat in their own space surrounded by a yard that held some small outbuildings and fields. Occasionally, there was a newer, perhaps nicer house painted gray or made of brick that sat by itself all alone without even a barn to keep it company. Where the combines had already crossed the fields, the bean fields looked flat and empty but the corn stalks stuck up, looking sad and defeated as the rain soaked them. There were also fields that hadn't been harvested yet, where the ears of corn hung down, waiting to be grabbed by the header and stripped of their kernels. The row of telephone poles, helping to separate field from road, led the way. Their arms stretched out to hold the threads of wire against the gray sky.

The rain had slowed to a sprinkle and the windshield wipers swiped at the glass intermittently, matching the flow of their conversation. She asked how the harvest was going. He told a few things. He asked how she was feeling. She said not good, but better. For reasons that she couldn't explain, she didn't volunteer the fact that she had been to the doctor.

"Thanks for telling me about the soda cracker trick. It really does help." If they would have looked at one another, they each would have seen the other blush at the remembrance of that first personal interaction in the women's restroom.

When they had driven about fifteen minutes, he pointed to a farmhouse on the left. "That's where my folks live." The house and its surroundings were typical of the homes of the well-established farmers of the area. The house was larger than average and well-landscaped but it was the buildings and grain bins that defined the homestead, indicating that it was the home of someone who had accumulated a sizeable amount of land and equipment.

Jack pulled into the next house on the right, a modest ranch with white siding that sat in front of one equally modest outbuilding. He pulled out of the rain and into the attached garage saying, "Well, this is it." She wasn't sure what to say. His house seemed fine, perfectly acceptable, but nothing to which she could honestly say "Oh isn't it lovely!" So she said nothing.

Luckily, he quickly hopped out and showed up at her door before she could find the handle to open it herself. She hopped out unaided and he awkwardly stretched to open the door into the house for her, pressing himself against the doorframe so that she could get past him and enter the house first.

She stepped into the kitchen. To the left was a small table that was already set for supper and to the right was a u-shaped cooking area. One side of the U was a counter that divided the kitchen from the living area that she could see straight ahead, directly across from the doorway. The overwhelming colors of the house were gold, orange, and brown: colors that had been in style several decades ago. The furniture was mismatched and well-worn. But the house was tidy and had a comfortable feel. The smell of supper filled the air.

She was now able to say, "It's nice." She meant it sincerely and hoped her voice reflected her sincerity. It wasn't beautiful, well-decorated, or large, but it was nice in a homey kind of way.

"I haven't done much to it. I guess I don't care much for redecorating. Not when it's just me," he apologized.

"How long have you lived here?" Annie asked.

"I bought it off my grandparents about five years ago when they moved into town. They used to live where my dad lives, then they built this when he took over the farm about twenty years ago," he explained.

"Do you like living so close to your parents?"

"It works out well since I help farm and all. They have their faults, but they really are great. I guess you already know my dad. You'll like my mom, too."

"Something smells delicious," she said.

"I wasn't sure what you liked. I made a pot roast with some potatoes. It's ready whenever you are."

"Now's fine, if you'd like." They were still standing in the middle of the kitchen and it seemed awkward to remain where they were and equally awkward to move to someplace more comfortable. She hoped that the meal and the activities surrounding it might break the ice.

"Oh, I forgot. I picked up a few groceries in town. I'll go out and get them." He disappeared out of the door and into the garage.

While he was gone, she stood in the middle of the kitchen and looked at his fridge. There were snapshots of children held up by cheap magnets that sported names and phone numbers of seed corn dealers and hardware stores. A prayer card was held in place by a plastic clip. There was also a paper with torn edges on which he had written an address and phone number but there was no name to tell who it was for.

He came back in and she guiltily looked away from the display that she had been studying. "Can I help?"

"Will you microwave the corn?" He gestured to the glass bowl and the baggie of half-frozen corn on the counter.

As she did the task, she inquired, "Did you grow the corn?"

"Yep. That's my project. I grow a big patch out back and then when it's ready my sisters come over and we all put it up together. The kids help, too." He busied himself opening a jar of gravy and pulling the roast out of the oven. She helped put a few things on the table and they sat down to eat.

He dished up hers and then his and there was an awkward moment while each waited for the other to start. He looked down briefly and then made a fast gesture. She recognized it as a Catholic sign of the cross even though it looked more like he was waving a fly away from himself. He picked up his fork and they both began to eat.

As she ate the nourishing food, she found herself comparing the meal to the man who had put it in front of her. He wasn't fancy, or especially interesting. But he was wholesome and old-fashioned and predictable. There was a lot to be said for that. And a pot roast took a long time before it was ready. Yes, she thought, smiling to herself, if he were a food, he would definitely be a pot roast dinner. Unexpectedly, a picture of Eric came to her mind. He was sitting with the greasy burger and fries that had turned her stomach that day in the restaurant. Funny. Same ingredients but totally different - just like Jack and Eric were so different from one another.

She complimented him on the meal and he offered that the potatoes were from his mom's garden and that the roast was from a steer that they had raised to be butchered. "But I cheated on the gravy and rolls. I can't do either one of those. I can do dessert but I didn't. I figured that my time was better spent catching up on some housework that I got behind on since we've been in the fields. So I bought some ice cream instead."

After they were done, they both agreed to wait on the ice cream and she insisted on helping to clear the table. They made wide circles around each other as they worked.

When the kitchen was clean except for the roast pan soaking in the sink, they moved into the living room and she claimed one side of the couch, not sure of where he would sit or where she wanted him to sit. He sat down in a chair perpendicular to the couch, allowing them to face one another for the talk that they were about to have.

She was surprised when he was the one to begin, even if his beginning was really only an invitation for her to start. "So, have you come up with anything we need to talk about?"

"Do you want me to start?" she asked.

"It doesn't matter."

She took a deep breath. She skipped to the bottom of her list, needing to get the most difficult part over with. "I guess the first thing I want to talk about isn't really an issue about marriage in general. It's more about, well, I guess, just this marriage."

He encouraged her to go on with an "Okay."

"I've thought a lot about it and I've decided that I want to be honest about who the father is. I don't want to lie about anything and I don't want to keep anything a secret." She looked at his face for a reaction and all she saw was a pensive expression. "What do you think?" she prompted.

He thought for what seemed like a long time. "No one would believe the baby's mine anyway. No one that can put two and two together. Or count to nine. We weren't even dating last summer." He stopped. "You should know that I know who the father is." She couldn't hide her surprise at this. Although others would figure it out when they heard she was pregnant, she had assumed that a thirty-year-old farmer

Offerings

wouldn't know a thing about what went on among the younger town kids. "Elizabeth told me," he explained.

"You told her I was pregnant?" she asked incredulously.

"No, she doesn't know you're pregnant," he reassured. "But she told me you were running around with that Keaton kid this summer and so I figured that must be who it is."

"It is. Do you know 'the Keaton kid'?" She wondered if he considered her a kid, too.

"No, not really. I go in there to buy shoes like most other people in town so I know the family a little. I think it was Eric that sold me my last pair when he was working in there this summer." His words ended but she could tell that his thoughts didn't. She wondered when Jack had bought the shoes and if they had been seeing each other yet. She knew that Jack's thoughts were going in the same direction.

"I don't know if we were really 'running around'. We weren't serious. We just hung out and, well, I guess, we started fooling around a little and got carried away." She was looking down so he couldn't see the shame in her eyes. She had justified her behavior last summer by telling herself that everyone else did it. But that seemed like a poor excuse right now.

"I don't know if that makes it seem better or worse," he grimaced. "But that's over and I don't need to know any more about it."

She waited while he was quiet for a while, thinking. Finally he stated, "We'll need a lawyer. I hadn't thought about it until now. I'll want to legally adopt the baby. And I suppose a lawyer can help us draw up papers to define Eric's role in all this. I don't know what rights or obligations he has."

Things seemed very complicated and a having a lawyer sounded both intimidating and expensive. "I'm sorry," was all she could think to say.

"It's okay. We'll get it sorted out." But in spite of his words, his face now reflected the cloudy sky that was visible through the window.

She took a deep breath. "Well, that was the most important thing on my list. What about yours?"

"The first and only thing on my list is religion." This was something that hadn't even crossed her mind. "I'm Catholic and I want the baby to be, too." She slowly nodded her head up and down in agreement.

"That's fine."

He smiled weakly. "That was easy." He leaned forward in his chair and his eyes bore into her. "I mean I want the baby to go to Mass every Sunday and learn about God and say his prayers every night."

"That's fine. I don't know anything about being Catholic, or any other religion, as far as that goes, so you'll have to be in charge of that, but it's fine with me." She wouldn't understand until later what she was agreeing to. She had no way of knowing what Jack knew: that if they did it well, her "That's fine." would shape the child's whole life and identity. And, because she was the mother, it would influence her, too, in untold ways.

Moving down her list, they talked about "money" and "children" and they were pleased to find a lot of common ground with both subjects. They both had grown up knowing that money was something that needed to be worked for, saved, and spent wisely. He wanted a large family like the one in which he had grown up in and she wanted a large family like the one that she had always wanted but never had.

As they talked, several hours passed quickly. By ten o'clock they were both feeling the effects of a long day, magnified by, in her case, pregnancy, and, in his case, having gone to bed late and gotten up early. They both agreed to skip the ice cream that had been waiting for them in the freezer and they got in his truck and headed back to town.

Offerings

As they rode, it was Annie who asked the same question that she had in the park. "So now what?" The words bounced off the dark windows of the truck cab.

His answer surprised and scared her. "Will you come over on Sunday for supper with my family?"

Her first instinct was to say no. What they had been planning was too crazy to share with anyone yet. And she wasn't sure if she was ready for the commitment that would come with other people's knowledge of their relationship. "I don't know Jack. I'm not sure. What if we change our minds and decide not to do this?"

"We won't make any big announcements. It's just Sunday supper. No obligations. Lots of people come to supper at my parents' house and never come back again."

She laughed out loud and the seriousness which had hung over them all evening lifted. "You're making it sound real appealing!" His laughter joined hers, filling the dark space of the truck.

She agreed and they talked about the details. When they pulled into her drive, he opened her door for her and walked her to the door. He stood with his hands in the pockets of his jeans and said, "Well, I'll see you Sunday, then."

"See you Sunday." Did he want to kiss her? It seemed like he should. She thought about taking the initiative and kissing him on the cheek but he turned and hurried down the steps before she could decide whether or not to act on that thought.

As expected, her mom had lots of questions and she answered them honestly but didn't offer any information that wasn't requested.

Less than a half-hour later, she crawled between the sheets. Her body was exhausted but her mind ran in circles. She replayed their conversation and marveled at how easily they had agreed on so much.

Tina Williams

Her last thought was his laughter blending with hers in the darkness of the truck cab and she fell asleep smiling.

Chapter 18

Jack

The rain kept them out of the fields through the next morning. Instead of going to the diner for his coffee, he drove down to his parents' house. He wanted to tell them that he had invited Annie over on Sunday while he still had the nerve.

When he walked in, his mom was just coming out of the bathroom. Her hair was damp and she smelled like some type of flowery powder or lotion. "Well, hi Jack. You want some breakfast?"

"Sure."

Without asking, she put two slices of bread into the toaster. "So what brings you down here? I thought you might be enjoying your morning off."

"Oh, I wanted to talk with Dad about a few things," Jack lied.

"He went to town for some coffee." Jack had already figured as much when he had seen that his side of the garage was vacant.

"Mind if I hang around until he gets back?"

"Not at all. I think Kate's coming over with the kids to help can some applesauce, but it takes her a while to get around so I don't know what time she'll make it."

This was a good lead-in to a topic that always provided lots of conversation, especially when talking to Meg. Jack asked about his new niece and then they talked about the other grandkids for a while, how the older ones were getting along in school this fall and how the younger ones were singing the ABC's or counting to 10.

When the topic had been exhausted and the toast had been buttered, served, and eaten, Jack finally asked, "You mind if I bring someone over for Sunday supper?"

His mom's face lit up with hope and he cringed. He didn't feel like what was going on between he and Annie deserved such a look.

"Of course I don't mind. You know that. So who is she?"

"How do you know it's a girl? Maybe it's just a friend of mine." It wasn't uncommon for him or his sisters to invite a friend to be a part of their Sunday evening ritual.

"I can tell by the way you were all nervous when you asked."

"Okay, it's a girl."

"Girlfriend?"

What was the answer to that? "I guess we haven't really established that yet. We've gone out a couple of times, though." He was satisfied with that answer but when he thought about it, he realized that she wasn't his girlfriend at all but they were almost engaged.

"I was hoping that you might start dating one of these days."

"I know, Mom. You've mentioned it just a few times over the years." He tried to joke with her but his voice held a trace of bitterness.

"Well I just want you to be happy." He knew that to be true. What mother doesn't want her son to be happy? But she had never understood his uncertainties about the direction of his life and his need, until now, to leave his options open.

"I'm happy, Mom." He didn't want Annie to feel as pushed as he did, so he warned her. "Look, Mom, just please don't embarrass me on Sunday. We're just starting to date. Don't talk about wedding rings or spend a lot of time telling her what a great husband I'll be."

"But you *will* be a great husband."

"Mom!"

"Alright, I'll be good," she promised. And at that, the topic was dropped for the moment.

At odd times during the rest of the week, though, she would radio Jack while he was working and ask if his "friend" liked chicken or beef better or if she might prefer cherry pie over apple pie. Through the radio she couldn't see Jack roll his eyes before he started teasing her with comments like "She's vegetarian." or "She's from Pakistan; I don't think they have pie there, so I don't know."

At home alone that week, in the rare moments when he had time to sit in his chair and wind down from a long day, he remembered Annie sitting across from him on the couch, wearing her brown sweater with her hair hanging loose in the back.

He imagined what it would be like to have her at his parents' house on Sunday and decided that he was looking forward to it. His mom wasn't the only one who had been wondering when or if he would find a girlfriend. His sisters, also, had been encouraging him to find someone, often offering to set him up with someone they knew. He understood that they were just trying to help him to find the completeness that they had found in their spouses and children. But he knew better than to allow himself to be rushed into anything, so he had resisted their efforts, only rarely agreeing to be set up on a blind date and never following up for a second date. But now he was anticipating the moment when he would show them that he was finally taking their advice and that he was capable of finding someone without their help.

Chapter 19

Annie

As they had agreed, Annie drove herself out to his parents' farm at about five o'clock on Sunday. She pulled in the drive and was relieved to see his truck there. She walked up the concrete steps to the side door and rang the doorbell. Through the sliding glass door, she saw a boy, about 8, run full-speed towards the door, stopping himself almost, but not quite, in time to avoid running into the glass. He opened the door for her, giving her a panicked look before he turned his head and yelled, "Grandma, someone's here!" His cheeks were rosy, his hair was messed up, and the sleeves of his white turtleneck were pushed up past his elbows, an obvious attempt to make himself cooler.

She looked past him into a large family room. It was simply decorated in muted shades of blue and beige. A few toys were strewn about and Annie noticed a boy-sized sweater that had been thrown over the back of one of the two sofas as well as three pairs of boys' shoes in varying sizes beside the door.

A woman appeared from around the corner, drying her hands on a dish towel. "Curtis, for heaven's sake! Mind your manners. Invite the lady in out of the cold." It was easy to tell that her harshness went no further than her words. She looked at Annie and smiled warmly and gestured her into the house. "You must be Jack's friend. He told me you would be coming." She looked back at Curtis. "You need to stop running around. Why don't you take her coat for her? Go throw it on my bed with the others. Then go upstairs in the drawer where I keep extra clothes for you boys and see if there's a t-shirt that fits you."

He took off with her coat, dragging the corner of it on the carpet. He was running in spite of his grandmother's orders. Meg turned back to Annie. Skipping any introductions, she said, "Jack's in the shop with Frank. I've been babysitting Sarah's boys since church this morning. She went to a baby shower and Tim was busy this afternoon so I said I could keep the boys, but they're both coming for supper. Mary and David won't be here this week but Kate said that she and John would be here after the baby wakes up and she feeds her. Elizabeth's running around with her girlfriends but she'll be here too."

Annie tried to pull out names from the whirl of words. Annie knew Elizabeth from school. She had heard Kate's name at the diner and knew her to be Christopher's mother. She realized that until now she hadn't even known the names of the other two sisters. The men's names were obviously their husbands. "The boys have kept me hopping this afternoon. I'm a little behind for supper. Could you peel these carrots?"

Being given a task made Annie feel at ease. She suspected that Jack's mom knew it would. She immediately liked Meg, who was so different from her own mother. While her own mother seemed to be fighting a constant war with the aging process, this woman seemed to welcome it, or at least accept it. Unlike her mother's bleached blond hairstyle, Meg's hair wasn't completely gray but well on its way and there seemed to be no attempt to hide it. She was slightly overweight but not much, just enough to make her appear pleasantly soft. She wore a sweatshirt and blue jeans, both which fit her loosely and comfortably.

While Annie peeled the carrots, Meg ran around, taking things out of and putting things into the oven, as well as refereeing an argument between Curtis and one of his younger brothers, who had appeared from another room. When she was done with the carrots, Meg asked, "Could you go down the basement and get a jar of pickles? I would send the boys but I don't think they can reach. The door's right there." She indicated a door in the corner of the kitchen.

Annie found the light switch at the top of the stairway and descended the wooden steps into the basement. In spite of the bare light bulb attached to a beam overhead, it was dim and smelled musty. Cobwebs hung from the floor joists above her head. Piles of old Farm Journals sat on the floor, tied into bundles with twine. Shelves of canning jars filled one entire wall and her eyes moved across the jars that showed their contents in a beautiful mixture of colors: green beans, red beets, orange carrots, yellow corn, green pickles. Green pickles. She looked at the pickles that were, indeed, on a high shelf. There were two kinds, one light and one dark. She decided to bring up one of each.

By the time she came back up, Jack was standing in the kitchen and Annie was relieved that he would be present when the sisters started arriving. He smiled at her. "You found Mom's stash, huh? She's got a contract with the government to feed the army this winter." Although he was speaking to Annie, this was obviously intended for Meg's ears.

"Your shelves are beautiful," Annie said supportively as she handed Meg the two jars of pickles.

Meg was obviously pleased to have an ally in the ongoing battle that raged over her excessive canning. "Thank you, Annie," she replied, looking smugly at her son as if to say, "See; there are people who appreciate my handiwork."

The back door into the kitchen opened suddenly and a young woman walked in, placing an infant car seat covered in blankets on the kitchen table. Behind her were her husband and Christopher. Chaos ensued. All three of the boys that had been playing in another room came running to see their cousins. Meg stopped her supper preparations and came rushing over to uncover the baby and remark on her incredible growth over the past week. Jack took coats. In the midst of it all, four-year-old Christopher looked up at Annie, put his hands on his hips, and said "Annie! What the heck are you doing here?"

The grown-ups burst into laughter. Christopher's mother contained hers enough to say, "Christopher, that's very rude." But she looked equally puzzled for a moment, trying to figure out how her young son knew someone that she didn't.

Jack jumped in, introducing her by explaining, "This is Annie. Christopher knows her from the diner. She makes pretty good coffee, doesn't she, Christopher?" He put his hand on her shoulder and she realized that it was the first time that he had ever touched her.

Christopher was pleased to play the game again. "Yep. She makes great coffee."

The older two cousins looked at each other and said at the same time, "Coffee, yuck!"

As if that were a code phrase, all four boys simultaneously went running into the other room, leaving a calmer atmosphere in the kitchen. Now it was Jack's turn to admire his godchild. "Jeez, sis, what have you been feeding the kid? She's growing like a weed."

"A box of Wheaties every day," Kate said in reply.

Annie stood back and watched the baby as she lay in her seat. Kimberly, now six weeks old, stretched out her arms and opened her mouth in a yawn, observing with apparent disinterest the faces looking down at her. At the sight of this perfect, precious child, any lingering thoughts of adoption were forgotten and Annie let herself anticipate the time when the child growing inside her would be looking up at her the way that this baby was.

The door opened again and Frank appeared, taking off his dusty cap and laying it on the table next to the car seat. Annie noticed that Meg silently picked it up and took it into the adjacent laundry room. He stopped when he saw Annie, and proclaimed in a booming voice, "Annie. What in the heck are you doing here?" This echo of his grandson's earlier question had all the grown-ups doubled over with laughter.

Meg was the one to reply this time, "Annie is Jack's friend." The word "friend" was said with great emphasis and Annie wondered just what she meant by that.

"Is that so?" Frank was obviously pleased and surprised. It looked like he might have something more to say on the subject but, luckily, he was interrupted when the door opened again.

Sarah and Tim walked in, holding hands and smiling. John recognized the look and said, "Looks like you two took advantage of your empty house and squeezed in a little time for a nap this afternoon."

Sarah blushed and Tim grinned, "We do have a license for that sort of thing, you know."

Sarah asked Meg how the boys had been and then she and her husband took their turn inspecting the baby. The door opened again and Elizabeth walked in. She immediately saw Annie, rushed toward her, and hugged her. "Annie! It's great to see you!" Her greeting could have been considered to be overdone, given the fact that they had never been close in high school. But Annie knew her well enough to know that she was naturally exuberant and that the greeting was sincere. Elizabeth continued, "Jack said he was thinking about asking you out. I'm so glad he did!" Annie threw Jack a questioning look.

Everyone that was expected was now present and all the food was set out on the counter, thanks to Meg's continued moving of dishes. The children were called back into the kitchen and the family automatically gathered for the prayer. They all made the sign of the cross and bowed their heads. Meg gave thanks for the safe harvest so far and asked for the continued blessings on the harvest and the family. She also prayed for Mary and David and their kids, who weren't able to join them tonight. Then, as a group, they mumbled a prayer together and closed with another sign of the cross. Not being sure what to do, Annie didn't bow her head in prayer but rather observed the group around her. She saw with great clarity the beauty of this family gathered together for a meal. But she felt so far removed that she might as well have been outside in the cold peering in through the window.

After the prayer, they filled their plates and gradually sat down to eat, the kids in the kitchen and the adults in the dining room. Annie noticed how Elizabeth and Jack took a role equal with the parents in helping with the kids, being sure that everyone had what they needed to eat and drink before they took their seats, one on each side of her. The meal was simple but delicious.

As they ate, Jack coached her on the names of those present and told her about Mary and David, explaining that they had a birthday party on David's side tonight. They had three kids, two boys and a girl. As he talked, Elizabeth listened and interjected warnings about the mentioned family members in her animated style. "Don't even try to talk to Tim during a Bengal's game." and "Do NOT ask Mary about her job, whatever you do." and "Michael's getting better; he only bites once in a while now." Although they were talking about the people that were sitting with them around the table, something that Annie would normally regard as a rude thing to do, there was nothing impolite about their conversation, even Elizabeth's comments. They made no attempt to either lower their voices for discretion's sake or to raise them so that others would be sure to hear. There was a sense of peace that permeated the house, helping to ease Annie's nervousness.

Eventually the conversation expanded, and the others at the table began to talk to Annie, too.

"If you want to hear how Jack used to torture us when we were little, I'd be happy to fill you in on the details." This from Kate.

"I worked at that diner one summer before I got married." This from Sarah. "Leo had this guy named Nick helping to manage the place. I couldn't stand him, so I quit. He's not there anymore is he?"

"I have a new fish named Fin." This from 6-year-old Sam who, like the other kids, had finished before the adults and was wandering around the house, occasionally entering the circle of grownups with a comment, request, or complaint.

Just when Annie was wondering how long they could sit, Kate stood up, initiating the clean-up. The sisters were in charge of this and before Annie could wonder long about her place in the procedure, Meg handed her a soapy dish rag and asked if she would wipe off the tables.

Everyone left soon afterwards, with comments about school, work, and, in Elizabeth's case, the drive back to college yet that night. After Jack had held her coat for her and Annie had again thanked them for the supper and complimented Meg's cooking, she and Jack walked together out into the cold night air.

"Yes." Her single word came out in a cloud of breath, disappearing into the night.

She had no way of knowing that his heart stopped along with his footsteps. He turned to her. "Are you sure?"

"Yes." She said it a third time. "Yes."

They looked at each other, their faces illuminated by the glow of the security light that was mounted on the barn nearby. They both knew that after an acceptance of a marriage proposal, a passionate kiss should follow. Words seemed to Annie to be an effective way to avoid this.

"This is what I want. I want my baby to be a part of this. All of this. This will be the baby's Grandma and Grandpa and aunts and uncles and cousins. You're so lucky to have such a great family, Jack."

Jack looked down at his feet and pushed the gravel around a little with the toe of his shoe, making a mark, then making it deeper. "But you're not marrying them. You're marrying me. Do you want me?"

"Yes." She met his gaze when he looked up at her. "So now what?" It was her question once again. Once again he had an answer.

"Well, we need to tell our parents and, I guess, we need to set a date for the wedding." A date for the wedding. These were words that should have caused a nineteen-year-old girl to begin dreaming about gowns and flowers but they only brought a sense of dread to Annie. During the previous week, when she had considered agreeing to Jack's marriage proposal, she had also considered what kind of wedding they might have. She pictured herself standing at an altar with a protruding stomach and white dress that she didn't deserve trying to pretend that she was in love with the very nice man that stood before her.

"I don't want a big wedding. I mean, not that you were suggesting one, but I don't want any wedding, really, just whatever we have to do to make it official."

"I don't need a big wedding either, but take some time to think about it, Annie. You only get married once." Annie immediately recalled her mother's three weddings, and was very much aware that many people did, indeed, have several weddings in their lifetime. But she didn't argue the point.

"Okay. I'll think about it, but I know I want to keep it very, very simple."

"I want it performed by a priest."

"That's fine."

They both looked down at the stones now.

"Can I take you out this week so we can talk about it more?" Jack asked.

"You mean to a restaurant?"

"Sure."

They decided on Friday and that he would pick her up at her house. And then, without any sort of physical contact to seal their new engagement, they got in their vehicles and drove away.

When she got home, a car was parked in the driveway. She recognized it as belonging to the man her mother had been seeing. She let herself into the house to find the lights on but the living room and the kitchen deserted. She wasn't surprised to find her mother's door closed. Although it was still early, Annie quietly got ready for bed and lay down in the darkness, wide awake. She had been in this situation before but this time she didn't turn on the radio to drown out any sounds that might carry into her room. Instead, she listened to the soft voices and laughter drifting into her room from across the hall.

Tears slid from her eyes, making a small stream down the sides of her temples and into her ears. She was nineteen, pregnant, and now engaged to be married and she didn't have any idea of what it was like to be truly intimate with a man.

Chapter 20

Jack

The new week brought with it new thoughts for Jack as he and his dad resumed the process of filling and emptying combine hoppers, truck beds, and grain bins with the golden kernels of corn, separated from their reddish cobs by the corn header. In Jack's mind, the routine of the harvest contrasted with the newness of the plans that he and Annie had made. The result was a constant, drastic leap in his thoughts from the harvest to Annie and back again.

To add to Jack's unrest, Frank was now pestering him. All fall, Frank had thought that the only thing that would make a man as absentminded as Jack had been lately would be a woman. Now that Annie had been Jack's guest for supper, his suspicions were confirmed and the comments began. Jack knew that his dad loved to be on the giving end of a good-natured ribbing, so this was not unexpected. Frank began teasing Jack about his "cup of coffee", giving the phrase a sexual innuendo. Jack had learned from years of experience that his father wasn't going to let up anytime soon, so he began to play along, dishing out some good-natured teasing in return.

Frank would say, "My golly, boy, you're thinking about something else again. Maybe you need to go to town and get yourself a 'cup of coffee'".

"Yeah, a cup of coffee sounds real good. Have you had one yet today?" Jack would reply.

"Come to think of it, I haven't had myself a decent cup of coffee since harvest began." Frank's eyes would sparkle, enjoying the joke.

One day, when Frank was in a particularly foul mood, Jack's mom radioed to see if they needed anything and Jack radioed back from the combine, knowing that it was an inside joke that his mom wouldn't get. "Yeah, Mom, I think Dad needs a nice warm cup of coffee to improve his mood."

Frank, who was heading back from town with the empty truck, joined in the conversation through his end of the radio. "You know, he's right, dear. I'm headed home right now. I think I'll come in and get some."

Jack grinned. His mom would be surprised, but not too surprised, when the fresh pot of coffee that she was probably already making went untouched. His parents had a great marriage, which still included an active sex life that wasn't vanishing as they aged. On the contrary, Elizabeth's departure from the house a little over a year ago seemed to have sparked a renewed interest in that aspect of their marriage. He and his sisters had all noticed the way that they had been flirting with each other the past year.

Since Jack worked closely with Frank, there were a few times when Jack knew for certain that they were taking advantage of their empty nest. Once when Jack had planned to come over for an afternoon of working on the farm software, his dad had called and told him not to. When asked why, Frank said, "Well, um, your mother wants to take a nap," after which he heard a not-too-loud slap and Frank's wheezy laughter as he hung up the phone. Another time he had stopped in unexpectedly to talk to Frank. He was surprised when the truck and car were both there and the lights were on but no one was around. Realizing what was likely going on, he quickly retreated to his truck and went home.

    Jack wondered how things would be between him and Annie. The kind of relationship that his parents shared seemed to be light years away from where he and Annie were now. He understood that the easy way his parents got along hadn't happened overnight nor was it always as easy as it seemed. Even now, after all the years that his parents had spent learning to live with one another, they had trouble seeing eye to eye on some things. It was comforting to know that he and Annie didn't have to have things worked out perfectly right now. Marriage was a skill they would learn over time and a journey that they would travel together.

    It rained again on Wednesday, so he went to town to shop for a ring. Nothing had been said between them about a ring but, of course, she would need one. He had debated on whether to drive the forty-five minutes to the nearest mall to shop anonymously at a jewelry store there. But he knew from his rare trips to the bigger town that the jewelry stores there all looked too upscale. He decided that he was more comfortable at the local jewelry store. The rumors would be flying soon enough, so he might as well start the speculation.

    He parked his truck on the main street in downtown, directly in front of the store. He had bought his class ring here how many years ago? It must be about fifteen by now. Although he had certainly had no occasion to buy jewelry for himself since then, or for any girlfriends, he had been in several times over the years, running his sisters in to order their class rings or picking up a repaired piece of jewelry for his mom.

Offerings

The bells that hung on the door jingled as he walked in. The building was at least a hundred years old. Constant updates kept the atmosphere pleasant and the squeaky and sagging floors, plaster walls, and high ceilings were all part of what Jack liked about shopping downtown instead of in the newer stores that had popped up on the edges of town.

Mrs. Heister was spraying the showcases with Windex when he walked in and she looked up at him over her half glasses and gave him a half smile. "Good afternoon. Let's see, I'm trying to place you…"

Jack wasn't surprised by this. The downtown merchants were first concerned with who you were and only when they had this figured out could they effectively help you with what you needed to purchase. "I'm Jack Schroeder, Meg Schroeder's boy." Frank was the more common reference that Jack used and, although it was needed less and less as his age gradually made him an established member of the community, he still introduced himself as "Frank Schroeder's boy" occasionally at some of the places around town. But here in the jewelry store, his mom's name seemed to be the more appropriate.

"Oh, yes. A Schroeder boy!" Her face darkened just a moment before she began to conduct business. "How can I help you?"

"I'm looking for an engagement ring." He was proud of how smoothly the words flowed from his mouth, like he said them everyday.

"Oh, my, how lovely!" She looked over his shoulder and said the words as though his romance was an imaginary portrait hanging somewhere behind him. Her manner was as shiny but as transparent as the glass counter that she stood in front of as she asked the inevitable question, hoping for a piece of juicy gossip. "Who's the lucky lady?"

"She's not from around here." This was a lie but, other than telling Annie's name, which he wasn't ready to do, he knew of no other effective way to drop the matter.

Her smile drooped just a little. She was obviously disappointed, but tried to hide it. "Will she be helping you choose the ring?"

"No. I'd like to surprise her."

"All right. Then let me show you our selection." She cheerfully walked around the counter and began unlocking the display case.

For an hour, the woman explained to him the details of settings and bands and recommended various rings. She was delighted when he told her that money wasn't a concern but then was puzzled when he gravitated towards the smaller diamonds. He didn't want something flashy and was sure that Annie wouldn't either. In the end, he chose a modest ring that was neither too large nor too small, he hoped. Several small diamonds were embedded in the band on either side of the center diamond and there was a matching wedding band that also had embedded diamonds.

She let him take the ring engagement with him but explained that the "lucky lady" would need to bring it in for sizing after he had given it to her. He wrote a check for the entire amount, put the receipt in his jeans pocket and refused a bag so that he could stick the ring case deep into the inside pocket of the coat that he wore.

He walked out onto the sidewalk and on a whim he walked past his truck and jaywalked across the street to Keaton's Shoe Store. Over the years, he had frequented the shoe store more than the jewelry store, so Mrs. Keaton, who worked part time at the register, greeted him by name when he entered.

"Hello, Jack. Do you need a new pair of shoes?" Although, like most of the business people in town, she was known to be somewhat of a busybody around town, she had genuine warmth about her. Because of the callousness of her son, Jack wanted to be angry at the whole family but her friendly smile kept that from happening. It was easy to picture her directing that same smile to a grandbaby and he was sorry that her son's decision wasn't going to allow her to be a grandmother to Annie's baby.

Because of his thoughts, he was just a little late in answering her question, but she didn't seem to notice. "Yep. I think it's about time to start thinking about a new pair of work boots." He didn't need a new pair just yet but he could always stick them in the closet for next year. He had bought tennis shoes in the summer and was wearing them now, so he couldn't say he needed a pair of those, and he rarely wore anything besides these two types, except to church.

"I think we can set you up." He told her the brand and size that he always wore and she disappeared behind the same brown curtain that had hidden the store room since his mom used to bring him in for gym shoes. She returned with a brown box and began to push buttons on the cash register. "Is there anything else?"

"No, I don't think so. How are you today?" The question was out of its normal place immediately following a greeting but she seemed glad to be asked.

"I'm great, thanks. We're having a lovely fall this year, aren't we?"

"Can't complain at all." He took the bag that she handed him and stuck his receipt in his pocket with the other one.

"Thank you and tell your mom and dad hello." His parents weren't friends of the Keatons but they were good customers, which was a close second.

"I will." He actually probably wouldn't bother but they both knew that the request and the agreement were just a matter of politeness. He walked out, not knowing what had made him go in, but feeling a little more connected to the baby than he had before.

When he arrived home, he carefully took off his coat and hung it over the back of the kitchen chair that Annie had used when she had come over for supper. He was very much aware of its precious contents, nestled deep in the pocket. He carried the shoes to his bedroom and put the box in his side of the closet. Then he opened the sliding door on the empty side and looked at the metal bar and the empty shelves waiting to be filled. He caught his breath, suddenly gripped by a feeling of intense anticipation.

He slid the door shut, lifting it up as he did so. When he moved in, he had chosen the other side because this side tended to slide off its track. Until now, he hadn't had a reason to fix it, but he would have to do that soon.

As he walked across the room to the doorway, he realized something else would need to be done before their wedding: he would have to get a bigger bed. His twin bed wasn't big enough to share. He stopped and looked at the little bed and his breath came out in short puffs. He was both nervous and excited as he thought about sharing a bed with a woman for the first time in his life. He flopped down on the narrow bed and looked up at the swirled ceiling. He closed his eyes and reached his arm out, his hand moving through the air past the edge of the bed. He let himself look forward to the time when he would no longer reach out into the emptiness but rather would reach out and touch his wife, the flesh of his flesh.

Chapter 21

Annie

Annie and Jack had decided that he would pick her up at 5:30 on Friday, giving her mom time to arrive home from work so that she could meet Jack. Annie didn't want to announce the engagement just yet, wanting to introduce Jack just as a boyfriend before she sprung the rest of the news, and Jack agreed.

Thursday night Annie asked her mom about her plans after work the next day. Cindy confirmed that she planned to come right home. Annie explained that a man, the same man to whose house she had gone for supper, was coming over to pick her up for a date and that she wanted her to meet him. Annie was prepared for her mother's questions but her own emotional reaction was a surprise.

"Annie, does he know you're pregnant?"

"Yes, mom."

"How'd you meet him?"

"He comes into the diner."

"The diner! You always say it's only a bunch of old farmers in there."

"Well, he's the youngest old farmer."

"A farmer, Annie? What in the world do you want with a farmer?"

"I guess the same thing he wants with an impregnated waitress." After that brief exchange, she stomped out of the room, something that she hadn't done to her mother in the last few years; not since her teenage rebellion had subsided. Her mother's skepticism about Jack stirred up her own doubts and, at the same time, her guilt made her want to argue that, given the circumstances, she was lucky that anyone would want her.

On Friday, she dressed in the same skirt that she had worn to his house just a week and a half ago. Her shrinking wardrobe caused by her expanding waistline was becoming an increasing problem but she wasn't about to make the leap to maternity clothes yet. She dug through her mom's closet for a different shirt than she had worn with the skirt before and found a bright turquoise blouse that seemed more elegant and, more importantly, hung down to hide the rise of her abdomen. Although she usually didn't bother with make-up, she decided to apply a light amount of lipstick and blush and she let her hair hang loose, curling the ends under in a soft, flowing style.

Her mother arrived home at 5:15 as she usually did. They hadn't spoken since Annie had shut herself into her room the night before. As Annie had come to expect, Cindy was the first to make an effort to smooth things over. Cindy would be the first to admit that she needed the love and support of her daughter more than her daughter needed her love and support. Their arguments, few though they were, always weighed on her and she did whatever it took to set things right between them. There were times when Annie was growing up that she had used this to her advantage, asking for a new CD or permission to stay up late, knowing that her mother would give her anything in order to get back on Annie's good side. Cindy was fortunate to have a daughter that stopped at small requests because they both knew that larger requests would also have been granted.

But Annie's recent maturity made demands and bribes unnecessary these days. Cindy's apology instantly restored the friendship between mother and daughter. To Annie's surprise, her mother also complimented her appearance, which was a rarity due to their different styles. Years ago, they had agreed to disagree on topics such as make-up, skirt length, and cleavage. Although such disagreements were common between mothers and teenage daughters, their debate was uncommon in that Cindy was always urging Annie to dress less conservatively. Cindy's motto wasn't exactly "If ya got it, flaunt it." but perhaps rather "If ya got it, attractively display it."

Jack rang the doorbell and Annie opened the door, inviting Jack to step in. It was obvious that Jack, also, had spent some time preparing for the evening. He was wearing freshly-pressed navy slacks and a white shirt and a tie. The smell of cologne came in with him.

This was the first time that Jack had been inside Annie's house. Jack looked around the room. She knew that he was contrasting their home with his. Even though their house was older and smaller than his, the womanly touch was obvious. The furniture matched and was color-coordinated with the carpet and drapes. A floral painting hung over the couch with brass sconces on each side. A silk vase with flowers sat in the middle of the coffee table.

Annie handled the introductions. "Jack, this is my mom, Cindy. Mom, this is my date, Jake."

They shook hands and Annie was delighted with Jack's air of confidence as he said, "Pleased to meet you Mrs. Norton."

Cindy laughed and said, "That was several husbands ago. My last name's Kraft now. But just call me Cindy."

He smiled shyly. She had told him the day in the park that her mom had been married several times and Annie knew he was embarrassed by the slip-up but he hid it well. "Cindy it is."

Cindy was a little too quick with the next line, making Annie wonder about her mom's plans for the evening. "When do you think you'll be back?"

"We won't be late. We've both had a busy day and Annie needs her rest."

With that, Cindy ushered them out the door and they climbed into his pickup that still had beads of water on it from the car wash.

As he backed onto the street and headed away from the house, he glanced over to her and said, "You look beautiful."

The sensation in her stomach had nothing to do with morning sickness and she replied, "And you look handsome."

Looking at his profile, she saw the corner of his mouth lift in a satisfied grin before he asked, "How was your week?"

She told him about it, glad to be talking to him casually. Throughout the past year when she had poured his coffee, they had often talked casually, but briefly, about such things as the weather or current events. But since the morning in the restroom, each word between them had been measured and judged. Their conversations had been exhausting in their intensity but now the words were light and easy. She told him about who had been in the diner lately and a few things about her evenings, although there wasn't much to say about them. He listened attentively, keeping his eyes on the road and adding a comment or a chuckle.

She, in turn, asked about his week and he told her about finishing a field and moving to the next and about equipment and grain prices and bushels per acre. He took into account her lack of knowledge by speaking in generalities at times and explaining things at other times. He was pleased when she asked a few questions, eager to understand everything that he told her.

By the time that he had finished talking, they had passed the mall that Jack had shunned a few days earlier and pulled into the parking lot of the restaurant. It was a fairly expensive restaurant known for its pasta, seafood, and romantic atmosphere.

Annie was pleased to be there and commented, "Wow, good thing I dressed up a little. I've heard that this is a really nice place."

"John took Kate here for their last anniversary. They liked it. Well, no, she liked it. John said that he didn't know what half the stuff on the menu was and they put weird things in his salad. So I thought it must be pretty nice."

Jack told the woman at the hostess station the name and time of the reservation and she showed them to a small table by the window. The table was covered with a table cloth and a lit tea light was floating in a glass globe half filled with water. A shade filtered the sun that was beginning to set outside and the lights of the restaurant were dim, giving the dining room a relaxed atmosphere. There was ample space between tables and soft music was playing so that the only voices they heard were those of each other.

They studied and discussed the menu and Annie waited until they had ordered before she said, "I went to the doctor a few weeks ago." She felt guilty about not bringing it up earlier and was glad when Jack didn't seem to mind that she hadn't told him sooner.

Jack was immediately inquisitive. "Is everything okay?"

"Everything's fine. He gave me a due date. April 24th."

Jack laughed and quickly explained, "Right during planting. My parents have an ongoing joke. My dad says that my mom always insisted on having her babies during planting or harvest. My mom always replies that he should have thought of that nine months before planting or harvest." Then he assured her, "Don't worry. I won't complain - as long as you have it on a rainy day." His eyes teased her and she felt her eyes sparkling back.

"I'll see what I can do."

"Did the doctor say anything else?"

"No, not really. He gave me a prescription for some vitamins that I've started taking. I bought a book about pregnancy and I've been reading that. It's been really helpful." She paused. "Jack." Saying his name to get his full attention was unnecessary but she did it nonetheless. He looked worried at the seriousness of the way she spoke his name.

She continued, needing to tell someone about what she had felt in the doctor's office and surprised to find herself telling him. "I was scared when I went to the doctor's office. You know what I was scared of?"

He briefly imagined a few of the possible things that a pregnant woman seeing a doctor might be scared of and was sure there were others of which he had no clue. "No. What?"

"I was scared that he would tell me I wasn't pregnant after all. That there wasn't a baby." She felt tears come to her eyes but held them back. "I was so happy when he told me that I really was pregnant." She smiled apologetically at him. "Isn't that crazy?"

He smiled back at her, a smile that was comforting and understanding. He wanted so much to reach out and take one of her hands but they were tucked away safely in her lap. "That's not crazy. That's God telling you that it's good." Suddenly there was a tension between them.

Their food came and as they ate, they began to discuss the wedding. Jack would call Father Bill to arrange a meeting and to, hopefully, reserve the church. They decided, because of increasingly obvious reasons that, with Father's permission, the wedding should be soon and that mid-November would be ideal. That would give them a month to plan. Annie was quick to restate her desire for a very simple wedding, so a month would be plenty. Annie would be four months pregnant by then but, hopefully, a loose-fitting gown would help to make her pregnancy less noticeable. They both agreed that it was useless to hide anything but it would be nice if it wasn't so obvious.

They also decided that they would announce the wedding to their parents and to Jack's sisters after a date had been set with Father Bill. They talked about who else should know and be invited and they added grandparents to the guest list and decided to limit the guests to these close relatives only.

They discussed the maid of honor and the best man and they were both undecided. Annie had had a number of good friends in high school, but they had gone off to college after graduation, reappeared during the summer and then deserted her again. They rarely found time in their busy schedules to call or drop in on weekends, even when they were home. Jack friends had, one by one, gotten married and were busy with their own families so he, too, had little contact with friends lately. In his case, his large family filled this void well, but left him with few options for best man.

After the waiter had cleared their plates, he blurted out, "I bought you something."

Her eyes widened in surprise and then her mouth dropped in astonishment as he produced the small gray case. He offered it to her unopened. She took it and lifted the lid slowly. Tears filled her eyes and this time spilled down her cheeks. "Oh, Jack. You didn't have to do this. I wasn't expecting this." In truth, she hadn't even thought about a ring. "Is it okay? I don't know much about jewelry."

"It's perfect."

"If you don't like-"

"It's perfect." The tone of her interruption told him that there would be no discussion of an exchange or return.

"Try it on."

She looked from the ring, nestled in the black velvet lining, to his anxious face, and back again. "Will you do the honors?" She handed the box back to him.

With steady hands and calloused fingers, he plucked the ring from its soft nest. She placed her left hand on the table and he slid the ring onto her finger. It fit her slender finger exactly. She captured his hand in hers before he could withdraw it and they sat, holding hands for the first time. "It's perfect," he breathed. And she knew that he was talking about not only the ring but of the union that was being formed between them. She held onto his hand and, in the silence of the moment, she agreed with him.

Chapter 22

Jack

The next day, on Saturday, Jack called Father Bill. The office was closed and Jack knew that on Saturday Father himself was likely to answer rather than the church secretary. Perhaps it was rude to interrupt Father's time to schedule an appointment, but if he called the secretary during the week, she would be far too interested in the details and far too ready to share what she knew with anyone who would listen. It was important to him that he would be the one to announce the engagement to his parents; therefore he wanted to continue to be discreet until he had done so.

As expected, Father answered. Jack asked for an appointment and Father asked the reason. Father knew Jack and his family well enough to know that Jack wasn't dating anyone seriously, so he was surprised when Jack told him the purpose of the meeting, but asked for little explanation over the phone. He set up an appointment for him and Annie on Tuesday, in the late afternoon.

Next he called Annie. It was the first time that he had called her and he had to look up her number in the telephone book. He sat a moment with his finger poised beside her number and thought about the night before. He looked at his work-worn hand resting on the names and numbers listed in the book and remembered what it had felt like to have her hand covering his.

After that moment of closeness, they had ridden back to her house the same way they had ridden away from it: on opposite sides of the bench seat, not touching. He had walked her to the door, wondering if she would welcome a kiss and she gave him the answer to that question by quickly thanking him for everything and telling him to call her when he had made the appointment. Then she had disappeared into the house, closing the door behind her.

He returned his thoughts to the present and dialed her number. She answered before the second ring. He could picture her sitting in her living room on the pretty sofa under the painting of the flowers.

"Hello." Like the smile that she greeted everyone with at the diner, her voice was warm and genuine.

"Hi, Annie, it's Jack." He felt beads of perspiration gather on his forehead. The easiness of the night before was gone.

"Good morning, Jack." She sounded pleased to hear from him.

"Can you meet with Father Bill on Tuesday at 4:00?"

"That's fine. Do you want to pick me up again?"

"I'd be happy to. About 3:50?" he asked.

"Sounds good," she agreed.

"I'll see you then."

Accustomed to using the phone for arrangements rather than discussions, he was ready to hang up when he heard her voice telling him to stay on the line.

"Jack, wait a minute. Is he mean?" She sounded worried.

"Who? Father?"

"Yes." There was a hint of exasperation in her voice.

"No." Jack was surprised by the question. "He's not mean at all. You'll like him."

He was ready to hang up again when she asked, "Could you tell me a little about him so I know what to expect?" The hint of exasperation had grown into annoyance. He tried to think of another time when he had heard her annoyed and couldn't remember one.

"Well, he's about my dad's age. A little younger, probably. He reminds me of a teddy bear, soft and a little chubby. Does that help?"

"Yeah, I guess. I was expecting a mean old guy."

"He's not mean or old. Well, not too old, anyway." he assured her.

"Okay. I'll see you on Tuesday then."

It was she that was just about ready to hang up when he was the one to prevent it this time by saying, "Annie."

"Yes?"

"Are you wearing your ring?"

"Yes. I was sitting here looking at it when the phone rang." He wondered if she, like he, had been thinking about the night before and how it felt when they had sat with their hands joined.

"Has your mom seen it?"

"No. She hasn't been home yet. She spent the night out. I think I might take it off until we have a date set and we're ready to tell everyone. Would you mind? It'll only be for a couple of days, right?"

"Hopefully we'll be ready to tell everyone after Tuesday. You're right. It's probably best if you don't wear it until we tell everybody." His agreement was accompanied by a sense of disappointment. Although the circumstances were sure to raise eyebrows, he was looking forward to finally being able to announce the coming end of his bachelorhood.

"I can't wait to get it over with." Jack didn't know if Annie's words referred to the announcement of their engagement or to their appointment with the priest or to the wedding. He thought probably all three and he was sorry that things weren't easier for her.

"It won't be so bad," he replied. He wished he could find the words to share with her his joy and anticipation and his wish that she might feel these emotions also.

This time, he thought he better ask before he hung up, "Anything else?"

She thought a moment. "No. Just thanks again for last night."

"You're welcome. Bye then."

"Bye."

Tuesday came and Jack picked her up at exactly 3:50. Although Jack was a parishioner of St. Mary's in the small village just two miles from where he lived, the rectory and offices of Father Bill sat beside another larger church in town that Father also was in charge of. The church was called St. Peter's, but his family referred to it as "the church uptown". The church and rectory were only a few blocks from Annie's house so, although Annie had several questions about what to expect, she kept these to herself during the short drive.

Jack parked along the curb in front of the large Victorian-style house which served as both office and rectory. When they walked into the front office, Carolyn, a heavy-set lady wearing a sweater with embroidered leaves, was sitting at a folding table stuffing envelopes. "Jack! Hi. What can I do for you?"

"We have an appointment with Father." As he told her this, she was openly looking Annie up and down, knowing that when a single man brought a young woman to meet with Father, it was almost always a prenuptial appointment.

"Are you sure? I don't have anything on my calendar."

"I called on Saturday. Father and I set it up."

Not accustomed to many things happening without her knowledge, she unwillingly conceded with a sigh. "Well, if you're sure, then he's in his office. You can go on back."

When Jack and Annie entered the priest's office, the man typing on the computer stood up as though this interruption was a welcome relief. He was dressed in standard attire for a Catholic priest: black shirt and black slacks with the small square of white showing under his chin. But in spite of his dark clothing, his cheerful smile made him seem anything but somber. He came around his desk and shook each of their hands, shaking with one hand and using the other hand to cover theirs, making the handshake a warm embrace as he greeted them with a full smile.

"Jack! Good to see you. And you must be Amy."

Jack quickly corrected him. "Annie."

"I'm sorry." His apology was sincere and Annie could tell that he had made the correction in his mind and guessed that he would call her Annie, not Amy, from now on. "Sit down, sit down." He gestured and they sank into the two roomy chairs that sat near each other in front of the desk and Father walked back around the desk and sat down himself.

In spite of his gentleness and unpresuming manner, Jack always felt that Father Bill had an air of authority that was impressive but not intimidating. He knew that much of this feeling came from the respect of priesthood that had been engrained in him since birth. He wondered if Annie could sense it, too.

Father looked at Annie and said, "So Annie, Jack tells me that you two are recently engaged."

"Yes, we are." She was obviously nervous. Jack knew that Father saw this and was sure that his manner would continue to be warm and welcoming even after the difficult details of their engagement were revealed.

"That's wonderful. I know Jack pretty well, and I'm looking forward to getting to know you, too" he now looked at both of them, "and to helping both of you to prepare for your marriage."

This preparation had been a concern of Jack's. He knew it was customary for engaged couples to participate in months of preparation during which time they attended classes to help them understand the sacrament of marriage. Given the circumstances, Jack was hoping that these rules could be bent so he jumped in, wanting to establish their need for special arrangements immediately.

"Father, we have some circumstances of our engagement that you should know about," Jack said.

Annie was looking down and Jack could see that she was looking at her engagement ring that she must have put on for the occasion. She was moving it back and forth and the late afternoon sunlight from the window beside her was making it sparkle.

She surprised him by suddenly looking up and telling Father herself. "I'm pregnant." Her cheeks flamed at confessing this to a priest. Although Jack winced at the blunt words, he was proud of her for volunteering the information. He reached out and grasped her hand.

"There's something else you should know, Father," Jack began in a strained tone. "The baby…"

Father interrupted quickly and decisively. "I don't need to know anything else." He looked at Jack in an uncharacteristically serious manner. "I would make my job easier if we just kept it simple."

Father rested his elbows on his paper-covered desk, linked his hands together, pressed his index fingers to his lips, and thought for a long moment with closed eyes before he spoke to Annie, "Have you considered the possibility of adoption?"

"Yes, I have, but I feel ready to be a mother and I believe that Jack and I can provide a good home for the baby." Jack was proud of her good answer to Father's question.

He went back to his thinking pose, fingers intertwined and index fingers raised to form a steeple. He let out a rush of air through his nostrils and spoke again, "Besides the obvious difficulties that you face as a couple in this situation, there are problems that we will have to deal with in order for you to be married in the church. First, have you prayed about this and do you truly believe that this marriage is God's will for you?"

"Yes, Father, I have," Jack answered easily and honestly.

Next Father looked at Annie, expecting an answer. Annie looked down at her ring again, which was on the hand that Jack wasn't holding. "No. I'm not religious." Jack wished that she could have lied or, better yet, wished the truth was something other than it was.

"I see." Although the enthusiasm with which he had greeted them had been replaced with gravity, his voice remained kind. "Are you a member of any church?" Annie shook her head. "Have you considered joining the Catholic Church, Annie?"

"No."

"I understand that you have other concerns right now that are, perhaps, more urgent. I hope that as you see Jack practicing his faith you might be motivated to explore it as an option for you, too."

He now directed his attention to Jack. "One of the requirements of the Catholic Church is that you, Jack, as the practicing Catholic, recommit yourself to your faith and agree to raise your children in the faith. I know that you have a strong faith and I believe that you will be able to do this, but it will be considerably more difficult with a non-Catholic spouse." He looked back to Annie. "And Annie, contrary to what most people think, as a non-Catholic, the Church doesn't require you to make this promise. However, from a practical standpoint, you will need to provide support to Jack and the child by having a positive attitude toward their religion. Can you do that?"

"Yes. We've already discussed this, and I'll be supportive," Annie replied quickly and easily. Jack knew that she was sincere but he again found himself questioning whether she understood all that she was agreeing to.

The conversation continued. Father asked them about how long they had known each other. Jack was glad to tell him that it had been over a year and didn't bother explaining that it had been quite casual until recently. Father already knew Jack's family and so he asked only Annie about hers. Jack listened as she gave a summary and Father responded. Gradually, they all began to relax. He was kind to Annie, just as Jack had promised that he would be, listening intently to all they said and not judging them in any way.

After they had chatted for a while, he explained the procedure for marriage in the Church "when things aren't so rushed". Then he explained what he would be willing to change and what he was unwilling or unable to change. With the bishop's permission, he could shorten the time of preparation in the case of a pregnancy. There was an all-day PreCana conference that they needed to attend. He turned to the computer, typed in a few things and announced that the next one in the diocese would be the Saturday after next.. He wrote down a number on a neon green sticky note that they were to call as soon as possible to register and to let him know if it was full. He could pull some strings if he needed to.

Finally, he moved some papers to the side to reveal a large calendar covering the front of his desk. He lifted the top sheet out of the black corners that held it in place. Jack read an upside-down "October" on the sheet that he held up and he could see from the scribbles on every box that Father was in the middle of a busy month. "Let's see here, I'm assuming you would like the wedding to be in November?"

Jack told him that they were hoping that they might marry around mid-November if possible, less than three weeks away. Father studied his page for November and, given his wrinkled brow as he did so, Jack guessed that November must already have its share of markings as well. The only Friday or Saturday available was the weekend after Thanksgiving and they had hoped to have the wedding before that.

"What about a weekday?" Annie asked. She looked at Jack as well as Father Bill and explained, "I just want a simple ceremony and no reception or anything. It seems like we could do that on any day. Maybe in the evening so Jack's sisters and their families could come."

Father looked at his calendar again. "Thursday evenings are the most free for me. What about the third Thursday in November? That would be the 17th."

They agreed and the time was set for 6:30. Father requested another meeting with them the following week to further discuss the sacrament of marriage. That was arranged and they left.

Daylight Savings Time had just passed and had shortened the days. It was dark already as they stepped off the porch and walked down the sidewalk to his truck. Jack asked, "Are you hungry?"

"I'm starved," she replied, to Jack's satisfaction.

"Wanna grab a bite to eat?"

Not wanting anything fancy, but deciding against fast food or pizza, they went to the other diner in town, the one that Annie didn't work at. Its appearance was a little nicer than the one that Annie worked in and the food and service were adequate. They ate and once again talked easily. They discussed their meeting with Father Bill and both wondered aloud about the PreCana meeting. They made plans for telling her mother and his parents about the engagement.

They also talked about the wedding and Annie agreed that, even if she didn't want a big wedding, a gown and a bouquet were essential elements. They agreed to expand their guest list to include the men at the diner. They discussed whether printed invitations were possible on such short notice and if they were even necessary because of the small guest list. Jack was grateful for her easy-going attitude about the details of the wedding, knowing that most young women hold on tightly to the ideal of a picture-perfect wedding and resent anyone that tries to pry it away from them.

As she ate, Jack noticed that she still wore the ring and he wasn't about to tell her take it off.

Chapter 23

Annie

Over supper, they decided two things about telling their parents. The first was that, given the fast-approaching date of the wedding, they needed to tell them as soon as possible. The second was that both Annie and Jack should be present for the announcements on both sides.

So, although they hadn't said that they would start tonight, when Jack pulled up to her house and her mother's car was in the drive and the lights of the house were on, they looked at each other and said simultaneously, "Ready?" Their nervous laughter mixed with the pleasure of being of the same mind.

They walked to the porch and Jack stood behind Annie as she opened the door. Her ring sparkled conspicuously under the porch light and she had the sensation that she was on a roller coaster, at the top of the first big hill. Things would go fast from this point onward.

Cindy was watching TV and quickly switched it off and stood up as they walked in. Annie felt Jack watching as she held out her hand and let the ring speak for itself. Cindy hugged Annie and started crying, her mascara running down her cheeks, making little dots on Annie's white shirt. She hugged Jack next, a quick hug that left a little space, appropriate for two people, like themselves, that barely knew one another.

She told Jack to take off his jacket and sit down and he complied. Cindy was bubbly, not revealing any concerns about the brief engagement or the pregnancy. Annie knew that this would be her reaction but she wondered what Jack thought of her unreal optimism. Instead of delving into the deeper issues of their engagement and potential problems with it, she was full of questions about the wedding arrangements, staying on the surface of things like she tended to do. She was eager to help Annie shop and she listed out loud the various items that would be necessary and where they might get each thing. It was obvious that her mom didn't share Annie's desire to keep the wedding low-key.

Jack was very quiet as he listened and Annie knew that he was as unconcerned about the details as she was. After a while, she rescued him by standing and saying, "Well, Mom, I think we better let Jack get back home. He's been busy with harvest and I'm sure he's tired. And I need my rest, too."

She walked with him out to his truck. "She took that well," he said.

"She takes things well," Annie replied. "And she loves weddings. She's good at them. It's the marriages that always seem to cause her problems."

They agreed that tomorrow evening Annie would drive out to his place and they would go to talk with his parents. She insisted that this would include telling about the pregnancy and the fact that Jack was not the one who had caused it. Tonight had been easy because her mom had already known these two things. Tomorrow night wouldn't be as easy.

Chapter 24

Jack

Harvest was slowing. Thanks to the generally dry fall, by Wednesday Jack and his father were down to only one field left to be combined and had already done all the sowing of the winter wheat as well as some of the fall plowing. A cold front had come through which, thankfully, had brought little more than a sprinkle but had cooled things off considerably. A cold north wind insisted that they keep their jackets zipped and their hands tucked in the pockets of their Carhartt jackets whenever possible. In the fall when they were busy, their mother customarily brought them a cold lunch which they ate either on the tailgate of the pick-up or in the cab of the combine. But today, when her voice came over the radio asking if they would have time to come to the house today for a bowl of chili, they both responded with an eager "yes".

At lunch, as the three sat at one end of the large kitchen table enjoying the warmth of the soup, Jack's mom asked about Annie. Jack was hoping that she might do so. It gave him a good lead-in to inform them of the upcoming visit.

"So, Jack, your father tells me that Annie's a very nice girl." Indeed, Meg had been surprised at how Frank, usually a man of many opinions but few words, had gone on and on about how wonderful Annie was. He had laughed heartily as he recounted several times when she had played practical jokes on farmers. He also talked about how she was so pleasant and hard-working "not like the rest of the town girls these days". Meg had brought up her concerns about the age difference and Annie's unknown religion but these were disregarded completely by Frank. Annie had passed his inspection and that was that. In fact, over the past year that Annie had been working in the diner, Frank had hoped that she and Jack might hit it off. But knowing the age difference and his son's past reluctance to date anyone, he had thought that it would be unlikely.

Jack took advantage of the opening that his mom had given him. "She is nice, Mom. We're still going out." He knew that this statement was unnecessary. Although his parents weren't nosy, the teamwork demanded by the farm this time of year made it necessary for Jack to inform his father when he wasn't available. He hadn't told them where he was going or what he was doing each time he had cut out for a meeting with Annie, only that he needed to go uptown, but they knew that ever since the Sunday she had come over that he was seeing Annie during these times. He also knew that it was expected and assumed that anything that would take him away from farming at this time of year was fairly serious.

As if reading his thoughts, his mom asked, "Is it serious?"

It would have been so natural to answer his mother's question with "Yes. In fact, we're engaged." But, because they had agreed to make the announcement together, his reply was necessarily deceptive, "Yes. It is. In fact, she's coming over to my place tonight. I'd like for her to get to know you two better. Do you think I could bring her over tonight, maybe after supper?"

Jack saw his mother and father look briefly at one another and, for once, couldn't read their thoughts. Was it as obvious as it seemed that there must be a reason behind the visit and, if so, what reason could there be other than to announce an engagement? His dad answered. "Why, sure, bring her over. We'll be here."

Jack and Frank returned to work but, unlike earlier in the fall, they stopped working at dark, an hour before Annie was scheduled to arrive. When he walked into his almost-dark house, he was greeted by the chirping of the answering machine. He pressed the button and Annie's voice broke the silence, His initial reaction was a mixture of pleasure and worry. The worry disappeared as he heard her announcing that she could bring supper if he wanted and to give her a call to let her know.

He called her back to take her up on the offer if it wasn't too late and then jumped in the shower, letting his cold body be soothed by the warmth of the spray. Afterward, as he dried and combed his still-thinning hair, his eyes met the eyes in the mirror and he stopped a moment to marvel at the excitement that was easily seen in them.

"You're in love." He said the words to the man that was in front of him and they were a revelation. Until this moment he had known that he liked Annie and certainly he had thought of little else this fall, but really admitting that he was in love with her was a step that he had not taken before now. And this wasn't a small step. The tightening feeling in his stomach made this step feel like a step off the side of the Grand Canyon. He was delighted to realize that, although scary, it was much better than the view that he had been taking in from the edge for the past ten years as he watched everyone else take the leap, falling in love and getting married while he remained safely on the edge.

After he was dressed, he roamed nervously around the house, somehow finding in his sparsely decorated home a hundred things that needed to be picked up or brushed off or rearranged, even though he had thought everything was in order the night before. When the doorbell rang, he didn't know if he wanted to answer it or run and hide from all the crazy changes in his life and his heart. But when he opened the door and saw her standing there, he was glad that he had opened the door that had been closed for so long. He wondered how he had managed to wait so long.

He helped her carry a few things in and in no time they sat down to a pasta casserole, salad, and garlic bread. He thought about the stack of frozen burgers in the freezer from which he would have pulled his solitary supper, and thanked her for her thoughtfulness.

After supper, they had just started to clear the table when she said, "Jack, do you mind if we go right now? I'm ready to get this over with. Maybe we can come back and clean up afterwards?"

He looked at her pale face and instantly agreed. They stuck a few things in the fridge and left everything else for later. They put on their coats and before they stepped out the door, he grabbed both of her hands in his and looked her in the eyes, hoping to give her the gift of reassurance. "It'll be fine," he said, knowing that it was true and wanting her to know it, too.

"Don't be so nice. It makes me cry." Indeed, tears were once again in her eyes.

Without thinking, without worrying about whether he should, without questioning whether or not she wanted him to, he wrapped his arms around her, embracing her. He felt her arms slide around his waist in return. They stood like that for long minutes. He drank in the feel of the embrace and the scent of her hair and the wonder of it all. She accepted from him the strength that he offered to help her regain her composure before facing his parents.

He breathed her scent fully in one last time and reluctantly broke the embrace, taking her hands once again and, like the night before, they both said at once, "Ready?" Tonight there was no nervous laughter, but rather their eyes and mouths smiled weakly at one another in acknowledgement that they had again spoken in unison. Then they turned and walked out the door, she more confident than before and he even more in love than before.

As usual, Jack entered his parent's house through the garage and walked into the kitchen without knocking. He held Annie's hand as he announced himself, as always, with "Anybody home?"

This was greeted by the standard "Come on in," even though he was already in. Although the verbal response was standard, the immediate click and thud as the foot of Frank's recliner was released and pushed down was not, nor was the fact that both of them came into the kitchen to greet them.

"Did you two have supper?" his mom asked. Being sure that everyone around her was well fed was a priority for Meg.

Jack was happy to tell her that Annie had brought supper and he gave her a few details, happy to increase Annie's approval rating before its imminent plunge.

Jack thought there was no point in delaying things. "Mom, Dad, Annie and I have something that we wanted to talk to you about. Do you mind if we all have a seat at the table?"

They sat on the sides of the oblong table; Frank across from Jack and Meg across from Annie. Jack silently and quickly prayed for the right words and for their acceptance and began, "I've asked Annie to marry me and she's agreed." He paused to take in the effect of this bomb before he dropped the next one.

In that pause, Meg said, "I was wondering if that might be why you wanted to come over. But it's so sudden that I thought it must be something else."

He wasn't about to drag this out. "Well, there's a reason that it's sudden. Annie's going to have a baby."

They were both speechless and he went on quickly, the way that one pulls off a band-aid or swallows nasty medicine. "And we both want you to know that the baby's not mine."

Their silence continued as they absorbed this. "Well?" Jack finally asked.

Frank was the first to find his voice, and it was gruff. "Do you mind if I ask a few questions?"

Annie answered, "No, I don't mind." Her voice was appropriately humble but not fearful or timid. She made it clear that she was willing to speak for herself in response to any questions. Jack admired her.

Frank wasn't one to step around the issues. Jack knew that he would bluntly ask what he wanted to know. "What was the timing on all of this? Were you done with this other fellow before you and Jack got together?"

"Yes. We - the father and I - dated a little last summer. Jack and I didn't start dating until September, after I knew I was pregnant."

"So you found out you were pregnant and started looking around for someone that you might be able to talk into marrying you?" Jack winced at his fathers words.

Needing to defend Annie and make it clear that he had not been talked into anything, Jack answered. "I was the one that did all the persuading. I could tell she wasn't feeling well and I guessed she was pregnant and I asked her to marry me. The only thing she did was say yes."

"Maybe she should try saying no," Frank said.

"Maybe *you* should try saying *less*." Jack's words warned Frank to be careful. Jack, who was always obedient to his parents, felt uneasy in his new role as the one giving the orders.

Their words hung in the air above the table while tempers silently flared and then cooled.

Jack's mother waited patiently while this happened. Jack had watched his parents together for all of his life and he knew that she often had opinions that differed from her husband's. He was familiar with the way that her lips drew into a thin line when Frank said one thing and she thought another. He was also familiar with her amazing silence in those situations. But she wasn't silent now.

She looked down at her hands that rested on the table in front of her and said carefully, "I've been praying for the past few years that you would find a wife and have a family, Jack. I guess God answered both prayers at once." Her words were matter-of-fact. They lacked any trace of the joy that might have accompanied them had the situation been different, but they were words of acceptance and peace.

"Thank you." Annie whispered and looked up at the woman across from her while avoiding Frank.

Frank grabbed a seed corn business card that was on the table and tapped the edge of it against the table, slid his thumb and index finger down the side, and then picked it up, turned it a quarter turn and repeated the process. He finally put it down and firmly put his hand down on top of it like he was playing slapjack. He leaned forward and looked directly at Annie, and said, "Annie, I like you, but it seems to me you got yourself in a little bit of a mess here." Jack watched Annie's eyes meet those of his father. "And I don't think it's Jack's problem to solve."

Then he turned to his son and conceded. "But I trust you, son. You usually have good judgment, so maybe this isn't as dumb as it seems.

You're too old for me to be telling you what you should and shouldn't do, anyway. So if you want to take on this responsibility, I don't have any choice but to go along with it."

They remained at the table for another two hours and, unlike Annie's mother, Jack's parents asked the tough questions that went way beyond the wedding ceremony. They talked about whether Annie would keep her job, about Annie's plans to talk more to the father of the baby, Annie's future life as a farm wife, how they would handle the issue of religion, and on and on. The tension gradually eased. They were kind but concerned, and together the four of them explored things realistically.

Only after they had discussed the issues of the marriage did they switch to the practical details of the wedding. Meg was slightly panicked by the approaching date but recovered quickly as they talked more about how simple it would be and that Father himself was the one who had helped them decide on the date. Meg offered any help that Annie needed, declaring herself an expert, having planned the weddings of her three married daughters. Annie thanked her and restated her desire for a no-fuss ceremony.

By 9:30, all four knew that they could sit and talk for days and still find more to discuss. But it was at this time that Meg abruptly stood up and said, "You know what? I think we all need a good night's rest. Let's call it a night."

To Jack's delight, Meg congratulated them and welcomed Annie to the family. Frank was colder, but his "I just hope this all works out okay." was accompanied by a hug for each of them.

They drove back to Jack's house and did the dishes together, Jack washing and Annie drying. They briefly revisited several of the topics that his parents had brought up. When Jack had drained the water and Annie had hung up the towel and they were both afraid that she might have to leave, she said, "What happened to that ice cream that you bought for me a few weeks ago?"

"I've been eating it without you, but I think there's a little left." He grabbed the carton and she found the bowls behind the second cupboard door that she opened. He dished the remaining ice cream into the two bowls and they went into the living room. She kicked off her shoes and sat on the middle of the couch with her legs tucked under her, sitting at an angle to face Jack, who had sat down at the corner of the couch, angling toward her. They began to eat their ice cream and Jack sensed that she had something on her mind and guessed what it was.

She began to speak, searching his face for a reaction as she did so, "Jack, I'm going to get in touch with Eric soon. I need to let him know about the wedding and I need to talk to him about giving up any rights to the baby."

"I've been wondering if you'd talked to him yet." He took another bite but his ice cream seemed to have lost its flavor and now it was nothing but a lump of cold in his mouth.

He got up and walked into the kitchen with his unfinished ice cream that was melting into a puddle. He walked back and sat down on the chair where he had sat that first night that she had been over, safely distancing himself from her.

"If you need help, I can help. Are you going to see him in person?"

"I think I probably will meet with him in person. And no, I don't need any help."

He offered again, but not because he wanted to. He didn't want anything to do with this man who had fathered the baby that should have been his.

"Are you going to be alone with him?" He questioned whether he was jealous or insecure and decided that they were one and the same and he was, indeed, guilty of being both.

"We met at a restaurant in Columbus before and that worked out pretty well. I think I'll suggest the same thing again."

He tried to stop himself but couldn't. "Annie, what if he's changed his mind and wants you and the baby now?"

"He hasn't." She said this in the same tone of voice she would have used to tell him that the sky was blue or the world was round.

"But what if?"

She gave him the words that he so desperately needed to hear. "I'll tell him he's too late. My baby and I are already spoken for." At that, she unfolded herself and walked her empty bowl to the kitchen.

She slipped her shoes and coat on, grabbed a grocery sack that contained her clean dishes, and stood at the door in the place where they had embraced earlier, unsure of how to say goodbye. Talking about Eric had created a wall between them that neither was about to step through. Jack put on his coat and walked her out to her car.

"Good-night. And good luck with everything." And with that he closed her car door for her and she drove away.

Afterwards, Jack stood at the kitchen window where he said his morning prayers each day and stared out into the darkness. He couldn't remember a time in his life when he had ever had so much to be thankful for and, at the same time, so much to ask for God's help with.

Chapter 25

Annie

Not wanting to put it off any longer, Annie prepared to make the call to Eric the very next day. Over a month earlier, after she had called him, she remembered sitting in her room, holding the slip of paper on which was scribbled his hard-to-get phone number, and looking around, trying to decide where she should put it. She had needed a place that would be out of sight but not lost. She had laughed to herself as her eye caught a paperback copy of *The Scarlet Letter*. She had extracted the book and slid the paper between the pages, knowing that such a hiding place would be easily remembered when she needed the number again.

She vividly recalled holding the book in her hand and thinking that it seemed like ages ago when that high school girl that she used to be had stuck the dog-eared novel on her book shelf after she had finished reading it with her senior English class.

And so on Thursday, exactly two weeks before the wedding date, she pulled the book out once again and thumbed through the highlighted pages, smelling the faint odor of newsprint that cheap paperbacks give off. She let the small paper with torn edges fall out onto her bed. On it she had written his first name "Eric" and then the number.

She looked at that name and thought about Jack's question from the night before. What if he would say that he had changed his mind and wanted do the right thing – to marry her and raise the baby? When she had told Jack that it wouldn't happen, she had been sure that what she said was true. She was positive that after having time to think about it, he still wouldn't want her or the baby. But, as Jack had persisted, what if? What if she could give the baby what she herself had never had: a life with his or her own father? Would she do it if she had the chance?

Last night she hadn't seen the importance of her response to a situation that was never going to happen. But now she knew why Jack needed to know. Eric wouldn't make the offer but if he did, would she truly say that she had been spoken for? Had she walked away from what had pulled her toward Eric and was she committed to a life with Jack?

Over the course of the last few weeks, she had begun to imagine life with Jack. What they would watch on TV together. What they would eat. What it would be like to crawl into bed with him. Now she replaced Jack with Eric and willed the same types of images to run through her mind. It didn't work. It wasn't that she didn't like what she envisioned; it was that she couldn't create any mental image of life with him, positive or negative. When she tried, her mind put Jack back in.

But what about the baby? Was Jack the best choice for the child? Was he better than the biological father? The picture of Jack taking Christopher's hand and leading him to the restroom the morning that she first knew she was pregnant had, for some reason, embedded itself into her mind. She also thought about the way that he had been with all of his nieces and nephews when they had gathered for Sunday supper; how he had helped them fill their plates and had lovingly teased them. Jack had a combination of strength, gentleness, humor, and patience that would make him a terrific father. Again, she tried to picture Eric in the same situations and it didn't work.

"My baby and I are spoken for." The repetition of the words that she had said to Jack the night before was both a confirmation and a rehearsal, just in case they became necessary. The night before, she had known that these words were true in a formal sense, signified by the ring that she wore. Now, however, the words seemed to resound deeper.

She got up and walked into the living room carrying the slip of paper. She had a phone in her bedroom, but calling while she sat on her bed seemed too personal. Sitting on the sofa, she dialed, and was surprised to hear a young woman's voice answer. "Is Eric there?" Annie asked.

"Yeah. Just a sec." She now recognized the voice as Jenny's.

His voice came on the line. "Eric here."

"Hi Eric. It's Annie."

"Hi." She could tell he was thinking about what to say to her in the presence of Jenny. She smiled at the sticky place that she had put him in.

She was determined to continue. "I was wondering if we could get together sometime soon."

"Yeah, I know, it's going to be a tough project." His attempt at disguising the conversation for Jenny's benefit was amusing. "How about 7:00 tomorrow night at the library, you know, where we met before?"

"You mean tomorrow night at the same restaurant at 7:00?"

"Yep, sounds good. Don't forget your research notes." He wasn't going to get an Emmy anytime soon.

"I'll be there, Eric."

"See ya then."

She hung up and let herself acknowledge for a brief moment the immature thrill of sneaking around behind Jenny's back. Then she stopped herself and started thinking about tomorrow night and what she was going to say to him.

Her mom came home and over supper, as Annie expected, they began planning all the places that they would go on Saturday as they began to arrange the wedding. They were interrupted by the telephone.

Annie answered and was surprised to hear Jenny's voice on the line.

"Annie?" she asked tentatively.

"Yes?" she tried to sound like she had no idea who it was or why they were calling.

"This might be silly, but I'm just going to ask. Did you call Eric this afternoon?"

"Yes, I did." She refused to lie to her.

"Oh." She only said that one utterance that was barely even a word, but the sadness with which it was said meant, "Oh, so he's lying to me and what I've heard about you and him is true and you might still be seeing each other behind my back."

She didn't want to hurt her but couldn't provide honest consolation, either. "Jenny, it's not what you think. But it's not good, either."

"Can you tell me?"

If there had been a thrill in plotting a secret meeting a few hours earlier, there was a greater thrill in planning a secret trap for Eric now. "Why don't you join us? Of course, you know that we're not working on a project, but we are meeting tomorrow night at seven." She named the restaurant and described its location. "Eric will be surprised." She hoped that this would be interpreted as "Keep this a secret."

Jenny hesitated, knowing that whatever was to be talked about between them was not for her ears. After a pause, Annie continued,

"Jenny, I promise I won't start a cat fight. I'm asking you to come because I really don't want there to be any secrets or lies. Please come."

Jenny and Annie hadn't been friends in high school but their paths had crossed enough for Jenny to know that Annie wasn't manipulative or vindictive. And, of course, as Eric's girlfriend and, most likely, future wife, she needed to know what was going on. "Okay, I'll try to make it."

Annie hung up and saw her mom looking at her. "What are you doing, Annie?" She had been listening and had heard enough to have an idea of what the answer to her own question was.

"I'm just getting everything out in the open."

"Some things shouldn't be in the open," Cindy warned.

"I guess we'll find out tomorrow night."

On Friday, it was dark by the time that she left her house and headed for the restaurant. Traffic was fairly heavy in both directions. It always seemed that the people who were in the city wanted to get out for the weekend and the people who lived outside of the city wanted to spend the weekend in the city.

As she drove, she questioned what she was about to do. She put herself in Jenny's shoes and decided that if she were her, she would definitely want to know about her boyfriend's illegitimate child. Perhaps it wasn't the best way to break the news to Jenny, but Annie couldn't think of a good way.

Having Jenny present solved another problem also. At their last meeting, she had been deeply hurt, although not shocked, by how he had reacted to her news. She needed someone to act as a witness to how callous he was being or, hopefully, to prevent him from being so callous again.

She pulled into the lot about ten minutes early. It was more crowded tonight but not extremely so. The restaurant was not expensive or trendy, two requirements to draw a large weekend crowd in the city.

Eric pulled in a few minutes later. They walked in together as before and, as Annie hoped, Jenny arrived before the hostess got around to seating them.

Eric unsuccessfully tried to hide his shock. "Jenny, what are doing here?" He strived for his easy-going mannerisms but he fell short of the mark as he leaned forward and kissed her cheek.

"Annie invited me. Wasn't that nice of her?" Jenny's voice was the audible equivalent of honey laced with arsenic.

Annie saw him glance nervously toward the door and wondered if he might just dash out of it but he stayed and she found a little admiration for him as he resigned himself to a meal sure to cause indigestion. "Well, we better let her know we need a table for three, then," he said.

The hostess appeared, grabbed some menus and asked, "Booth or table?"

"Table," Annie replied quickly. When she was waitressing earlier in the day, Annie had thought about the three of them in a booth and laughed at each possibility of who would sit together on the one side and who would sit alone across from them. Would it be the women versus Eric? Eric and Jenny against her? She and Eric against Jenny? That didn't seem likely. Yes, she definitely wanted a table.

They shed coats and Annie sat down quickly, not wanting her still-small but expanding stomach to announce anything before she did. Annie started. "Eric, I don't want you to feel like I'm tricking you. I just really believe that Jenny should know."

"Maybe we should go someplace else," Eric suggested, looking around at the other diners nervously.

"No," Annie countered, feeling very much in charge. "No one here is listening or knows who we are. And I think it's good that we're somewhere where we have to keep ourselves calm."

"Annie! What's on your finger?" Jenny asked. To Annie's surprise, it was the ring, not her stomach, which was starting the flow of information.

"Oh, well, I'm engaged." She blushed and wasn't sure why.

"To who?" Annie saw the relief on Jenny's face when Eric asked the question with a puzzled look on his face.

"To Jack Schroeder, Elizabeth's big brother." Her blush deepened.

Eric looked at Jenny's hands and asked, "Where's *your* ring?"

It was Jenny's turn to blush, "I wasn't sure if…" She started over "I wanted to see how things went tonight."

"We're engaged, too," he told Annie. For good reason, he didn't sound too sure of that fact.

"Eric, I'd like you to be the one to tell Jenny what we talked about when we met here before." The friendliness of her voice contrasted with the awfulness of the request.

He spoke in a quiet voice and it was as if he was forcing his lips to move. "She told me that she was pregnant with my baby."

Annie and Eric braced themselves for an outburst, either of tears or anger, but there was none. Jenny only replied, "I was afraid of that."

"At that time, I hadn't decided what I was going to do yet, but now I have. I wanted to meet with Eric tonight to let him know what I've decided."

"Can we back up a minute?" Jenny asked, doing a remarkable job of keeping her composure. "I have two questions. First, is it completely over between you two? And second, Eric, did you know about the baby when you proposed to me?"

Annie answered, "I can answer the first one. Yes. Completely." The words were filled with joy and unmistakable finality.

Jenny looked at Eric. "And the second?"

Eric hung his head and closed his eyes. "Yes, I knew."

Only her quivering bottom lip gave anything away. "Okay, go on."

Annie continued, "So, Eric, I wanted you to know about the engagement. Jack's a great guy and he wants to raise the baby so it looks like we'll both be well cared for and I won't need any support, financial or otherwise, from you. Jack and I will meet with a lawyer and talk about how to arrange an official adoption and all that, if you're in agreement."

"I am." He was listening but was also obviously thinking about Jenny's reaction to all this.

The waitress came and wanted to take their order but they hadn't yet opened their menus, so they sent her away. With controlled movements, Jenny placed her menu on top of the placemat. "Look, you two, this is overwhelming. I'm going to go. Talk about whatever you have to without me. Annie, thank you for inviting me." She stood up and plucked her coat from the back of her chair. "Eric, give me a call, but wait until at least tomorrow. I need to sleep on this." She turned and left.

For a second, Annie was afraid to be alone with him, afraid of how angry he might be at her for inviting Jenny. But when she looked at him, she saw that he was watching Jenny as she walked away from him and that he was much more afraid than she was.

Chapter 26

Jack

Jack suffered through a miserable day on Thursday. It rained, which left him alone with his thoughts of Annie and he couldn't think about her without wondering if she had spoken to Eric yet and what had been said between them.

On Friday, when he woke up to more rain, he decided that he needed to do something productive. After having his coffee in the safety of his own kitchen, he drove into town to shop for a bed that would comfortably accommodate the two of them. What he found in the local furniture store was nice to look at but poorly made, glued together and covered in cheap veneer. And even if he would have found something he was happy with, he wasn't sure what Annie would like. He went home without purchasing anything.

On his way home, he stopped in at his parents' place. It was lunch time and he often found himself there at lunch time. He liked eating his mom's cooking as much as she liked feeding him. As the three of them ate, he told her about his disappointing shopping trip. After he had endured Frank's comments about the necessity of a bed that would stand up to a lot of motion, his mom suggested that he buy something from Amish country.

He went home thinking about his mom's advice. He knew that he would find outstanding workmanship by traveling to the opposite side of Ohio where the Amish lived, but didn't know if he wanted to make the trip that would take an entire day when he was so busy with harvest. And the wedding was approaching so quickly. They would need a bed by the time they got back from their honeymoon, the planning of which was another thing that needed to be done.

"That's it." His words interrupted the silence of his empty house. He went to the computer and began researching.

He was lost in thought until hours later when his stomach told him that the lunch that his mom had served was long gone and it was time for supper. He made himself one of the frozen burgers that Annie had rescued him from just two nights ago and thought about that night and their conversation again. After he finished eating, he finally gave up and picked up the phone. He looked at the fridge where his favorite John Deere magnet was holding up her number and dialed.

Her mom answered. "Is Annie in?" he asked.

"No, she's not." Her voice was careful and he knew without asking who she was with.

"Okay, well, could you tell her I called?"

"Sure, Jack, I'll tell her." She sounded apologetic.

"Thanks." He hung up and turned on the TV, praying for something to hold his interest. He gave up and opened his Bible and began reading, forcing himself to pay attention.

She returned his call about an hour later. She immediately told him where she had been and described the meeting for him, including the interesting twist of his girlfriend being present. He was silent through it all and she ended with "So what do you think?"

"I think you did what you had to do. What do you think?"

"I think he's a jerk and I made some very poor decisions last summer." Her voice broke and he knew she was crying.

"I wish I was there to hold you again." The honest words spilled from him before he had time to decide if they should be said.

There was silence for a long moment while each held the receiver to their ear, feeling at once close and painfully far apart. He could hear her swallowing as she fought the tears.

He broke the spell by saying in a rough voice, "So what are you doing tomorrow?"

"My self-appointed wedding coordinator has the day planned." She sniffed loudly.

That meant another day before he could see her again. "How about Sunday?"

"I'm free."

"Do you want to spend the day together?"

"The whole day?" She sounded surprised by the idea.

"You gotta get used to it sometime," he teased. "I go to 9:30 Mass in Kirby, the little town out by where I live. You can go with me or, if that's too early, we can get together afterwards."

"Afterwards sounds good, if you don't mind. I am so tired right now. I'd really like to catch up on some sleep this weekend before Monday rolls around."

"You do sound exhausted. What if I cook lunch and we spend the afternoon watching movies and then go to supper at my parents'?"

"That sounds great. I take it that supper with your parents includes telling your sisters the big news?" Her tone told him that she wasn't looking forward to it.

"The wedding is less than two weeks away, you know," he reminded her gently.

"Believe me, Jack, I know!"

"Have you thought about the honeymoon?" There was silence on the other end and Jack realized that she thought he was asking about the consummation of their marriage rather than travel plans. He quickly added, "I mean where we're going on our honeymoon?"

"No, I haven't. Have you?"

"I started to today. I haven't arranged anything definitely but I have some ideas. Do you mind if I handle it?"

"I would love for you to handle it, Jack." She drug out the word "love", making her statement emphatic. "But I don't want anything…"

He interrupted her, "Anything fancy. I know. I'll keep it simple, I promise."

They talked a little more and by the time that Jack hung up, the worries about Eric that had plagued him for the last few days had once again faded into the background.

He returned to his computer and began to make more definite plans for the honeymoon. He smiled when he thought about her silence when he had asked about the honeymoon. And now he found himself thinking about more than hotel reservations. He willed his body not to react so readily to the thought of what they would be doing in just a few short weeks.

Chapter 27

Annie

After Annie hung up with Jack, she forced her weary body to go through the motions of getting into her pajamas. She slept without dreaming or even moving until her mother woke her the next morning, anxious for their day together.

They drove into Findlay, which provided more selection and more privacy than shopping in the small town where they lived. Cindy was by now an expert at planning weddings, and they had a very productive day. They started with dresses and, although Cindy had to be pulled past the elegant bridal gowns, in the end she approved of Annie's choice of a simple two-piece suit that hid her stomach well. Self-conscious about white, Annie insisted on cream. Because the gown was designed for a mother-of-the-bride, the shop didn't have cream, but it could be ordered and would arrive in just a few days.

Also at the bridal shop, they spied the satin pillows designed to be carried by a ring bearer. An image of Christopher immediately came to mind and she wondered out loud if a ring bearer would be appropriate for such a simple ceremony. Cindy immediately grabbed the pillow and purchased it before Annie could convince her to wait.

From the bridal shop, they went to a craft store. One of Cindy's many previous jobs had been at a flower shop, so she offered to put together Annie's bouquet. They selected an array of fall colors that would blend fabulously with the cream of Annie's suit. They also bought extra flowers and containers needed to make two arrangements for the church.

By this time, it was mid-afternoon and they were hungry. They went to a trendy restaurant and over lunch they summarized and evaluated what they had done so far and listed other things that needed to be arranged.

Cindy convinced Annie that they should provide some sort of simple supper for their guests afterward, although they came to no conclusions about where this would be or what would be served. Their next stop was a bakery where they ordered a small but beautiful cake that, like the bouquet, would showcase the colors of fall. By the time they took the freeway back home, they both felt good about what had been accomplished.

In spite of the relief of having things underway, Annie was glad to walk out of the house the next morning. They had scattered their purchases the night before and every room seemed to contain evidence of the impending wedding and all that there was to do in connection with it.

She had slept in, so it was late morning by the time that she climbed the two front steps and Jack opened the door in jeans, a pullover sweater, and his stocking feet. He invited her in, asked how she was feeling, and, like his mother had a few weeks ago, set her to work chopping vegetables while he made the other preparations for the meal.

Offerings

He asked about yesterday and she told him each detail, asking after each if it was okay and he reassured her each time that it sounded good to him.

When they sat down and began eating, Jack looked at her and said, "You look good." The way he lifted his eyebrows and said it in a higher-than-normal tone made it sound like he was surprised by the fact.

She laughed, "Don't I usually look 'good'?"

"No, I mean, yes you do, but today you look…rested, I guess. You looked pretty tired on Tuesday and Wednesday. And you sounded really tired on the phone Friday."

"Yeah, I have been tired. It's a little harder to keep up these days." That was an understatement. Lately she felt that life was going at top speed and she was crawling behind, trying to catch up.

"Are you going to keep working?" The topic had been raised by his parents that night at their kitchen table but not yet answered.

How had something so important not found its way to the list that she had jotted down on the green paper? "Do you want me to?"

"No, I don't. At least not after you have the baby."

"Will we have enough money?"

"I can support both of us pretty well."

She thought about spending long winter days with nothing to do and she thought about the men whom she loved to serve and tease. "In that case, I'd like to keep working for a while and quit maybe a month or two before the baby comes."

"Sounds good." His brow wrinkled as he led into the next topic. "There's something else that I wanted to ask you about your job. Just something I've been wondering about."

"Go ahead," she encouraged.

"Why do you work there? You do a great job and I know you like it fairly well, but why didn't you go to college? Elizabeth told me you're really smart."

Whether she was smart or not hadn't been noticed or mentioned for over a year now. "Well, I'm not sure I'm 'really smart', but I got good grades, anyway. I was always interested in a lot of things that we studied."

"So why are you working at a diner?"

She thought a moment. "Well, Mom was in the middle of her most recent divorce the spring and summer that I graduated and she needed me around to help her. So I decided to wait a year. Then when it was time to think about it for this year, I was already, well, I guess comfortable, with my job. I was planning on taking some night classes this year at the community college in Findlay, though."

"You should do that. I guess it's too late for fall semester and the baby will be born in spring. But next year you should. I could watch the baby."

She was more excited than she showed. "I might. But right now I have enough to think about." She changed the topic by announcing, "Okay, now it's my turn to ask *you* a tough question."

He commanded her to ask by stating, "Shoot."

"Jack, why didn't you ever get married?" Her heart pounded. This was the one thing about the man across from her that worried her.

He stopped chewing for a moment then started again, taking his time before swallowing, giving himself time to think. "Well, I guess the same reason a lot of guys don't get married. I couldn't find the right woman."

She persisted, not satisfied with his answer, sensing that there was more to it. "But it seems like if you were looking you would have been able to find someone. You're attractive and intelligent."

"I'm glad you think so." He poked fun at himself by saying, "You may not have noticed this, Annie, but I'm not exactly an outgoing guy."

"You don't say?" Her response was an acknowledgement of his admission.

She knew that he was withholding something from her and wondered for a moment whether her outward acceptance of his explanation was a result of trust, denial, or need. Knowing that the answer would forever remain elusive, her mind moved to the next question that she needed to ask.

She took a breath in and was just about to speak when he saved her the embarrassment of formulating the words.

He put his silverware down and directed his full attention on her. "No. Or yes. I know what you want to ask but I don't know how you were going to phrase it. No, I've never had any serious girlfriends. Yes, I'm a virgin, although I always thought that that's a term that's more for women than men. Does that answer your question?" he asked. His manner was confrontational.

"Yes. I'm sorry, I didn't…"

He interrupted her and said apologetically, "It's okay. We're getting married. That's something that you should know about your future husband." He picked up his fork and pushed the potatoes around his plate, a good way to avoid looking at her. "Do you mind?"

"Mind that you haven't slept with anyone?" she asked.

"Yes," he replied.

"No, I don't mind. Why would I mind?"

He blushed beneath his tan and stumbled over his words. The assertive man that had briefly sat across from her a moment ago was now once again uncertain and shy. "I, well, I guess I wish I had a little practice. I don't know if I'm going to know how to, well, you know, if I'm going to know how to make things good for you."

It was her turn to blush. They had finished eating and she stood up to begin clearing the table, hoping to feel more at ease when they weren't face to face. But after she had moved her plate from the table to the sink, she knew that she needed to face him for what needed to be said. She returned to the table, moved her chair closer to him, sat, and took both of his rough hands in hers. Now that she knew about him, she told him what he needed to know about her.

"Jack, you've been honest with me. Can I be honest with you?" She continued, not waiting for an answer. As she spoke, she looked down at their four hands, not able to look at his face. "I have had sex a total of three times. Each time was, well, rushed and, I don't know, maybe mechanical. I don't know if that's the word I want but, you know, it wasn't like what you see in the movies and not even close to what I hoped it would be. So don't think that you're the only one who has a lot to learn. Just because I've done it doesn't mean that I've done it right." She looked up and met his eyes that had been looking at her as she spoke. Their eyes said things for which there are no words.

He squeezed her hands gently but firmly in his and said only, "Thank you, Annie." He kept her hands captured in his for a lingering moment. Where the backs of her hands touched his pants, she could feel the rough fabric of his denim jeans and the warmth of the man inside of them. Then he released them and, with a jagged breath, broke the spell by saying, "Well, I guess now that we have that cleared up, we better clear the table."

As before, they worked together well. Since this was her third meal in his kitchen, she was beginning to know where things were kept and, as in the diner, worked quickly and efficiently.

Offerings

As they were putting away the last of the evidence of the meal and were both secretly worrying about where their conversation might go next, there was a knock at the garage door, startling them both. Jack opened the door to find Elizabeth, who, because of Annie's car in the drive had thought it best to wait for the door to be opened rather than barge in, as was her custom.

"Elizabeth!" Jack exclaimed. Annie heard in Jack's tone the same relief of having been rescued that she felt. Annie watched as he wrapped his strong arms around his sister and was surprised at her sudden shortness of breath when she remembered herself in his embrace.

"I'm not interrupting anything, am I?" Elizabeth asked with a grin.

Annie jumped in, joking back, "No, unfortunately not. If you only would have come a few minutes earlier you would have interrupted us - doing the dishes."

She hung up the towel that she had been using. As she did so, Elizabeth noticed the ring. Her mouth opened wide and both hands flew up to cover the opening. Her excited eyes looked from her brother to Annie and back again. Annie marveled at how observant everyone seemed to be.

"Jack!" she finally said, pulling her hands away from her mouth just enough to talk. "I hope that ring on her finger is from you!"

"It is," he responded with such pride that Annie, for the first time, believed that he truly felt fortunate to be engaged to her.

Elizabeth slapped him on the shoulder and said, "I can't believe you proposed without even calling for my advice. I want to hear all the details." She went in and sat down on Jack's recliner, leaving the sofa for them. Annie started, telling her about the night at the fancy restaurant when Jack presented the ring. She left out the preliminary discussions and made it sound like he had suddenly proposed.

"So when's the big day? Have you decided yet?"

There was a pause. Annie knew what had to be said and knew that Elizabeth would figure out the rest, including who the father was, quickly and easily.

"In a few weeks. November 17th," Jack answered.

"What! My God, Jack, you've waited all these years! What's the rush for?"

Jack turned his head to glance at Annie again and she nodded for him to go on. "It's about what you'd expect a rushed wedding to be for."

Her head cranked forward and her eyes widened. "What? You mean you *have to*? This is too much! When's the baby due?"

"In the spring." Jack hoped that a vague answer might postpone the inevitable.

"April 24th," Annie clarified. Once again, she was determined to have this matter in the open, and soon.

"Wow! Jack once you make your mind up, you don't waste any time." She looked at Annie, "So are you sick?"

"I was for a while but it's better now."

At this, Elizabeth stopped to think, "Already? But you two have only been dating for, what? a month?" Now they could see her mentally counting backwards from April. "Oh," she said softly when she landed on last July.

Jack said what she had obviously just figured out. "It's not mine."

"Oh." she said again. "Is it Eric's?"

"Yes." Now Annie could ask what she had been wondering for a while. "Do you think a lot of people will figure that out?"

"I think the tongues will be wagging in that direction once everyone knows you're pregnant." Her brow wrinkled as she imagined the gossip that would go around. "But you know, I think that since you two are getting married, they'll all just decide that it must be Jack's. Maybe it won't be a big deal. Does Eric know?"

"Yes," Annie replied.

"And Jenny?"

"Yes," Annie replied again.

"I heard they were engaged."

"I heard that too." Annie thought it best not to share any information from two nights ago.

Elizabeth leaned back in the chair, soaking in the news. A smile began at her mouth and spread across her whole face and then seemed to fill the entire room as she beamed at Annie. Apparently unable to contain the joy that she felt, she got up and went over to where Annie was sitting, bent down, and hugged her. "I'm so glad you're going to be my new sister!"

Just as quickly as she had embraced her, she released her and remained standing, preparing to go already. "I don't want to stay. I really didn't want to interrupt, but I just had a feeling that I should pop in."

Jack and Annie stood and the three of them inched toward the door as they talked a little more. She hugged them both again and took off down the road toward her parents' house.

Her presence had added a lightness that had been lacking before she arrived. When the door closed behind her, Jack and Annie smiled at each other and Jack said, "Well, one sister down, three to go."

Jack clapped his hands together and said, "How about a movie? I picked up a few at the video store yesterday." The casual statement gave no hint of the time that he had spent agonizing over what she might like and eliminating dozens of movies because they were too silly, too violent, or too sexy.

"That sounds great. But first, I was wondering if you could give me a tour," Annie replied. "I've never been beyond the living room and I just wanted to have a better idea of where I'll be living soon."

This hadn't occurred to Jack and he immediately looked sheepish for neglecting to do it earlier. "Sure. I'm sorry. I didn't think about that." He looked around. "Well, this is the kitchen. I guess you know that." He walked into the living room. "And this is the living room. I guess you know that, too." Her only reaction was a grin.

He led the way into a narrow hallway. He stepped through an open door into a small room and she followed. "This is my office." She stood in the center of the room and looked around. Closet doors indicated that the room was originally intended to be a bedroom. There was a computer sitting on an ancient desk and, beside the desk, a cheap metal filing cabinet. On a little table on the other side of the desk he had a small sturdy cardboard box that contained what appeared to be a few bills. There were also a few papers lying on the table and on the desk but overall the room was tidy. The only decorations on the wall were a metal sign with a feed logo and his name on it and a clock on the wall that announced the seconds passing.

He stepped back into the hallway and showed her the bathroom. "This is the bathroom. There's another one in the laundry room." He stayed in the hallway but motioned her to go in. The small room smelled of Zest soap and some kind of aftershave. He watched as she surveyed the standard tub and shower combination and the two sinks separated by a few toiletry items. She imagined her things sitting next to his and wondered which sink would be hers. She caught a glimpse of her image in the mirror and she thought about how the girl looked out of place.

He led the way down the hall, opened a door to the right, and stepped in. It was completely empty, which was a surprise to Annie. She and her mother had lived in numerous houses of various sizes over the years and they had never had an empty room. Any room that didn't have a purpose became a catch-all for boxes and miscellaneous clutter. Annie's mother was always holding on to as much as she could. Annie marveled at Jack's apparent lack of any sort of need for all the extra stuff that the rest of the world couldn't live without.

"I thought this would be the baby's room," Jack said. His words bounced off the blank walls and caught Annie off-guard. The words echoed in her mind. The baby's room. She looked at the empty space and imagined a crib and a rocking chair. And little fire trucks and baseballs. Or maybe baby dolls and dresses. As she thought about it, mild panic ran through her veins and she was at once both impatient and unready for all that the baby would bring.

Seeing the emotion on her face, Jack gave her some time for her thoughts but then interrupted them by walking out and into his bedroom which was at the end of the hallway. "And this is my bedroom." Although a modest size, it was the biggest of the three bedrooms. He walked over to the closets and opened what would be her side. "This will be your closet. Unless you want the other side. I can move my stuff if you do." She assured him that he didn't need to. He slid the door shut again, struggling to keep it on its track. "I'll fix that for you before the wedding," he said embarrassedly. She knew he would.

Although this was the biggest room that they had been in, as they stood there together, they both felt the walls pressing in on them, not giving them room to breathe properly. Annie's eyes circled the room. They ran to the dresser with a pair of folded jeans sitting on top, to the crucifix that was hanging on the wall across from the bed, to the pajamas on the knob of his closet door, and finally to the small bed, which had been neatly made. Her mind pictured him in his lonely bed wearing the pajamas. Would he still wear them in a few weeks, when his bed wasn't so lonely?

Seeing her gaze and incorrectly guessing her thoughts, he said, "We'll have to get a bigger bed, of course."

"Yeah, that one might be a little crowded." She strived for the lighthearted teasing tone that she was usually so good at, but her voice sounded uncharacteristically tense.

Making a wide circle around her, he led the way back out of the room. In spite of the narrow space of the hallway, they both felt freed from the suffocating confines of the bedroom.

He led the way back through the hallway, living room, and kitchen. Nearly opposite the door that led to the garage, was another door that Jack now opened to reveal a fairly large utility room that held a washer and dryer, a coat rack, a series of shelves filled with caps, and a chest-style freezer. To the side of the room was a door that Jack opened to show her a half-bath.

Next he led the way down steps covered with thin carpeting into the basement. As she descended the steps, she was surprised to find a gigantic room that must have been the size of the entire house. There was a pool table covered with a sheet and another large table, both of which were lost in the large space. In one corner was a small kitchenette, complete with oven, sink, and refrigerator.

"This is awesome, Jack."

Jack explained, "My grandparents built this house after my dad and aunts and uncles were grown up. So they built the upstairs small for just the two of them but they made the basement big enough to hold all the family get-togethers." He went on, "I have a lot of great memories of this basement." He walked over to one of the metal poles that ran down the center of the area and caressed it with his hand. "My cousins and I used to spin around this and then shock each other." He walked over to a space at one end of the room. "And this is where Grandma and Grandpa always put their tree with all the presents." He walked over to the pool table. "And Grandpa could hear someone scratching the felt on his pool table no matter how loud it was in here."

He walked back to where she still stood at the foot of the stairs and they both sat down side by side on one of the steps. "And sometimes we would sit on the steps up there where the grown-ups couldn't see us," he pointed behind him where a half wall concealed the top steps from the main area of the room, "and listen to what our parents would say about us."

She asked him about his grandparents, aunts, uncles, and cousins and, in turn, he asked about hers. They sat on the step for quite a while, sharing both information and memories with one another.

When they finally went back upstairs, the clock told them that there wasn't time for the planned movie before they needed to go to supper, but Jack insisted that Annie lie on the couch and catch up on her rest. She agreed and gladly accepted the blanket that Jack offered her. As a shorter alternative to a movie, they decided on some old re-runs that were showing on television.

As she curled up on the couch, with Jack in his nearby recliner, her eyes were on the black and white television screen but her mind was elsewhere. She was thinking about how comfortable the old couch was, how warm the fuzzy orange blanket was, and how this house felt like home.

Chapter 28

Jack

As planned, they made their announcement to the sisters, including the pregnancy and the fact that Jack had not caused it, over supper. After a respectable amount of time, Annie had left, leaving Jack with his family to further discuss the matter without her.

She called Jack on Monday night. "So what'd they say after I left?"

"What, no 'Hi, how are you?' That's no way to start a phone conversation," he teased, making her wait for his response.

"What they'd say?" she persisted.

"They said more of the same thing that they said when you were there. How happy they are to finally have a sister-in-law, how nice you are, blah blah blah. You know, girl stuff." He didn't tell her of the concern that his sisters had voiced or that, after they had finished with all their urges to be careful and think about what he was about to do, they had begun plans for a surprise bridal shower. He thought that both could technically be classified as 'girl stuff' and it was better to not inform her of either topic.

"So they're fine with it?"

"Yes, they're fine with it." And, in spite of their concern, they really were. They, like his parents, knew that Jack used good judgment and that, even if this wasn't good judgment, he was old enough to make his own mistakes.

He heard her breathe a sigh of relief before she changed the subject. "Jack, I wanted to ask you something."

"Sure, go ahead."

"I have a doctor's appointment tomorrow. Do you want to go along?"

His intake of breath communicated through the phone line that she had caught him off-guard. "Do you want me there?" His answer depended on hers.

"Only if you want to be there." They were stuck, each unsure of the other.

"I want to," he said hesitantly. "It's just that I don't know anything about this stuff. I always leave the room as fast as I can when my sisters start talking about amniotic fluid and dilating cervixes and babies dropping and, well, I guess I listened enough in health class to know what all that means, but I'm not sure that I'm going to be much good in a woman doctor's office."

She laughed out loud. "It's not a 'woman doctor', it's an obstetrician, and he's a man, not a woman."

"See, I told you. I wouldn't even be able to find the office in the yellow pages, let alone know what I'm doing once I get there."

She laughed again, "You'd be fine." She became serious again. "But I don't want to force you to go if you don't want to."

"Are you going to have to take your clothes off?" he asked innocently, concerned about respecting her privacy.

"Would that convince you to come?" He blushed, glad that she couldn't see over the phone.

"It might." Were they really flirting with one another? Jack told himself that she might have the same type of conversation with any one of the old men at the diner.

"Well, I'm sorry to disappoint you but they told me last time that I could keep my clothes on this time."

"I guess I could come anyway." He tried to read her thoughts over the phone. "I take it since you invited me that you wouldn't mind."

"If you're going to be the daddy, you might as well start now, don't you think?"

He wished he would have started from the very beginning, but better late than never. They agreed to meet at the doctor's office and said goodbye.

Jack arrived early the next day and waited in his truck until Annie pulled in. The walked in together. He watched her sign her name in loopy letters on the list at the receptionist's window. They sat down side by side, separated by the wooden arm of the waiting room seats. He picked up a magazine about pregnancy and thumbed through it nervously, turning the pages so quickly that it was obvious that he wasn't reading even the titles of the articles. In just a moment, Annie was called back and the nurse invited Jack back also.

While Jack watched, she stepped on the scales and got her blood pressure checked. He waited awkwardly in the hall when she went into the bathroom to provide a urine sample. Then the nurse led them to the examining room and left them alone. Jack looked around the room. He walked over to a table where plastic models of nine fetuses in various stages of development were displayed, each nestled inside a plastic uterus that had been cut in half like an apple. Each uterus was cradled by a metal wire that stuck up from a base that announced the month of development. He picked up the one that said "The Fourth Month". He carefully brought it over to where she sat on the table and said, "So this is what your baby looks like now." The word "your" left his lips without thought. In his mind, it was her baby. It didn't yet feel like theirs.

She studied it for a moment before she whispered, "You better put it back. I'm not sure you're supposed to be touching those."

He replaced it, being sure to put it back as he had found it.

The doctor knocked and then walked in. "Hello, hello. And how are we today?" He shook Annie's hand and then shook Jack's. "I don't think we've met," he said, prompting an introduction by Annie.

"This is Jack Schroeder. We're engaged. I thought he might like to hear the baby's heartbeat."

"That's great." He probably assumed Jack to be the father and neither one corrected him. Even though Dr. Walton had not been in town long, he must have already picked up the need to figure out everyone's place in the world. "Let's see… Schroeder…You wouldn't be Meg Schroeder's son?" Although Meg was past childbearing years, Jack knew that she saw him for her yearly exams and for some problems that had developed with menopause, the details of which Jack was thankfully ignorant. Jack nodded. The doctor wrinkled his brow, thinking. "That must mean you're Kate's brother." Jack nodded again.

He got out his chart and asked questions about the various aspects of pregnancy. Was she over her morning sickness? Any pains in her abdomen? Spotting? Swelling of hands or feet? He asked if she were taking her vitamins and getting enough rest. He looked at the chart and declared her weight, blood pressure, and urine to all be satisfactory. Then he invited her to lay back so that he could measure her uterus and listen for the heartbeat.

"You'll need to pull your shirt up and your pants down so I can see your tummy." She did as was instructed. Jack looked on, seeing for the first time a part of her that was usually covered. He looked at the smooth stomach, just beginning to be nicely rounded, and marveled at the beauty of her skin. He pictured the plastic model that he had held in his hands a moment ago nestled inside of her.

The doctor pressed gently on her stomach and measured with a tape measure the distance from the bottom to the top of her uterus. As he did so, he pulled her pants down slightly more than she had, revealing some of her pubic hair. Jack noticed that as soon as the doctor turned to record the measurement on his chart, she quickly pulled her pants up to cover this part of herself, embarrassed that Jack had seen it. Jack wished that he could tell her that it was okay, that it was beautiful but not sexual right now.

"Okay, let's see if we can hear that baby. We should be able to pick up a pretty good heartbeat by now." He squirted some gel on her abdomen and picked up a device that was hooked to a speaker. He glided it over her abdomen and they heard some random swishing sounds. Jack wondered if this was the heartbeat or, if they listened close enough, they might be able to make out a heartbeat within the noise. The doctor looked at the far wall as he continued running the device over her stomach.

Suddenly, the unmistakable sound of the baby's heartbeat filled every inch of the room, incredibly loud and strong. The baby was speaking to them with the only voice that he had, announcing to them that he was alive and well. It was as if another person had entered the room and vivaciously announced "Here I am!"

The discomfort that Jack had felt at being in this place for women now vanished. This was the baby that he would raise and love along with her. He *did* belong here, standing beside Annie as she went through her journey toward motherhood. He grabbed her hand that lay beside her on the table and the three of them were joined.

Jack looked down at Annie and saw in her eyes all the awe that he was feeling in his own heart. She squeezed his hand and he knew it was an unspoken "thank you". Thank you for coming today. Thank you for agreeing to be this child's daddy. Thank you for seeing the wonder in this. Thank you for holding my hand.

He squeezed back his own thanks. Thank you for inviting me. Thank you for letting me be a part of this miracle.

Too quickly, the doctor put the device back in its holder and wiped the gel from her stomach with paper towels. She covered herself and sat up while he recorded a few more notes and then asked if there were any questions. He wanted to see her back in six weeks and promised to do an ultrasound the visit after that, at six months.

Jack walked Annie to her car. Because there were no words for what they had experienced, they remained silent except for a brief goodbye.

As Jack drove home, he worked to grasp the magnitude of what he had witnessed and couldn't. It was then that he knew what he needed to do. He drove past his house and continued on before arriving at his church and letting himself in. In the late afternoon, the stained glass windows lacked their Sunday morning glow and the organ sat silent. But the holiness of the sanctuary didn't depend on the streaming sunlight or music filling the air. He walked down the center aisle, letting his hand caress the curved wood that stuck up on the ends of the empty pews. When he reached the front, he genuflected deeply and made the sign of the cross before the crucifix that hung behind the altar.

Then he turned and walked to the statue of Mary that sat in the front corner keeping watch over several rows of votive candles. He knelt before the Blessed Mother and prayed to God, imagining Jesus as that tiny plastic fetus that he had held in his hands, and thanked God for coming to earth as such a vulnerable child. He looked up at the statue above him and reflected on Mary's role in salvation and what it was like for her to have both the privilege and duty of giving birth to Jesus. And he thought about Annie and her privilege and duty to carry this precious new life. He thought about Joseph and what a great responsibility he must have felt to care for both mother and child, the same responsibility he now had.

He stayed on his knees for a long time. He didn't notice the darkness fall around him. He didn't hear the man who lived next door and who locked the door each night at dark, peek in and then discreetly disappear, not wanting to interrupt his prayers.

Finally Jack stood, took the box of ordinary kitchen matchsticks that sat on the metal stand in front of him and struck the dark red tip. The match lit the corner of the now nearly dark church. He touched the match to the tips of three dark candles in their red glass holders, bringing them to life. First he lit a candle for the baby, praying that the child would grow strong and healthy. Then he lit a candle for Annie, praying for her health during the pregnancy and delivery. And, finally, he lit a candle for himself, praying that he might be worthy of the task that God had blessed him with, that of caring for and loving both mother and child.

Chapter 29

Annie

Four days later, Annie was a bundle of nerves as she put on the larger pants and oversized sweater that she had bought a few days before. She looked at the clock. She still had fifteen minutes before he would pick her up. As she returned to the bathroom to brush her hair again, she coached herself, "It's just another hurdle. You can do it."

She thought about all the hurdles that had been jumped since she and Jack had decided to enter this race just a few weeks ago: all the things that they had discussed, the meeting with the priest (twice now), telling her mom, telling his parents, talking to Eric, numerous wedding preparations, telling his sisters. Each one had been difficult but had gone better than expected, leaving no scars, only a sense of accomplishment and an increasing belief that this crazy scheme would work. She hoped that the marriage conference today would be the same.

She went out into the kitchen where her mom was sipping coffee and reading the paper, still in her silk pajamas that had been a gift from her most recent husband. "Hey, honey." She looked her up and down. "New outfit?"

"Yeah." She moved around the room, straightening the already tidy kitchen.

Her mother looked at her and said, "Sit down, would you? Good grief, you're making me nervous."

She went to obey, but just before her bottom hit the chair, she heard his pick-up pull into the drive and stood back up. She moved to the door and opened it before he could ring the bell. Her mom remained seated but put the paper flat on the table, waved, and greeted him through the small living room that separated the front door from the kitchen where she sat. "Good morning, Jack."

"Good morning, Cindy." There was the slightest pause before he said her name, indicating that he wasn't yet completely comfortable with that level of familiarity. "Thanks again for supper on Wednesday." He had come over after they had seen Father Bill for the second time.

"Your welcome, Sweetie."

He stood with his hands in the pockets of his coat. Annie grabbed her coat and gave her mom a kiss on the cheek and stepped out into the cold November morning through the door that Jack held open for her.

As they began the long drive, both were quiet. "How are you?" he asked.

"Good. How 'bout you?"

They drove on. "Do you know your way to this place?"

"No, not really, but I looked it up on MapQuest. The print-out is there on the dash."

She unfolded the piece of paper and looked at the directions but wasn't able to focus on them.

Sensing her tension, he asked, "Do you wish we were just getting married by a judge?"

"No. No, not at all. I know this is important to you. It's fine, really."

"I appreciate that."

After an uncomfortable silence, Annie asked him about the farm and gradually their tongues loosened and the minutes went by quickly, like the telephone poles and fields that were now stripped of their crops. Soon Annie was reading the directions that had been forgotten in her hand and they were in the parking lot of Our Lady of Sorrows. It was a former convent that had been converted to a retreat center. They joined the stream of other young couples entering the front door.

In spite of her nervousness and professed lack of interest in religion, Annie found herself enjoying the day. It was the closest thing to a classroom that she had experienced for over a year and, having always been an eager student, she missed it.

Throughout the day, married couples talked about their experiences and shared the Church's teaching on various aspects of marriage. Then, after each talk, couples spread out and Jack and Annie had time and space to talk privately about what they thought and how to apply it to their marriage. Besides listening intently to the formal talks, Annie willingly participated in the private discussions with Jack and they found themselves working out the details of marriage that they hadn't yet discussed, such as budgeting and division of household chores.

At the end of the day, they climbed a curved staircase up to the chapel and Annie experienced her first Catholic Mass. She silently read the readings in the missal as several selected young people read them aloud at the lectern. She sang along with the hymns in a shy voice. She listened and watched as the priest blessed and broke the bread.

Before communion, the priest reminded the couples that non-Catholics didn't receive communion and Annie was relieved to have the company of other non-Catholics as she remained in the pew and let Jack squeeze by her. While she waited in her seat, Annie watched the others. In general, the non-Catholics who remained in their seats seemed bored and Annie had to admit that it had been a long day with a lot of sitting. Of those who received communion, there seemed to be two groups: those that seemed to take it seriously and those that didn't. She watched Jack as he inched his way toward the front of the line and waited for the priest to hand him his wafer. She noticed how he bowed deeply beforehand and made the sign of the cross afterwards. When he returned to his seat he kneeled and prayed fervently. Jack was definitely in the serious group, Annie decided. She looked at the back of his head that was in front of her as he knelt in prayer and she wished that she knew what he was thinking and, perhaps more importantly, what he was feeling.

Driving home, they had lots to talk about. "So what did you think?" Jack asked.

"It was good. It was really good. They covered a lot of really useful stuff."

"So how long do you think Roger can put up with Ashley?"

Annie laughed. At lunchtime, they had sat with Ashley and Roger. Ashley had interrupted Roger's meal at least five times by requesting that he get out of his seat to get something for her. Each time, she criticized what he did or how long it had taken him to do it. Annie feigned surprise at the question, "Why do ask that? It looks like the perfect relationship to me." She changed her voice to imitate Ashley's sugary-sweet tone. "Oh, by the way, honey, do you think that you could drive just a little faster, please? And I would just love it if you would stop somewhere to get me a fresh squeezed lemonade." Jack laughed, appreciative as always of her sense of humor.

"Speaking of stopping, I'm hungry. I don't know why, but that chicken salad just didn't stick with me," Jack said. They had served a meal that seemed to be geared more toward the women than the men and Annie knew that Jack had missed his usual meat and potatoes fare. "Are you hungry for anything in particular?" Jack asked. "We'll be going through a town soon. But I only noticed fast food when we went through this morning."

Annie said that was fine and they stopped at McDonald's where Annie ordered a hamburger for herself and yogurt and salad for the baby. They sat down at their postage stamp-sized table and opened their wrappers and containers.

Annie took a breath and asked, "So the priest is pretending to be Jesus?"

Jack's Big Mac stopped on its way to his mouth so he could answer before he took the next bite. He seemed surprised by the question. "Yes, I guess you could say that. It's a reenactment of the Last Supper."

Annie wondered about the Last Supper. She had seen the famous painting but other than that knew nothing about it. She considered asking more questions but knew that any more answers would just lead to more questions. "Oh, okay," she replied.

"What did you think of Mass?" Jack asked.

"It was okay, but there was a lot I didn't understand." She had felt like she did the first time she had been at his house for grace. Just like on that day, today she had marveled at the beauty of the moment but hadn't felt like a real participant.

"It'll take time." He paused, then said, "Thank you for going with me."

He sounded so hopeful and she didn't want him to expect more than she was prepared to give. "I didn't have a choice, remember? It's part of our agreement that I go along with your religion."

Jack searched her face. She knew he was looking for bitterness or anger, but there wasn't any. "Yeah, I guess it is," he said, disappointed that the interest that he had witnessed throughout the day and just now when she asked about the Mass seemed to have disappeared as surely as their supper.

Chapter 30

Jack

When they returned to Annie's house after the conference, Jack accepted Annie's invitation to come in. They stepped into the living room to find her mom and Ray cuddled up under a blanket on the couch. It was obvious from their flushed cheeks, the disarray of Cindy's clothes and hair, and the guilty look on Ray's face that their return was not particularly well-timed. Annie was mortified and ushered Jack quickly to the kitchen, saying that she needed a drink of water.

Jack tried hard to control himself but he couldn't resist a comment. "Wait a minute. Isn't it supposed to be the *mother* that catches the *daughter* making out?" Jack asked good-naturedly. Although Annie was still mortified, his response lightened the situation. They waited in the kitchen and quietly sipped their water, giving the couple on the couch time to tidy their clothes and smooth their hair.

When they returned to the living room, Ray began making small talk and both Jack and Annie found him quite likeable. Although Ray himself didn't farm, he had grown up on a farm and this provided a steady stream of conversation between the two men. The conversation eventually turned to the wedding and Cindy shared some details of errands that she had run in Annie's absence that day.

Time passed smoothly and it was quite late by the time that Annie walked Jack to door and sent him home with a kiss on the cheek.

Jack drove home and thought about the day. He had been delighted by Annie's attentiveness during the long day. He remembered her beautiful but quiet voice as it had joined his in the hymns in church. He evaluated his answer to her question about the Mass and realized anew how inadequate it had been.

As he prepared for bed, he chuckled to himself as he thought about their interruption of whatever Cindy and Ray had been doing on the couch. But his chuckle stopped and his brow wrinkled as he remembered the peck on the check with which Annie had said goodnight to him. He was suddenly jealous of the kind of affection that made it difficult to keep your hands off of one another. He and Annie seemed to find it extraordinarily easy to be good.

Chapter 31

Annie

Annie opened her eyes slowly on Sunday morning, enjoying the luxury of waking up slowly, a luxury that the early mornings at the diner hadn't allowed her since the previous Sunday. The morning sickness had faded weeks ago and had left her with a wonderful awareness of how well she felt each morning. She lay in bed and thought about the day before. In her mind, she put together the information that she had received, the people that she had met, and the feelings that she had felt and experienced a sensation of satisfaction. Yesterday had been a surprisingly good day.

Annie stretched in bed. As she did so, her abdomen resisted slightly, reminding her that she was not alone. Having thought about the previous day, she now turned her attention to the day ahead. She had told Jack that she needed the day to herself to catch up on wedding stuff, some household chores, and rest. He had agreed to give her the first half for those things but begged her to come for Sunday supper. She smiled at the realization that she was actually looking forward to sharing another meal with Jack's noisy, joking, welcoming, wonderful family.

After she reluctantly pried the covers off, rolled out of bed, and readied for the day, she and Cindy spent time arranging the fall flowers that they had bought a week earlier into two bouquets, one for Annie and a smaller one for Cindy, who would be her matron of honor. They then made two flower arrangements to adorn the church and had enough left over for a few centerpieces for the tables at supper.

Jack had informed her that Meg had eagerly volunteered to make the arrangements for a simple dinner after the wedding ceremony. She had also suggested the church basement, which was used occasionally as a small hall and volunteered to arrange it if they wanted to eat there. Annie had agreed, grateful for the help, on the condition that the meal and any decorating of the basement be kept simple.

It was mid-afternoon when Cindy looked at the clock and said, "Wow, look at the time. Ray wants me over at his place this afternoon. He's taking me out for dinner. I better get ready." She disappeared into the bedroom and came out wearing a skirt and blouse and perfume.

"Wow. I take it you two aren't going to McDonalds," Annie commented.

"No, we're not going to McDonald's," she replied, a smug smile on her face.

Shortly after her mom left, Jack called. He was in town getting a few groceries and asked if he could pick her up. She agreed and they headed out of town once again. She had expected to go to Jack's house before stopping at his parents' for supper, so she was surprised when they pulled into Jack's parents' drive. She was even more surprised to find that there were about ten cars lining the large gravel area in front of the machinery buildings. Annie looked at Jack, who looked guilty.

"What are all these cars doing here?" she asked. She saw one that she recognized. "What's my mom's car doing here?"

"It wasn't my idea," was Jack's only reply, coming around and opening her door. He took her arm gently; leading her up the steps to the front door like an orderly might lead a reluctant patient down the hall for a painful medical procedure.

Meg opened the door and repeated Jack's words, "It wasn't my idea."

Behind her, women of various ages shouted "Surprise!" They stood to do so with the exception of three elderly women who shared the sofa and appeared unable to comfortably unfold themselves to participate in the greeting. The paper wedding bells and the stack of gifts told her that she was at her own bridal shower. She looked around at the fifteen or so faces and recognized Jack's four sisters, her mother, and no one else.

Jack saw her dismay and put an arm around her shoulder, pushing aside her emotions with a flood of introductions. "Well, everyone, this is Annie. Annie, this is my cousin Julie, my aunt Betty, Grandma…" He went on, pointing to each woman who in turn gave an acknowledgement with either a little wave or a "Nice to meet you".

When he was done he said, "Okay, well, I don't know what goes on at these things but I DON'T want to find out. So I'm outta here. Annie, whatever they tell you about me, it's all lies." He gave her an awkward, apologetic peck on the cheek and literally ran out the door and back to his truck so fast that Annie didn't have time to follow him and climb in before he put the truck in reverse and stranded her in this house full of women.

Meg, in the manner that Annie had so quickly grown accustomed to, quickly worked to make her feel at ease. She took her hand and led her to an easy chair that had been moved in front of the television for the event. Next to the chair, a folding card table that had been covered with a table cloth acted as a gift table. Folding chairs had been brought in and those along with the sofa and love seat formed a circle around the room. "The girls and I just thought that you might want to meet everyone before the wedding." In the silence of her own mind, Annie adamantly disagreed with this and hoped that her feelings weren't evident on her face.

Elizabeth chimed in, "And we also thought that you might want a set of dishes that matched and bath towels that weren't faded orange." Having eaten off of Jack's mismatched dishes and seen his orange towels, Annie laughed in spite of herself.

Each of Jack's sisters had planned a game. Sarah went first. Still trying to keep the sisters straight, Annie reminded herself that Sarah was the mother of the three boys and was the oldest of the sisters, closest in age to Jack. Sarah had each of the guests write an interesting but little-known fact about themselves on a slip of paper. The slips were collected and Annie had to read them out loud while everyone guessed who had written the item. Annie appreciated the opportunity to learn about her new extended family and was grateful for Sarah's thoughtfulness in her choice of game.

Mary, who Annie had just met once, had a paper that on the left side had the rooms of the house and on the right blanks where the women had to give a piece of advice for a new bride about that room. When they were done, they passed them to the left and that person chose one piece of advice that could be applicable to the bedroom. They went around and read the advice and everyone laughed until they cried when the piece of advice intended for the kitchen became, "In the bedroom, always preheat the oven before you put something in it," and the piece of advice intended for the bathroom became, "In the bedroom, don't take too long, whatever you do!"

Cake and punch were served and then Kate, the mother of Christopher and baby Kimberly, conducted a trivia game about Jack. Kate had requested answers from Jack during the week, so Kate asked the question, Annie answered and then Kate read Jack's answer. She had a combination of the expected (What's Jack's favorite color?) and the unexpected (If Jack was stranded on a desert island, what is the one thing he would want with him?). Annie did surprisingly well, which was a result of both Jack's predictable nature and the fact that Kate had mercifully made the questions multiple-choice.

Fun-loving Elizabeth's game was last. A show-person by nature, she gave a lavish introduction, saying that Annie had packed a suitcase full of lingerie so that she could dress up and impress Jack on her wedding night. Elizabeth then handed Annie a plaid suitcase which must have been made in the 1950's and was itself a source of laughter, especially among the sisters for whom it brought back memories of family vacations and sleepovers. She went on to say that just when she was ready to get all dressed up for their romantic night, the lights went out in the hotel and Annie had to get dressed in the dark. At this, Elizabeth pulled out a blindfold and put it over Annie's eyes, tying it behind her. The ladies then watched as Annie pulled out items that she couldn't see from the suitcase and put them on over her clothes. They included men's boxer shorts, a huge bra, lipstick, slippers, and rubber gloves. By this time, Annie had relaxed enough to actually enjoy this comedy in which she was the star.

When she had "undressed" from the last game and was just starting to open the gifts, the men and kids arrived. They had all gathered at Kate's house, the men watching football and the kids drinking sugared drinks and wrestling without interruption in the absence of their mothers. When Meg saw them walk in, she looked at the clock and exclaimed, "My, where did the time go?" and hurried to the kitchen to pop a few things in the oven for their usual Sunday night meal.

Jack stood in the kitchen, looking into the living room and taking in the scene. Annie sat amidst his family, and everyone was glowing from the laughter that they had just shared. When his eyes met hers, the light in hers told him that she had had a joyous afternoon. The light in his told her of the delight that he felt to see her relaxed and happy with his family.

"Jack, you're just in time to use those muscles of yours to break some of the stubborn ribbons." Cindy's words broke the look that they were sharing and Jack walked over to the table, and stood awkwardly in the middle of the circle of women without a place to sit, like he had just lost a round of musical chairs.

Meg came in with a kitchen chair, Jack sat, and Jack and Annie opened gifts together. Annie had never been one to gush over gifts, but her sincere appreciation of these women's thoughtfulness on such short notice was evident with each heartfelt "Thank-you" that was said. They did indeed get dishes and towels as well as a variety of other useful gifts to replace Jack's collection of hand-me-down household supplies. Annie's favorite gift was a beautiful afghan that Jack's grandmother had crocheted. "It's been in the closet waiting for you, dear." Annie got up and went over to the old woman who had a cane propped beside her on the couch. She grabbed her hand and gave the woman a kiss of thanks on the cheek as Jack looked on.

When the pile of wrapped gifts had been transformed into a stack of items for the house, Meg declared it time to eat. A few of the women excused themselves, needing to get back to their families. Some stayed and joined the usual Schroeder gang for grace and the meal, which gave Annie more time to get acquainted with them. Cindy stayed also, easily making friends with everyone there.

When the plates had been cleared and last piece of pie was gone, the extra guests cleared out, leaving just Jack and his sisters and their families. Cindy also stayed, enjoying the company of this new family with whom she would share her daughter.

The men, except for Jack, gravitated toward the television and the sisters remained around the table, talking about how the shower had gone and then discussing the wedding. Annie had asked Kate about Christopher's role of ring bearer last week when the wedding was announced and they finalized this now. In keeping with the casual nature of the wedding, he would just wear a button-down shirt and tie and slacks. Annie talked to Mary about a flower girl, or rather lack of one. Mary's daughter was Jack's only niece besides infant Kimberly, but because Annie wanted to keep it simple, Abby was a little too young, and Annie didn't have the prior relationship she had with Christopher, she had decided against using the girl as flower girl. To Annie's relief, Mary agreed and assured her that it was fine.

The sisters, who were each bringing a dish to the reception dinner, discussed their choices with Annie and Jack, making sure they approved of each dish. Cindy told them that she and Annie had made a couple of centerpieces for the tables. Annie reminded Frank and Kate of the brief rehearsal planned on Wednesday and invited Kate and her family and Frank and Meg to supper afterwards.

When it seemed like all the necessary details had been talked about, Cindy yawned, and then stretched her arms above her head, displaying her shapely figure which, Annie noticed, merited an appreciative glance from Jack's dad. "My goodness, it's late. Annie, would you like to ride back with me or is Jack taking you?"

Annie looked across the table at Jack, who didn't seem to have an opinion. "I might as well ride back with you."

She stood up and looked around the table at her future sisters-in-law and Jack's mom. Their kindness seemed to wrap itself around her, choking her and making her unable to say what she needed to. She opened her mouth to thank them but instead burst into tears. Immediately all five women surrounded her, asking if she were okay. This served only to intensify Annie's feelings and the tears continued to flow while an explanation of her tears stuck in her throat. Someone sat her back down on the chair, another brought her a drink, and all waited patiently for her to find words.

"I'm sorry. I don't know why I'm crying," She finally managed between sobs. Her eyes cleared enough to see the circle of understanding faces. Behind them, she spied Jack, sporting a look of complete panic.

Kate looked at her and smiled with empathy, "Well, I know why you're crying. You're pregnant. That's what pregnant women do. You don't have to apologize."

Sarah said, "We shouldn't have surprised you with the shower. It was too much."

Annie was quick to refute that idea. "No, no it was great. I loved it." Her tears started again. It was, more than anything else, the generosity of the shower that had overwhelmed her, making her question whether she deserved all that they had done for her and all the lovely gifts the women had given her. She tried to explain this to her new sisters. "It's just that you're so wonderful. I didn't expect all this. You really didn't have to do so much for me."

It was Mary who took Annie's hand and showed her understanding of Annie's doubts by saying, "But we did have to. You're becoming part of this family. And it doesn't matter how you got here. What matters is that you're part of the family and we want you to feel that way."

Annie smiled and nodded her acceptance of Mary's words while the tears began again. Elizabeth fetched a Kleenex, which Annie gratefully used on her eyes and nose. When the well had dried up for the last time, Jack said "Cindy, you can go on home. I'll bring Annie in a little bit."

Annie collected herself at last and was able to finally say thank you for the shower. Elizabeth joked about her tears. "If niceness makes you cry, don't worry. We're not always this nice. Just ask Jack." Jack heartily agreed and Kate gave him a playful slap as Annie smiled through her remaining tears at their playful banter.

Chapter 32

Jack

At last Jack and Annie walked out to the truck, breathing in the cold November air. Jack started the engine and put the truck in drive, making the gravel of the drive pop under the tires. Annie said, "I'm sorry."

"Don't be. It's okay. I was just worried that you might be having second thoughts." He had, indeed, seen the tears flowing and had imagined to himself the words 'I can't do this after all,' coming out of her mouth.

"No, it's not that at all. Not at all. Are you having any second thoughts?" Annie asked.

"No, not at all. I love seeing you with my family."

"Well, Jack, like you once told me, I'm not marrying your family."

"I know. I love seeing you alone, too." His voice was raspy and he considered the possible things they might do when they were alone together.

Offerings

Annie quickly changed the subject. "So, have things slowed down enough for a trip to town for a cup of coffee?"

He grinned. He had just been thinking about "coffee", the kind of coffee that his dad had been teasing him about all fall. "Sounds good. I just might come in for one. Speaking of work, did you ask off for a few days?"

"Yep. I have Thursday and Friday off."

"Think you could get Monday off, too?"

"I think so."

"Good, I'd like to get away over the weekend and it'd be nice if you didn't have to go back until Tuesday."

"I'll ask. It shouldn't be a problem. Do you have any hotel reservations made? Do you need me to do anything?"

"I've made all the arrangements. I hope you don't mind."

"That's great. Where are we going?" Annie asked.

"It's a surprise," Jack replied, then quickly added, "Not a big surprise, if that's okay, just a surprise."

"That's fine. Anywhere's fine. How's the farming going?"

"We're in good shape, thanks to the weather. Anything that needs finished up after Thursday Dad can do." The nervous excitement of the wedding being just a few days away made his throat dry.

They arrived at Annie's house and Jack made no move to get out of the truck. The dim light of the street lamp let them see each other in shadowy darkness. "So, the next scheduled event is the wedding rehearsal on Wednesday."

"I guess so."

"Annie?"

"Hmm."

Should he ask or should he just do it? He asked. "Can I kiss you?"

"I think it's probably past time you did," she consented. He leaned forward and pressed his lips politely but firmly to hers.

She kissed back but where he had hoped for eagerness, he sensed only obedience. And where he had hoped for desire, he sensed only duty. They separated and he looked in her eyes. He searched for any sign of love and saw only an apology for its absence. He quickly looked away and got out of the truck before she could see the disappointment in his own eyes.

As always, he opened the truck door for her and walked her to the step. He took her hand and asked one last time, "You're sure?"

"I'm sure." Looking in her eyes now, he could see her determination. He kissed her cheek and said good-night.

As he drove home, he thought about the kiss and all that it had lacked but he also thought about her unwavering confidence in the plans that they had made. "Determination might be better than love anyway," he said out loud, trying to convince himself of something that he knew wasn't true.

He continued to contemplate the two ideas of love and determination as he lay alone in his bed, trying to sleep. He decided that either one of the two might bring about the other. He prayed that this would happen and happen soon, because the success of any marriage depended on both.

Chapter 33

Annie

During the month that she and Jack had been planning the wedding, Annie had not breathed a word to anyone at the diner. Maggie had been quick to figure out the pregnancy and, because Annie had confided in her last summer, knew some of the details of how it had come about. But the wedding plans remained a secret and, while Frank could have easily started the gossip among the old men, it didn't seem that he had.

So Annie arrived at the diner on Monday morning with a short stack of invitations that she had printed herself and a giddy anticipation that she could barely control. Over the past year, she had listened to the old men's playful but persistent teasing of Jack's bachelorhood and, from time to time, the passing suggestion that she might be the cure for it. She smiled to herself as she put on her apron and noted that the strings seemed to have shrunk over the weekend. She hummed as she started the coffee, glad that it no longer made her stomach turn over.

Then she passed out the envelopes. In front of each upside-down coffee cup that waited on its saucer on the counter, she leaned an envelope with the hand-written name of the man who would soon be drinking from the cup. She imagined them finding and opening their invitations. They would be flabbergasted, indeed, to know that they would need to come up with a new target for their ribbing.

Annie heard Maggie let herself into the back door and knew that she was putting her purse away in the tiny break room. Soon her face peeked through the order window. "Good morning. You're looking wide-eyed for a Monday morning."

"I'm feeling good."

"Feeling good? God, when I was in your condition I never felt good."

"Maggie, I have something for you." She walked through the swinging door into the kitchen and pulled the last envelope from her apron pocket where she had put it a moment ago.

"What's this?"

Annie blushed. "Just open it."

Maggie slipped a rough finger into the flap of the envelope and pulled out the folded card made of cream-colored cardstock. Annie watched her eyes move back and forth over the words and her expression changed from puzzlement to disbelief to astonishment.

"You're marrying Jack? Jack Schroeder? When did this happen?"

Annie glanced at the clock that hung over the back door. "I gotta go open up."

Maggie grabbed her arm. "Oh no, you don't. They can knock if they need in. You're staying right here and telling me how the hell all this happened. I want to hear every juicy detail." Annie stayed put as ordered, knowing that the first customer usually didn't arrive quite this early, especially with the colder weather and longer nights of late fall.

She told Maggie the basic facts and Maggie hung on every word. Although Maggie hadn't joined in any of the coffee counter banter, she always listened to what she could through the order window. She had secretly agreed with the old men that Jack's bachelorhood had lasted way too long and that kind and industrious Annie would, indeed, be a good match for him. This fall when Annie had finally admitted to being pregnant, the older woman had been outwardly supportive, hiding her disappointment that, like other waitresses that had come and gone over the years, Annie had taken the wrong turn and was now headed down a rocky path toward no place in particular. And now the invitation that she held in her hand was an announcement that Annie had somehow found a way back to the main road.

The woman hugged the girl and then held her at arms length and looked at her. To Annie's surprise, there were tears in the older woman's eyes. "Annie, honey, you've been blessed. You hang on to that man. He's a good one. I know it. And don't you worry. I wouldn't miss the wed-"

They were interrupted by a knock at the front door. Annie looked at the clock. 6:17. She hurried to the door and let in a sleepy-eyed man that she didn't recognize. He made his way to the counter and she quickly whisked away the envelope with Ralph's name on it and put it on the mug that was the next one over, knowing that that seat was his second choice. A few moments later the first of the regulars started trickling in.

George, the oldest of the old men, who wasn't a day under 90, came in first, hanging his coat and hat on the rack before taking his place at the counter. He sat down and looked at his envelope, moving it away from him and back towards him again, trying to see the writing more clearly. Annie wondered that he was still able to drive himself here each morning. She heard the sizzle as Maggie dropped his daily sunny-side-up egg onto the griddle. "Well what do we have here? I don't think it's my birthday. Annie, you know what this is?"

"Why don't you open it and find out?"

"Well, yes, I guess that's a fine idea." He slid his bent finger into the opening and pulled out his invitation. He patted the pockets of his bib overalls, looking for his glasses which weren't there. Annie hoped that he had used them to drive with and then left them in the truck.

While he was still searching, Al walked in, shed his coat and took his place. He looked at the cards at each place and noticed that George had already opened his. "What you got there, George?" he asked.

"I don't rightly know. My spectacles walked off again. Maybe you can read it for me." He handed the card to Al, who held it at arms length and read out loud:

> You're invited to the wedding of
> Annie Norton
> and
> Jack Schroeder
> on the
> Seventeenth Day of November
> at 6:30 p.m.
> at St. Mary Catholic Church
> A light meal will follow

Al looked up at Annie and said what she knew he would, "Is that right?" Annie smiled and nodded as the door opened and Vince came in.

He made his way to his place at the counter and picked up his invitation. Annie moved George's egg from the window to the counter and

Vince grinned at her. "I hope this is what I think it is." He momentarily ignored his friends and opened his envelope, smiling sheepishly. "I was wondering when I could let on that I knew. Frank told me last week but made me swear not to know. Congratulations. I wasn't expecting to get invited, though. That's real nice of you, Annie." Annie knew that if any of the men here had a friendship that went beyond coffee and current events, it was Vince and Frank, so Annie wasn't surprised that Vince had known. Annie wondered how much Frank had told him and whether or not it had been presented as happy news.

A couple came in and Annie seated them and attended to them. While doing so, Ralph strolled in, patting each man on the back in greeting as he took his place at the far end of the counter. Everyone at the counter watched, even the stranger who was enjoying the interesting start to what he thought would be a dull day of travel. Ralph picked up the card and looked at it. "What the hell's this? An invitation to my own funeral?" He looked around and saw the others with theirs.

"Open it and read it yourself, Ralph," Vince urged.

He opened it and mumbled the words under his breath as he read them. "Is this some kind of joke?" Annie, who had returned to the counter, thought that it would have been a great joke. She should have thought of it earlier.

"No joke," Annie said, smiling and taking off with the two coffees requested by the couple at the table.

"Maybe it is a joke," Al said to Ralph. "It would serve you right for teasing them."

"Ah, hell, who doesn't like to be teased a little?" Ralph replied, still examining his invitation, trying to make sense of it.

His eyes lit up as a memory came to him, providing him with some material to work with. "So, Annie, you must have liked what Jack served you when you went over to his house for supper and skipped the supper."

Annie laughed out loud as she shoved the couple's order under a clip on the metal carousel that hung to the side of window and spun it around to Maggie. She had forgotten all about that conversation. "Best I ever had, Ralph. I decided he can cook for me every night, if you know what I mean."

"Who can cook for you every night?" Jack asked as he took his place at the counter. Annie turned and blushed bright red. She had been so absorbed with the order and the matching of wits with Ralph that she hadn't noticed his entrance.

"Why, you, Jack. Who else?" She regretted the direction that she had let this conversation go, not wanting to submit Jack to a game of sexual innuendo after the lukewarm response that she had given him to last night's kiss.

Al piped in, "Rumor has it, Jack, that she likes your, ah, cooking so well that she's going to marry you."

Jack noticed the invitations and remembered Annie once mentioning to him possibly inviting the men at the diner. He had forgotten all about it and felt like he had just walked into an ambush. He hadn't expected to be the topic of conversation.

It was Jack's turn to blush. As he struggled for something clever to say about his "cooking", Vince stood up, walked the short distance over to where he sat and extended a hand. "Congratulations, Jack." He gave Jack a hearty pat on the back with his left hand as he shook with his right. Al and George called their congratulations out from their stools.

"Thanks," was all Jack could say in reply.

"I don't know, Jack. You think you can handle her?" As always, Ralph was the one to give him a hard time.

"I think so, Ralph. If I need any advice, I'll let you know."

"My number's in the book. You can call anytime, even in the middle of the night if you get in a pinch."

"I hope she doesn't pinch," Jack replied. At this, Annie reached across the counter and gave him a playful pinch on the cheek.

The conversation continued in its pleasant teasing manner. The men all accepted the invitation, although George asked what was for supper before he agreed. Annie told them that it wouldn't be anything fancy at which Jack was quick to point out that wearing something besides overalls would be good.

They finally began clearing out one by one, everyone congratulating the future bride and groom, even the stranger who was now behind schedule for the day, having stayed longer than he planned. Jack sat on his stool until he was alone at the counter, watching Annie as she waited on a few tables and collected the pitchers of cream now that the coffee rush was over.

She smiled, feeling him looking at her and knowing that if she looked up she would see affection and, perhaps, even love in his eyes. She avoided doing so and kept her eyes on the clean counter she was wiping.

"What are you looking at?" she asked playfully.

"My future wife," he said simply.

She looked at him and saw the redness in the lining of his eyelids that told her that he hadn't slept well last night. She knew that her coldness had hurt him. "I'm sorry if I didn't seem very grateful last night," she apologized.

"I wasn't looking for a thank-you kiss."

"I know." She looked down, ashamed of what was missing in her heart. He reached over and put his hand under her chin, gently forcing her head up until her eyes met his.

"It's okay. It'll come." She felt the rough warmth of his fingers under her chin and looked into the deep brown of his eyes and she let herself accept the reassurance that he offered.

Chapter 34

Jack

On Tuesday, just two days before the wedding, Jack went to talk to his brother. It had been a long time since he had taken the time for a visit. As he stood there, with his head bowed and his cap in his hands, he realized that there was a lot to be said. He started, as he always did, with an update on the farm and family. He talked about harvest and what the crops had yielded. Although he was sure his mom already had, he told him of Kimberly's birth and talked about the other nieces and nephews.

And then he told him about the wedding that he would miss. He told his brother how much he regretted that it couldn't be him that would stand beside him at the altar as best man. He described Annie to him and longed for them to know one another. He shared with him the joy that he had found and his worries for the marriage that lay ahead.

He talked about how all that he had at one time planned for himself seemed to have changed. He cried softly when he realized that his brother was proof that things don't always go as planned. When the tears were finished, he filled his lungs with the cold autumn air and reflected aloud on the idea that what we plan isn't necessarily what God has planned. Fortunately, Jack had grown up being taught that, by God's nature, His plans are more perfect than anything we could come up with on our own. But standing where he stood, he knew this and doubted this at the same time.

Although his brother couldn't talk back, Jack knew that he heard the words that he spoke.

The day was cold and cloudy and by the time that he left the cemetery his feet were numb inside of his heavy brown work boots.

Chapter 35

Annie

Father Bill had requested that the three of them get together one more time before the wedding and they had arranged that this would be a brief meeting at the church, prior to the rehearsal and before the others arrived. She and Jack had agreed to meet at the church. Although the town was near Jack's house, Annie had never been there before so Jack had given her directions. They had turned out to be unnecessary because she had spied the steeple from miles away, poking up above the bare brown fields into the overcast November sky.

When she arrived only Jack's truck was parked in front. In another setting, the church might be considered small, but sitting among the small collection of tiny houses, it seemed large. She got out and looked up at the church, craning her neck to view the steeple now looming above her. She walked up the wide concrete steps and carefully pulled open the glass door and stepped into a darkening church. She walked quickly through the entryway, ignoring the bulletin board and the holy water font, both of which she felt weren't intended for her.

She stepped through another set of doors that were open wide, and found herself in the back of the sanctuary. The setting sun was illuminating the windows on one side of the church and creating colored pools of light on the pews. It was in one of these colored pools that she saw Jack. He knelt, head bowed, not hearing her silent entrance.

She tiptoed up to him, not sure whether this was to politely avoid interrupting him or to playfully startle him by sneaking up on him. He had left just enough space between himself and the aisle for her to slide in beside him. As she did so, he turned his head and looked at her, taking a moment to return from a place that was unknown to her.

"While you're at it, you might as well say a few for me, too," she said.

"That's just what I was doing." His eyes looked at hers and hers moved to look at the kneeler. He quickly made a sign of the cross to close his prayer and then moved backward to sit beside her.

"It's so quiet," she whispered. It was a silence that didn't beg to be filled but rather already was full of something that she could feel but couldn't understand.

"Yeah," he agreed.

"So this is where you go to church every week?" she asked in a quiet voice.

"Since I was a baby. Since before that, even, I guess."

"It's nice."

"Yeah," he agreed again.

Father shattered the quietness abruptly by opening the outside door widely and letting it close noisily behind him. He had warned that he was squeezing this meeting and rehearsal in between a diocese meeting and a youth group bowling party, which explained why it was immediately noticeable that his manner was more businesslike than in their past meetings in his office.

He flipped on a switch, illuminating the sanctuary and drying up the colored pools, leaving only the slightest hint that they had existed. He simultaneously greeted them and slid into the pew behind them. They turned to face him and each other, each with an elbow hung over the back of the pew.

He quickly confirmed that they still desired to marry and that they understood the commitment involved. Then he pulled out a sheet of scribbled notes from a cheap black portfolio that he had carried in with him. He read a few notes about the ceremony that he had taken at their most recent meeting, asking if he had everything right. He did.

When this was done, he leaned back and took a breath, signaling the change from business to small talk. "So are you two nervous?"

Jack and Annie looked at each other and said "No." in unison.

Father lowered the corners of his mouth and nodded, creating an expression that perhaps said "I'm impressed."

"And your parents, they're still okay with everything?"

"Yes," they both said together.

As if conjured up by Father's question, Cindy breezed in, carrying a floral arrangement in each hand, her cheeks red from the cold wind.

Annie jumped up and took one of the arrangements from her as she passed where they were sitting on her way to the front of the church. They each put one down on either end of the step that spanned the front of the church and led up to the altar. Mother and daughter quickly agreed on the placement and then stepped back in unison to judge them from a distance.

They walked back to where Jack and Father sat and introductions were made while Frank and Meg entered with Christopher and Kate.

They briefly walked through the ceremony. Once again, Father was businesslike, glancing at his watch once or twice. But he was also characteristically personable, commanding the rehearsal with humor and confidence. He was quick to compliment everything that Christopher did until he beamed with pride. He scooted Annie and Jack closer together as they practiced their vows, teasing that the guests would like to see both of them without having to move their heads.

When practice was over, they all stepped back out into the coldness. When they were in the church, day had turned to night and they talked quickly with hands in pockets and shoulders hunched up against the frigid air. Cindy announced that she had made reservations at the steakhouse in town. Father declined, explaining his prior commitment, and the others quickly agreed to meet there. So they all drove away from the village back to the town where Annie lived, Father turning towards the church and the other seven arriving at the restaurant.

The restaurant was the only place in town that could be considered fine dining and did a steady business, even on a Wednesday night. They all gathered inside the entrance while Cindy gave their name and then they were escorted to a large table on the far end of the dining area. On the way there, Frank stopped to say hello to an acquaintance and, when questioned, supplied that they were celebrating a wedding rehearsal dinner for "his boy". He then called Annie back from her trek over to their table to be introduced. The man, who turned out to be the owner of one of the local implement dealerships, sized her up and then congratulated her, telling her to keep her new father-in-law in line.

The waitress was a classmate of Annie's that was attending the community college in Findlay and waiting tables in the evening. They chatted a minute before she asked, "So is this your family?"

"Well, yes. This is my mom, Cindy," she gestured toward her mother. "And this is my…my fiancé, Jack, and his parents, sister, and nephew. Jack's Elizabeth Schroeder's brother." She gestured to each one, shy at having this private relationship now public. The girl congratulated her, showing no signs of shock or asking what sort of circumstances brought about the engagement and Annie relaxed a little.

After they were done ordering, a middle-aged woman approached the table and warmly greeted Meg. She introduced her to Frank as "Gladys from swim group." Then Gladys asked about the family and, for the third time that night, the engagement was explained and introductions were made. And, for the third time that night, no one questioned anything, but rather accepted the news with sincere good will.

When plates and glasses had been emptied, stomachs filled, and the dinner charged to Cindy's Visa card, they made their way back out to the parking lot and agreed to meet at the church the next day. They all got in their separate cars and went to their own homes. If anyone thought it was odd that the engaged couple didn't kiss goodnight or even say goodbye to one another, no one mentioned it.

Chapter 36

Jack

As usual, Jack woke up with the sun on Thursday, alone and in his twin bed. The peacefulness of sleep was gradually replaced with a nervousness that wouldn't let him remain in bed and anticipate the day ahead but rather pushed him to the bathroom and into the familiar routine of preparing for the day as though it were any other day.

And, like any other day, he showered and then shaved, with the towel wrapped around his waist. But today, after the razor had taken off the previous day's stubble, he took off the towel and stood before the reflection of his nude body in the large mirror.

For as long as he could remember, his body was something that was completely his own, intended to be kept to himself. He remembered how, as a boy, he had always locked the bathroom door to keep out his sisters, even when he was only brushing his teeth. He recalled a high school physical when he had had to "turn and cough" and the humiliation that that had caused him. He thought about times, the most recent was quite recent indeed, when he had found himself aroused and hoped that no one noticed. For so many long years he had guarded himself from physical intimacy, waiting to be sure of what God intended for him. Was the moment truly at hand? The moment when he could let his guard down and share himself completely with another person? He tried to convince himself that tonight, his wedding night, would be that moment, but he didn't believe it. He and Annie got along so well together but they still lacked the intimacy that he knew should exist between two people who married. While he presumed that Annie was willing to do her "wifely duties", he knew that that was exactly how she felt about it, that it was a duty and nothing more. He knew that tonight would be less than what it was meant to be.

He frowned at the direction that his thoughts were taking and refocused his attention on his reflection. The physical work of the farm was evident in the well-toned arms and chest. There was a little extra flab around his middle, but not much. The farmer's tan of the summer had faded some but was still there, making it look as if his chest and upper arms belonged to another, much paler, man. He looked lower, where the towel had been, and then quickly back up to his face. Once again the nervousness wouldn't let him stand there in anticipation, but rather pushed him back to his bedroom to get dressed in his standard jeans and flannel shirt. It would be many long hours before he could, at last, put on the suit that hung waiting on the closet door.

After he was dressed, he took his place in front of the window. Because of the extra time he had spent getting ready, the sun was higher than usual. He looked out across the bare fields and, like every other day, offered himself and his day to God.

Over the years, Jack had grown accustomed to the fluctuations of prayer. While he knew that God was always present, at times he felt this more than at other times. And while he knew that God always wanted something from him, sometimes he knew exactly what and sometimes he didn't. And while he always tried to do what God wanted, sometimes this was easy and sometimes it wasn't.

Today, as he stood at the window, Jack felt God's presence, knew precisely what God wanted, and knew it wouldn't be easy. God was asking him, once again, to wait.

Chapter 37

Annie

Annie took her time packing for the honeymoon. The clock was creeping along and it was a good way to fill the empty hours. "The next time I get married, it's going to be at 10:00 in the morning," she said to herself, laughing at the plans for her next wedding and, at the same time, finding the thought to be not funny at all.

She put all three pairs of pants which still fit her, more or less, in the suitcase. Jack had informed her that the trip had all been planned and, while he wouldn't tell her where they were going, he had said to bring comfortable, warm clothes and good walking shoes. "You won't need a snorkel, a parachute, or a rope for mountain climbing," he had teased her. He had also told her that he was honoring her request and keeping it simple and she had assured him that that was what she preferred.

She threw in her longest sweaters and sweatshirts, ones that covered her expanding waist, and then stood at a standstill. Would she need pajamas? She thought about lying naked with him all night long and decided that, yes, she needed pajamas. She grabbed her flannel pajamas from the back of her closet door, folded them, and put them in the suitcase. The puppy dogs on the flannel pattern looked up at her from the suitcase, their heads tilted to the side, questioning her, reminding her that it was her honeymoon. "All right, fine, you can stay here!" she told them and pulled the pajamas out of the suitcase and hung them back in her closet. After giving it some more thought, she decided to compromise and searched through her drawers for a skimpier summer pajama outfit that she hoped would say neither "Come and get it" nor "Keep your distance".

Her mom was working in the morning and then going into Findlay to pick up the cake they had ordered, so Annie ate lunch alone, pushing her food around and chewing every bite thoroughly, watching the clock hands move slowly around the face.

When each dish had been washed and she had loaded the suitcase into her car, she started dressing for the wedding early. She slid on the skirt of her cream-colored suit, breathing a sigh of relief when the zipper in the back slid up easily but then frowning at the bulge that hadn't been nearly as pronounced when she had tried it on at the store just two weeks ago. She didn't want to look pregnant on her wedding day, even though most of the people who would be there knew she was pregnant and the others, the men from the diner, wouldn't notice if she went into labor on the altar as long as they got their meal afterwards. She put on a silky brown blouse and then slid the suit jacket on, buttoning it so that it would conceal what the skirt didn't. She walked across the hall and studied herself from various angles in the full-length mirror that hung on the back of her mother's bedroom door. Then she stepped back and with a nod of approval she declared herself to look very elegant, mature, and not pregnant. Perhaps not as slim as she had been a few months ago, but at least not pregnant.

Offerings

She moved to the bathroom and plugged in the hot curlers. She and her mom had spent an evening experimenting with different styles and had together decided on an arrangement that was held back with ivory combs at the sides and loose curls down the back. When this had been accomplished, she once again surveyed herself and deemed her appearance to be quite satisfactory.

Not wanting to wrinkle her suit, she paced back and forth until her mother graciously walked through the door. Cindy looked at her daughter and tears filled her eyes. "Oh, honey, you're beautiful!" Warmth spread through Annie at her mother's words. There had been so many times over the years that her flamboyant mother had frowned at Annie's understated appearance. Compliments from her mother were rare and deeply appreciated.

With Cindy's presence, the hands on the clock moved more rapidly, perhaps trying to keep up with the older woman. Cindy ran from room to room, eating a bite in the kitchen, putting on her dress in her bedroom, and applying mascara in the bath. Then she started over again, eating a little more, digging for her shoes, painting her lips. All the while, she carried on a conversation with Annie about the details of the wedding and asked questions about the honeymoon plans that Annie couldn't answer. Finally they both stood in the living room, ready to go.

Jack and his parents were waiting when they arrived at the church. Jack walked up to her and carefully kissed her cheek. He told her that she looked beautiful and she told him that he looked handsome. Because the wedding was a weeknight and they didn't want to keep their guests later than necessary, they had agreed that some pictures would be taken before the ceremony. Sarah had insisted on a photographer, a friend of hers who was trying to get into the business and wanted the practice. She took all the usual shots of people involved in the wedding.

For most of them, Jack stood close, putting his arm around her waist, and Annie felt suddenly intimidated by this strong, older man who would soon be her husband. The photographer finished just as the first guest, George, arrived.

Cindy ushered Annie to the basement where, unnoticed by anyone upstairs, Jack's sisters had gathered. Sarah and Elizabeth were covering the last of the few tables that had been set in the middle of the room. Kate sat on a folding chair nursing Kimberly. Slow-cookers lined a table that sat against the far wall. The small floral arrangements that Cindy had made sat together on one table waiting for their final placement. A small table on the side held the cake which, as ordered, matched the flowers in the arrangements and in the bouquet that Annie held.

Sarah and Elizabeth stopped their work and greeted her warmly, commenting positively on her appearance. Then they resumed motion while they continued the conversation. They asked if she was nervous and, although she hadn't been when Father had asked yesterday, Annie realized that she now was and admitted so. They asked if Jack was, and she said simply no, she didn't think so. But the truth was that, while he didn't seem nervous, there did seem to be something bothering him and she wasn't sure what.

Chapter 38

Jack

Upstairs, Jack waited for the cue to walk to the front of the church and stand to wait on his bride. In the meantime, he talked with his father and greeted the few people who straggled in. After what seemed like an eternity, Father looked at his watch and then at him and asked, "Ready?" Although Jack really wasn't sure he was, he said, "Yep."

Meg poked her head down the steps, and called her daughters up to take their seats. Jack and his father walked to the front of the church and he stood there beside his father, feeling very alone. When the music started, Annie walked up and stood by his side. They both found themselves drawn into the current of the ceremony. They floated through the process, exchanging vows, trading rings, sharing a kiss, and walking out of the sanctuary as man and wife.

Although the guests were few, a traditional reception line was formed in the back. Meg predictably assumed the duty of being sure the men from the diner knew that supper would be down the basement. In just a few moments the last hand was shook and Annie and Jack followed the others down the steps.

In Schroeder style, a simple but filling meal was shared after which champagne was produced for a toast. When glasses had been filled, Frank stood and addressed the group.

"Well, as the best man, I guess it's my job to give the toast. I just want to say, Jack, that if you wanted me to have a really great speech planned, you should have given me a little more time to prepare." The group chuckled. He turned to his son. "Jack, ever since Annie started pouring my coffee last year sometime, I thought that she'd be a fine match for you and I'm glad you finally saw that, too. Better late than never." He now addressed Annie, "Annie, I hope that Meg and I did a decent enough job of raising Jack that he'll be a good husband to you. He's been a fine son to me." His voice broke slightly on the word "son", but he recovered quickly, raised his glass, and continued. "So, everyone, join me in wishing Jack and Annie all the best." Jack thought that the clinking of the glasses sounded like good wishes: bright and crisp and hopeful.

After the cake was cut and served, Jack whispered to his new bride, "Are you ready?"

She looked at him in surprise, "Ready to go?" He nodded. "So soon? Shouldn't we stay and help clean up?"

He laughed, "Annie, you're the bride. Brides don't clean up. My family will work together and have it done in no time."

Not having any other excuses, Annie agreed to go. Annie and Jack donned coats and everyone walked them out to the truck, hugging themselves against the night air. On the truck they found "Just Married" sprawled across the back window and strings of tin cans attached to the back bumper. Sarah's oldest two boys jumped up and down in glee. They had obviously had a hand in this. Jack walked over to them, squatted down in front of them and said with a twinkle in his eye, "You know, you really shouldn't do everything your uncles tell you to do."

Jack opened Annie's door and she got in, sliding to the middle of the bench seat. Jack knew it was for the benefit of those watching. Jack climbed in and kissed her on the mouth, also for the benefit of those watching. And so their journey began, with Jack navigating and Annie not knowing where they were going and the clang of tin cans the only sound that could be heard as they drove into the darkness.

Chapter 39

Annie

A few miles away from the church, Jack stopped and pulled a pocketknife from his suit pants. Without explanation, he slipped out into the night and sliced the strings that attached the cans to the bumper. Annie remained where she was and marveled at the practicality of a man that carries a pocketknife to his own wedding. She thought about sliding over to her side while he was out of the truck, but decided that doing so might be insulting to him, so she stayed put.

When they had driven a few more miles, Annie asked, "So are you going to tell me where we're going?"

Keeping his eyes on the road, he replied, "No. But I'll tell you that it will take a couple of hours to get there, so you can make yourself comfortable."

She took that as an invitation to scoot over, and she did so. "My suitcase!" She exclaimed, realizing that it was still in her car.

"I have it. Your mom moved it over for us," he reassured her.

Annie fought against the silence that threatened to swallow them up. "So it went well, don't you think?"

"Yes, I think it did," Jack agreed.

"I loved your mom's dress."

"Yeah, I guess it was nice."

"Kimberly's growing."

"Yeah. Annie?"

"Hmmm?"

"Do you want to listen to the radio?"

"I'd love to," she answered, so relieved by the suggestion that she didn't think to be insulted by his obvious effort to quiet her chatter.

He flipped it on and country music filled the cab, taking over Annie's job of filling the emptiness of the truck cab. But she soon found that this allowed her the freedom in which to think, something she wasn't sure she wanted to do. Although she didn't know where he was taking her, she knew it would have four walls and the main piece of furniture would be a bed. And she had less than two hours to ready herself for sharing that bed with this person that was now her husband.

She looked over at her new husband, who was lost in his own thoughts, and saw him for the truly good man that he was. Guilt filled her and her guilt was two-fold. She was guilty of giving herself so willingly to someone that was so much less than Jack was and now she was also guilty of lacking the eagerness to give that same gift of herself to someone who was so deserving of it.

Her thoughts were diverted when Jack turned off the interstate and onto a state highway, which surprised Annie. She had expected that they would be headed toward a city and this road didn't appear to lead to a city or to anywhere else, for that matter. Jack glanced over at her. Annie knew that he was gauging her reaction. She gave none. They drove for miles, winding around turns, and going up and down hills.

They drove through small towns, some big enough to require a traffic light and some not even big enough to slow down for.

They turned again, this time onto a country road. A few minutes later, they pulled into a small parking lot in front of what appeared to be a large restored barn. The sign that hung from a post in the yard told her that it was a bed and breakfast. She turned and smiled, momentarily forgetting her worries. "Oooh. I've never been to a bed and breakfast before." He returned the smile, but it stopped at his mouth and the familiar sparkle in his eyes was noticeably absent.

He pulled a cell phone and a paper from his glove box, dialed, and said, "Paul? This is Jack. We just pulled in…All right. Thanks." He closed the phone and explained, "They lock up at 10, so they said to call so they could meet us at the door."

He got out and pulled his suitcase and hers from the truck bed. A balding middle-aged man that Annie assumed to be Paul opened the door for them and welcomed them inside.

When she stepped across the threshold, Annie's mouth dropped. Where she stood was spacious but at the same time was perhaps the coziest place she had ever been in. To her right was an abundance of overstuffed furniture arranged in clusters with end tables and coffee tables, all holding lamps that worked together to cast a soft glow. A fireplace was in the center of the wall. Its glowing embers attested to the fact that the fire had recently died down. The left side of the large room was dark, but Annie could make out three large oak tables with doily table runners and candles in soft greens and mauves that coordinated with the colors of the furniture and carpet. In the dim light, she could see that the walls were painted a cream color with a wide dark green floral border running around the walls above a wooden chair rail.

Paul led them across the large room to a large desk that served as a check-in counter, made from oak and stained a honey color to match the tables. He opened a drawer and pulled out a key, led them down a short hallway, unlocked their door, and invited them to step in. Then he left them alone.

Annie looked around the room in amazement. The four-poster bed was covered with a quilt in a starburst pattern of blues and yellows, which matched the flowers of the wallpaper. Beyond the bed was a sitting area containing a fireplace with dancing flames and a loveseat where one could sit and enjoy its warmth. A coffee table between the loveseat and fireplace held a plate of homemade cookies. Jack interrupted Annie's assessment of the room, "Do you like it?"

She turned to him and said simply, "Yes." For the first time that day, her eyes smiled at his.

It was that look that connected them and brought them back to the moment at hand, their wedding night. She watched as he took off his coat and threw it over the suitcases that he had put against the wall. He then walked behind her and helped her slip hers off, his knuckles brushing her shoulders. Then he approached her again. She resisted the urge to match his forward steps with backward steps of her own. His face leaned down to hers and she made herself tilt hers upwards to his with closed eyes, expecting his kiss as he placed a rough hand on each of her cheeks. To her surprise, it was their foreheads and not their lips that met. "Annie?" he said.

"What Jack?" she asked with eyes still closed.

"Would you mind if we waited?" He lifted his head and removed his hands from her cheeks to grasp both of her hands in his, and looked directly into her eyes that had flown open in surprise.

"Until when?" she asked.

"I don't know. Until we're both ready, I guess." The bobbing of his Adam's apple told her that the words weren't coming easily. "It seems like we haven't had much time to, well, get to know each other real well, and I think we should wait." He added, "If that's okay."

She looked down to avoid his eyes that were seeing right through her. Her downward gaze gave her further evidence that it wasn't an easy decision for him. "It doesn't look like you want to wait." The fact that she was looking at his pants made it clear what she meant. They both blushed.

"I said that I wanted to wait. I didn't say that I took a vote of all my body parts and it was unanimous." The statement was made with humor. She smiled up at him and saw from the tenseness of his jaw and the controlled desire in his eyes that it was forced humor.

"You've been waiting so long. I can't ask you to wait any longer."

He squeezed her hands. "But you're not asking. I'm offering. It's completely different." As she was reflecting on that, he asked, "Do you accept my offer?"

For the second time that evening, she responded "I do."

Chapter 40

Jack

After she agreed to his offer, Jack immediately dropped her hands and let out the breath that he hadn't realized he had been holding. "How about some cookies?"

They sat on the loveseat in front of the fire and shared cookies and the thermos of milk that had been left beside the plate. Soon they were overcome by the weariness caused by the events of the day and the emotions that accompanied them. Annie gave a theatrical yawn, making the first move that would lead them into the waiting bed that loomed in the other part of the room.

"You can change first," Jack offered.

She went into the bathroom and emerged wearing the somewhat revealing summer pajamas that she had decided to bring. He took one moment to appreciate the way the fabric clung to her curves before he said, "Oh, Annie, I have my limitations. If we're going to share that bed, you've got to put on more than that."

He opened his suitcase and pulled out grey plaid flannel pants and a long-sleeved grey t-shirt. "I stuck an extra set of pajamas in my bag in case you needed them. I wasn't sure what type of pajamas a woman packed for her honeymoon but, given the circumstances, I thought that having an extra set along might come in handy."

She disappeared once again behind the bathroom door. When she came out again, he looked at her from head to toe, from the long loose brown hair that still hung in curls from the wedding to her painted toes that peeked out from under his pajama pants and then back up again. Even with nearly every inch of her covered, he still found her agonizingly attractive. "That's better," he said, but in truth the outfit that he had provided was only helping a little.

He took a similar set of pajamas from his suitcase and stepped into the bathroom, grateful for the momentary privacy. He changed quickly and mouthed the words "I hope you're happy." to God before he walked back out.

Annie was already in bed, the covers pulled up to her chin. She looked very small under the blankets. He walked around the bed and timidly lifted the covers on what would be, from now on, his side of the bed.

"I don't bite," she teased carefully.

He climbed in and covered his already-covered self. "I've never shared a bed before." Was that true? Pretty much, except for rare occasions when he was a kid. He thought briefly of Daniel with whom he used to share a room but not a bed. "At least not since I've been grown," he added.

"Neither have I," she said quietly, reminding him that she was more innocent than her pregnancy might indicate.

He longed to reach out and hold her but he didn't trust his body not to ask for something more and he knew that, if asked, she would comply.

"Good-night" was his only response.

"Good-night," she replied. The silence was close around them. "Thank you, Jack."

"You're welcome, Annie." And in a few short moments, with her name still on his lips, he fell asleep.

Chapter 41

Annie

Annie's eyes flew open in the middle of the night as if a noise had awakened her. But if that was the case, she had no idea what that noise was. She had been sleeping soundly and it took a moment to realize where she was and who was next to her in the darkness.

Now wide awake, she quietly made her way across the plush carpet to use the bathroom, something that she did more frequently these days. She flipped on the light and the sudden brightness made her eyes hurt. As she washed her hands, she caught sight of herself in the mirror and was startled for a moment to see her image in Jack's pajamas.

Last night she had rolled up the waist and the sleeves in an effort to make the large pajamas fit her smaller body. Now she tidied these folds that had come loose during the night. She lifted one sleeve to her nose and breathed in the scent of his laundry detergent. She marveled at how wearing his pajamas made her feel not only warm but also safe and connected to him in a way that was both intimate and platonic.

She snuck back to the bed where he lay sleeping. He didn't stir, unaware of her departure or return. She turned on her side to face him and studied his features made fuzzy by the darkness. His breathing was quiet, deep, and steady and the sound of it was calming and reassuring.

Annie had been grateful for many things in her life and was always quick to say 'thank you' to whoever had given her a particular thing. Birthday and Christmas presents. A ride to the mall. Help with homework. Now, as she lay there looking at Jack, gratitude for his gift of patience filled her and exceeded any gratitude that she had ever felt before. "Thank you." She whispered the words in the tiniest of voices, needing to speak them but not wanting to wake this man who was sleeping so peacefully.

In the darkness, she imagined the words floating from her mouth over to her husband, but they didn't stop when they reached him. She knew that they flowed over her husband and out into the night, beyond the walls of the room, winding their way up to the heavens. The thanks that she had just offered was not only thanks to Jack for his patience and so much more but it was also thanks to whatever or whoever had brought Jack to her. Although she wouldn't have called it such, she had just offered up her first heartfelt prayer of thanksgiving. And as she lay there wondering where her words had gone and if they had been received, they returned to her, transformed into a peaceful sensation that filled her completely as she drifted back to sleep.

Chapter 42

Jack

Hours later, Jack opened his eyes to the bright sunlight. He had obviously slept way past dawn. He looked over at the source of the light, a window that was at the back of the room beside the fireplace, covered by a lace curtain. He thought about sneaking out of bed to say his morning prayers in front of the window but decided that today the best way to see the glory and goodness of God was to simply turn his head to where Annie lay sleeping beside him.

He studied Annie's face and there was such softness there that he felt that it must be more than the effect of sleep. He saw in her a peace that he had never seen before, and he knew the wisdom of what God had asked of him just yesterday morning as he had stood in prayer. As much as he wanted the gratification that had been denied him for so long, he wanted her love and trust more. If a physical sacrifice would gain him that, then it was a sacrifice that he was willing and able to make.

Any worries about the difficulties of keeping his promise to her had been short-lived. He had fallen asleep almost immediately last night and had only now awakened; something that he thought could be nothing other than a blessing from God and he thanked God for this now. He prayed for the same blessing in the nights to come. He also prayed that it wouldn't be long before such prayers were no longer necessary.

Annie's eyes fluttered open and they smiled at one another. "Sleep good?" he asked. It was an effort to keep his hand from reaching out to stroke her cheek.

"Real good," she responded sleepily. "I'm not sure you're going to get your pajamas back. They're too comfortable."

"Well I hope you don't want to lie around in them all day. I've got things planned. Do you want to shower first or should I?" he asked.

"Would you mind going first? I promise I won't lie around all day but I wouldn't mind just a few more minutes. This bed is sooo cozy."

Jack hopped out of bed and went to the bathroom to shower, turning the water temperature so that it was just slightly colder than normal. As he stood under the flow of water, he let it wash away his reluctance of the night before and wake him for the first full day of his new life with Annie.

Chapter 43

Annie

While Annie nestled in bed and listened to the shower, she smiled. The same gratefulness and peace that she had experienced in the night was still with her now. She looked at the skewed rectangle of light shining on the wall across from the bed. The lace curtain made an interesting pattern of light on the wallpaper. The pane of the window divided this pattern into four sections. She lazily studied the familiarity of the intersection of these two solid lines created by the shadow of the pane.

It was then, while she was pondering the play of light and shadow on the wall, while she enjoyed the pleasant heaviness of the quilt above her and the softness of the mattress under her, while she listened to the pleasant sounds of Jack showering. It was then that she felt for the first time the unmistakable sensation of her baby moving within her. She put both hands on her abdomen that was covered in the softness of her husband's pajamas and tears of joy flowed down her temples.

She heard the bathroom door open and quickly wiped her eyes. Jack came out in a towel and apologized that he had forgotten to take his clothes in with him. She propped herself up with her elbows and watched him dig around in his suitcase with his back to her. It was the first time she had seen him in anything less than jeans and a t-shirt. She noted his muscled torso and smiled at the tan line just above his elbows. When he found the clothes that he needed, he turned and caught her looking at him. She felt the heat rise to her cheeks.

"Have you been crying?" he asked.

She knew her red eyes wouldn't allow her to deny it. "I'm just happy," she said simply and hoped he would accept this truth that she spoke.

"Me too," he responded, not asking for any other explanation than the one that she gave. They smiled at each other with mouths, eyes, and hearts and then he went back into the bathroom to dress.

Chapter 44

Jack

After they had both showered and dressed, they headed back to the common room through which Paul had led them the night before. One of the tables now held fruit and muffins and an older couple sat at one end, enjoying their breakfast. A woman wearing a rust-colored apron embroidered with fall leaves greeted them and introduced herself as Carol and apologized for not being present to welcome them the previous night. She urged them to sit down and told them that she would be right back with some bacon and eggs.

Jack sat first, choosing a seat at the far end of the table, leaving ample distance between them and the other couple to prevent conversation. He needed to discuss the day's plans with Annie. He waited until they had each taken a bite of muffin before he sheepishly confessed that their honeymoon was a working vacation. "I need your help shopping for a bed," he told Annie.

Her hand flew to her mouth. "Oh, my gosh. I forgot all about your little bed. You haven't replaced it yet?"

"Well, I went shopping once. But I didn't know what you liked and I thought a lot of what was in the furniture stores was junk. When my mom and dad want nice furniture, they come over this way to buy it."

He pulled out a piece of notebook paper from his wallet. He unfolded it to its full size, the creases making a checkerboard pattern as he reviewed the notes that he had taken over the past few weeks. "I made a list of places. Mom suggested a few and I have a friend that comes over here a lot and he told me about a few others." He handed it to her and she looked at his annotated list of six different places.

"I have a map in my truck that shows where they are," he explained.

"That sounds great, Jack." Annie responded sincerely, seemingly glad to have the day planned.

"Have you ever been to Amish Country?" he asked.

"So that's where we're at! And I thought we were in the middle of nowhere," she teased.

"That too," he grinned.

"No, I've never been here before," she answered. "My mom's more the big city type, so that's where we go whenever we take a trip."

Carol returned with their eggs. She pointed out the coffee carafes and cups on the table and asked if they wanted juice. She asked about their room and Annie quickly assured her that it was delightful. Noting the quality of the tables, Jack asked for her opinions on furniture stores and she gave three suggestions. Two were already on Jack's list and he made an asterisk beside them. The third he didn't have and he added.

After breakfast they set out. Annie navigated from a map of Holmes County that his mother had given him. Jack carefully passed the black buggies that shared the roads with the automobiles. A few furniture stores were in the country, down gravel roads. The others were in little towns filled with craft and antique shops. The normally busy streets were almost vacant, the summer shoppers disappearing for the winter with the leaves.

Jack insisted they take some time out from their search to browse the craft shops, knowing that that's what his mom and sisters enjoyed doing. He watched as Annie admired the varied and clever ways in which fabric came together in the quilt patterns. She smelled the candles and soaps. She commented on the colors found in the arrangement of silk flowers. Several times Jack urged her to buy something that she seemed particularly enchanted with but each time she refused.

Their search for a bed took them through huge furniture stores, some nicely decorated and some more like warehouses. All of them were filled with hand crafted furniture, mostly made of oak. Annie ran her hands over the smooth wood of each headboard that they stopped to consider, appreciating its workmanship. Each time they looked at the small white tags looped onto a spindle or post, she would say "Oh, Jack, that's too expensive." And, indeed, the price was as high as the quality.

But Jack would not be dissuaded. In his mind, somewhere along the line, the bed had begun to represent the marriage. It must be built to last and the price was not nearly important as the quality.

It was mid-afternoon when they walked into their sixth furniture store. Beside him, Jack heard Annie's intake of breath and the words, "Oh, Jack, look at that one!" Jack's eyes followed the direction of Annie's extended index finger and saw a simple but graceful bed. Across the top of the headboard, a double bow of light oak was supported by smooth spindles with a short post on each end. This was repeated in a shorter version at the foot of the bed. They walked across the store to the bed and, like each time before, her hand glided across the smooth wood of the headboard.

Jack looked at her and said, "Well, what do you think? Have we found it?"

"Yes," Annie replied. She knew by now that Jack wanted it to be her decision. She also knew that he didn't want to discuss the cost, so she didn't bother to look. A salesman soon arrived to help them and Jack began looking at the matching dressers. Before they left, he had arranged to pick up the bed as well as two nightstands, a dresser, and a chest of drawers on Monday. Annie could no longer keep silent about the cost of their purchases, but her protests were ignored and she was wise enough to know when to stop.

When they walked back out into the cold but bright November sunlight, Annie scolded him, "Don't you already have a dresser? I would have been happy using that one."

He stopped on the deserted sidewalk and looked at her. "I hope that our baby will wear more than diapers. We'll need a dresser for baby clothes so the baby can have my old one. I don't think he'll mind."

She smiled into his brown eyes and said, "You're right. *She'll* need a dresser and *she* won't mind."

He put his hand to his stomach and said, "Something tells me we missed lunch."

Annie looked at her watch. "Did you know it was three o'clock?"

Their breakfast had been so hearty and they had been so occupied by the shops that they hadn't noticed the hour. But now that they had accomplished their goal for the day, they realized they were quite hungry.

"So do you have a list of places to eat, too?"

"No, but I know we're not far from a really good Amish restaurant, if you want to try it."

She agreed and they drove the short distance to the next town and were soon seated at another oak table in a huge dining area. Their waitress seemed to be in her teens, wearing a plain dark purple dress with a white apron. Her brown hair was pulled back and tucked into a bun that rested on the nape of her neck. Above this was a light-weight white bonnet with the strings hanging loose. She brought them platters of fried chicken, roast beef, mashed potatoes, and noodles that seemed to melt in your mouth. Jack ordered a piece of butterscotch pie and a piece of coconut cream pie for dessert. When they arrived, heaped with golden meringue, Annie found room to sample some of each.

By the time they finished and walked back out onto the street, the shopkeepers were turning their signs from "Open" to "Closed" and a glance at Jack's watch informed him that it was five o'clock.

When they arrived back at the inn, Jack flipped his truck seat forward and pulled a duffle bag out of the storage space behind the seat, ignoring Annie's curious glance. Back in the room, they both made a wide circle around the bed and any issues surrounding it. Instead, Annie sat down on the loveseat, slipped her shoes off and rested her feet on the coffee table. Jack took a seat on an armchair that sat nearby, feeling out of place in the flowery room.

"So what's in the duffle bag, Mr. Schroeder?" Annie asked.

Jack scratched his neck under his soft flannel shirt collar. "Well, I thought that we might need something else to do." He felt the heat creep from his collar up to his receding hairline. "So I brought some games along."

Annie sat up in interest. "Games? Like what?"

He walked over to where he had dropped the bag and brought it over to her, sitting next to her on the loveseat. She opened it and found Monopoly, Sorry, and Yahtzee, as well as a couple of decks of cards and a jigsaw puzzle. The boxes were torn at the corners. The yellowed tape attested to the fact that repairs had once been made but hadn't lasted. "I raided the game closet at my mom's," Jack explained.

She leaned over and kissed his cheek, "This is great. I was wondering what we were going to do tonight."

Suddenly their proximity to one another and the privacy of the room was overbearing to Jack. "Wanna go out in the lobby and play?" he asked, successfully keeping the urgency out of his voice.

"Sure."

And so they passed the evening in front of the large fireplace in the lobby, playing board games like the good friends that they had somehow become, and watching the weekend guests arrive. When Paul locked the doors at 10:00, they went back to their room and readied themselves for bed.

When Annie was once again wrapped in his soft gray cotton pajamas and they were nestled in the soft bed under the warm quilt, she turned to her side to face him in the darkness. The inches that separated them seemed like a mile. "Jack," she said.

At his name, Jack turned to his side to face his wife. "Hmm." It was an invitation to say whatever she needed to.

"I felt the baby move for the first time this morning." Her words created a bridge between them, but he was silent, unsure how to cross over it. After long moments, he reached out and found her hand under the covers and held it.

And that simple connection was all that was needed for now. Jack felt the frailty and warmth of her hand in his and silently vowed once again to be a good husband and father. He felt his strength and faith flowing from his hand into hers. He imagined this strength spreading through her body, into her womb and to the baby growing within it. Then, with pleasure beyond imagining, he felt that strength flowing back into him, making him stronger than he had been before.

Chapter 45

Annie

Annie woke up the next morning to find Jack looking out the window. "How's the weather?" she asked.

He looked over and she could tell by the faraway look in his eyes that she had interrupted his thoughts. "Oh, uh, looks like it's clouding up," he replied.

She looked at the clock and saw that it was still quite early, which was not surprising, given the fact that they had went to bed early the night before.

"I thought maybe we'd go into the city today," Jack said, walking over to the bed and sitting on the edge furthest from her.

"What city? Is there a city in these here parts?" she joked, giving her words a hillbilly twang even though she hadn't heard such an accent from the locals.

"Canton's the closest. But we could go to Cleveland. That would be bigger. They have the Rock and Roll Hall of Fame there, if you're interested."

"What's in Canton?" She stretched her arms out to her side, waking herself up.

She saw Jack's jaw tense and he said, "You know what? I'm hungry. Let's talk over breakfast. I'll shower first." He quickly disappeared into the bathroom. She understood the reason for his quick getaway and she took a moment to appreciate his self-control before she got up and picked out her clothes for the day.

On this Saturday morning all three tables held muffins and fruit and a casserole was served to the dozen or so guests who sat at them. When Jack and Annie resumed their conversation about where to go that day, the woman next to them politely interrupted and stated that she was from Canton. On a piece of paper that they requested from Paul, she mapped out the best mall, the Football Hall of Fame, the art museum, and the McKinley Monument. She also told them about a play that was being performed by a community group and the best Italian restaurant in the city and put those on the map also. During all this, her husband was content to enjoy his breakfast silently, only occasionally correcting her driving directions.

After they had filled their stomachs and thanked their table companion, they drove the hour or so to Canton. It was still fairly early as they drove around the city using the inset of Jack's Ohio map and the woman's hand-drawn one. They decided to skip the Football Hall of Fame for which the town is famous but they did stop at the McKinley Monument and found that they both had an interest in history. They visited the city's art museum, where Annie enthusiastically admired the paintings and failed to notice Jack admiring her enthusiasm.

But, like the day before, Jack had a purpose. In the afternoon, he pulled the truck into the mall parking lot, led Annie through the light rain that had started to fall and into the large J.C. Penney store. He embarrassed her by asking the first clerk he saw where the "maternity ward" was. The clerk glanced at the still fairly trim figure of the mother-to-be and fought the urge to chuckle. First time parents, certainly. She pointed to her right.

"Jack, you spent too much yesterday," Annie argued as they walked in the designated direction.

"Annie, it's fine. I can afford it. And you need some clothes, for crying out loud."

"I can still wear my regular clothes."

"Oh, yeah, then why do you wear these black stretchy pants almost everyday?"

She gave him a not-so-playful whack on the arm. She had been hoping that he hadn't noticed her diminishing wardrobe.

The next hour was spent trying on clothes for length and guessing at possible future width. "Pull it out in front," Jack said when Annie stepped out of the fitting room to show him the blouse she was trying on. Annie obeyed. "That'll never fit you in April," he said.

"How big do you think I'm going to get, anyway?" she complained, not wanting to believe that she could possibly outgrow the large shirt that hung loose down the front of her.

"My sisters always grow out of most of their stuff by the last month," he countered.

By the time they left the store, Annie had three pairs of pants and five shirts, two that were huge and three that were just nicely roomy.

Annie suggested a late-afternoon matinee at the mall cinema and Jack agreed. Annie found it a relief to focus temporarily on the lives of the actors on the screen instead of their own. Afterward, they found the suggested Italian restaurant and enjoyed salad and pasta as they talked comfortably over a candle encased in a red globe.

By the time they arrived back at the inn, they immediately prepared for bed. As they pulled the covers up over themselves, Annie said, "Goodnight" and gave him a quick kiss on the cheek that she hoped would seem casual. Then she rolled away from him and stared into the darkness, wondering if he had taken it casually.

Chapter 46

Jack

"Annie." Jack nudged his bride gently the next morning. He had already showered and dressed in the suit he had worn to the wedding. "Do you mind if I go to Mass?"

Jack watched her eyes open and waited for his words to register. When she spoke her voice was deep and groggy. "No, I don't mind. What time is it?" He saw a tiny spot on the pillow case where she had slobbered in her sleep. He wondered how such a thing could be so endearing.

"About seven-thirty."

"What time's church?"

"Nine." He felt foolish for being ready so early. "I wanted to eat breakfast first and I wanted to leave lots of time to find the church. I thought I'd let you sleep in."

"Okay," she replied sleepily.

"Mind if I eat breakfast without you?"

"That's fine."

"Okay. I'll be back about ten-thirty, then." He brushed back her hair and gave her a peck on the forehead.

The dining room was empty when Jack arrived. Carol had made apple muffins today and Jack was savoring his first bite when the phone at the desk rang. Paul answered and, to Jack's surprise, walked over and told Jack that it was for him. Annie's voice on the other end asked, "Can you wait 20 minutes to leave?"

"Sure. I have plenty of time. Why?"

"Do you mind if I tag along?" It hadn't occurred to him that she would want to go with him and her question, asked in an insecure, childlike tone made him regret not inviting her along. He had assumed that she would prefer to sleep in.

"Not at all," he replied.

"Great. I'll shower as fast as I can and I'll meet you in the dining room."

True to her word, she joined him in the dining area just twenty minutes later. She stood in front of him and asked, "Does this match?" Not having packed any clothes for church, she had improvised and put together her suit skirt and a green sweater.

Because anything matched his daily denim, he had little knowledge of what matched and didn't match. Instead of answering her, he said seriously, "You know what, Annie?"

She frowned slightly. He knew that she was anticipating a negative comment on her outfit. "What?"

"I feel very married right now." The corners of her mouth turned up in a smile.

She wouldn't let him off the hook. "But do I look okay?"

"You look beautiful and your clothes aren't bad, either."

Her eyes lowered to the floor and she slipped into a chair with a quiet "Thank you."

After breakfast, they found the church with only a little difficulty. It was a small, plain building that lacked both the elaborateness of the convent chapel in which Annie had attended her first Mass and the traditional steeple and stained glass of Jack's church in which they were married. But the service was the same and Jack noticed that Annie seemed a little more at ease, knowing what to expect this time.

After services, they climbed back in the truck and were on their way back to the inn when Annie asked, "What's the stuff that you get at communion?" Annie asked.

"Bread and wine," Jack replied, not wanting to delve into the matter further.

"But it doesn't look like bread. Why's it so flat?"

"It represents the unleavened bread of Passover." Jack replied. Annie sat silent next to him. He knew that she was incredibly smart but he also knew that she had no knowledge of religion and, therefore, his answer must be unclear to her. But how do you explain thousands of years of history and covenants and prophesy in a 15-minute drive?

Back in the room, they changed into jeans, taking turns in the bathroom to do so. Annie put on the smallest of the maternity jeans purchased the previous day and borrowed a sweatshirt from Jack that hung down over her abdomen. Although he didn't say it, he thought that she looked pregnant today.

"So," Annie asked, "what's the plan today?"

"I don't have a plan. All the Amish places are closed on Sunday. Any ideas?" Jack looked at her hopefully.

She thought a minute and then grabbed her purse from the floor. She reached in and pulled out a dozen or so pamphlets that she had collected from a display at the Amish restaurant on Friday. She leafed through them, until she found a particular one, and handed it to Jack, asking "Would this be too far?"

It was for a historic village in a small town about an hour's drive away. The hours stated that they were open on Sunday and they quickly agreed that it sounded like a nice day.

And it was indeed. The drive both there and back turned out to be part of the fun. Although only a few brown leaves remained on the trees, the beauty of the hills was still evident. Never having visited the area before, Annie marveled at the Amish farms which could be identified in many ways. Jack explained to her that the plain white houses, large barns, buggies parked in front, remnants of large summer gardens, lack of power lines running from the road to the house, and clotheslines that were empty on Sunday were all indications that a farm was Amish and not "English."

The rain from the previous day had moved out and left the sky overcast and the air frigid, but they were dressed warmly and they stepped in and out of the shops and historical buildings that lined the cobblestone street.

In the pottery shop, they watched a potter demonstrate his craft. Jack watched as the man took the ugly lump of damp clay and spun it on the wheel until, under the guidance of his expert hands, a beautiful vessel had been formed. He was reminded of Jeremiah's image of God as the potter and he imagined himself as God's clay and joy filled him at the thought, glad that it was God's skilled hands and not his own that were molding and shaping him. He thought about God shaping their marriage, too, and, without thinking, he put an arm around Annie's shoulders and felt her lean into him.

After the demonstration, Annie browsed the shop and was delighted with the pottery of all shapes, sizes, and colors. Once again, she resisted Jack's urges to buy something, just as she had in the Amish stores, until Jack suggested they start their Christmas shopping early.

"Oh, let's buy gifts for your sisters and mom!" Annie exclaimed. "How much do you usually spend? Do you think they'd like something from here?" Her voice was animated, excited at the thought of purchasing a few of these unique treasures. Deciding what to get each sister turned out to be a fun challenge and they walked out with two large, heavy bags, which they stowed in the truck.

By mid-afternoon, they had their fill of history and shopping. The sun had come out and they found a walk path that led through a wooded area to a nearby park.

As they walked, their hands found one another naturally. The bare branches let the sun shine down on them, warming them. They could hear the sound of flowing water and the few birds that had not left for the winter sang to them. When Jack spied a bench overlooking a creek, he quickly steered them toward it. The river was swollen from the previous day's rains, the brown water flowing fast.

They sat in silence a moment until Annie said, "Just like our first date."

Jack laughed at the memory that was from a hundred years ago. "Yeah, our first date."

"So I guess it all worked out the way you imagined it."

Jack removed the cap that he wore and studied it, not looking at her. "Well, it's working out pretty good. But I wouldn't say it's all worked out yet."

Annie looked down at her lap, and Jack knew that she felt guilty for accepting his offer to wait. "No, I guess not."

"We need time, Annie, that's all. Time to really know each other and time to let this baby grow so I can be its daddy. That's why I proposed in the first place, you know. But we're off to a good start, I think."

He scooted over on the bench and put his arm around her again and she rested her head on his shoulder and they let some time pass before they resumed their walk.

They had supper at the historical village in a restored warehouse and returned to the inn early. Annie challenged Jack to a rematch of Yahtzee, which she won, and they crawled into bed that night tired from the walking and fresh air.

Chapter 47

Annie

In spite of her weariness that night, Annie was wide awake. It was the last night of their honeymoon and guilt overwhelmed her.

"Jack."

"Hmm…" It wasn't a sleepy 'hmm'. She could tell that he, too, was awake and thinking.

"I'm sorry."

"For what?"

"For wasting this beautiful room. For not making love with you." She swallowed back tears.

"Annie, I don't want you to feel bad." He rolled over to look at her but she continued to stare up at the darkness where the ceiling was.

"I know you don't want me to feel bad but I do. And you've been so wonderful. I should want to… to make love to you."

He put his elbow on his pillow and propped his head on his hand. With his other hand he reached out into the darkness and found her temple and the teardrop that she hadn't wanted him to discover.

"It's the baby," she continued. "I just want to guard it and protect it. I know pregnant women have sex and it's perfectly safe, but when I think about it, it seems so…I don't know, unsafe. Intrusive, maybe."

His hand moved to her pillow where he lifted a lock of her hair and rubbed it between his fingers. "Oh, Annie, why didn't you tell me?"

"Because it sounds dumb and it sounds like I'm making up an excuse."

He bent his head down to hers and kissed her gently on the lips. "I love you," he whispered. His words made her catch her breath. It was the first time that he had said them to her and while she knew that they were true, she hadn't expected to hear them now.

"Oh, Jack," she breathed as she exhaled. "This is where I should say I love you, too."

His face remained close to hers and his hand ran over her head, clumsily smoothing her hair. "That's not why I said it." Why had he said it? The last time that she had heard those words they had been from Eric and they had been an obvious attempt to get her to take her pants off.

She grabbed his hand and moved it away from her. "Jack, I don't know how I could have been so stupid." She sat up so that he was now staring at her back. It was a move that separated her from him quite effectively. She continued, her words traveling to the opposite wall. "Do you know that Eric told me he loved me? And I thought maybe he did. And I said it back to him. But when *you* say it, I know that it means so much more than what I thought it meant and I'm not sure that I can say it back to you yet."

"Annie…" She interrupted before he could say whatever comforting words he was formulating.

"And I told you I didn't want to sleep with you because of the baby. That's true, it is, but it's not *just* the baby. I think about sleeping with you and I know that sex means a lot more than I thought it did. And I'm not ready."

She lay back down and faced away from him, not looking at him and not allowing him to see her face. She curled herself up into the fetal position, fighting the tears. He moved over to her and shaped his body to hers, putting his arm around her and his hand over the swell of the baby. She had not asked for or known that she wanted any comfort, but his warmth provided what she hadn't realized that she needed. She relaxed into his embrace and felt sadness and the joy of sharing that sadness with someone else.

Chapter 48

Jack

The next morning Jack left early to pick up the bedroom furniture that they had purchased. At the restaurant the night before he had convinced Annie that she should sleep in and enjoy her last morning of relative leisure before returning to work the next day.

After the furniture was loaded onto his truck, he took advantage of his time alone to quickly do some Christmas shopping, this time for Annie, before he returned to the inn. By the time he returned, Annie was packed and ready. While Paul checked them out, Carol walked over to where they stood at the desk and insisted on feeding them even though the official breakfast hours had passed. By the time they finally said good-bye, it was almost noon. Jack squeezed the luggage into the back with the furniture, and they made the two-and-a-half hour trip home.

Annie's sadness from the previous night had vanished with the daylight, evidenced by her easy smile and flowing chatter during the ride.

When they arrived, Jack parked the truck and hurried over to meet Annie as she climbed down. Catching her by surprise, he bent to slip an arm under her knees and the other around her shoulders. He carried her up the garage steps and over the threshold. Her weight was pleasant in his arms. Her laughter and happy-scared "Jack!" were music in his ears.

When he put her down inside the kitchen, she fell silent and they both stood and looked around. In their absence, streamers had been hung and flowers and candles had been placed on the kitchen table and in the living room. On the counter was a note that Annie found first and read out loud to him, "Dear brother and new sister: Hope you don't mind that we let ourselves in. Jack, we thought we'd decorate your boring bachelor pad a little for your new bride. Annie, we thought perhaps you wouldn't mind waiting a day to cook for your groom. Supper's in the fridge. Love, 'The Girls'."

Jack smiled at Annie and said, "Don't cry!"

Annie smiled back with moist eyes and said facetiously, "What would make you think I'd cry?"

Jack looked at his watch. Although they had successfully bought the furniture, they didn't yet have a mattress. They had planned to make it to town yet today to buy one, but first what was on the truck needed to be brought into the house. They needed to keep moving. Jack didn't want to spend his first night in his house as a married man sleeping on the couch. His body remembered how it had felt to embrace her last night before his mind pushed the thought aside in favor of accomplishing the task at hand.

"Well, why don't we figure out where we want everything before I call Dad and see if he can help unload it?" He opened a kitchen drawer and pulled out a tape measure.

They went into the bedroom and laughed when they saw that someone had toilet papered the bedroom. White streams of bathroom tissue zigzagged the room, running from lamp to closet door to headboard to doorknob. The covers of the bed had been pulled back and Barbie and Ken dolls lie there in their pajamas on the little twin bed in a stiff-armed embrace. The newlyweds were delighted.

Jack started to take down the toilet paper, but Annie stopped him. "Who do you think did this?"

"That's easy. It's gotta be Tim and Sarah's oldest boys, with help, of course."

"We've got to take some pictures or something before we take it down. The boys would get a kick out of it. Do we have time?"

He agreed and they got out the camera and used the delay feature to take a picture of themselves together with shocked faces in the middle of the toilet paper. At Annie's insistence, Jack lay down on the bed and covered up with Barbie and Annie took their picture, knowing that the boys would laugh hysterically at the picture of their uncle in bed with the doll.

Then they quickly cleaned up the mess, measured for the furniture, and radioed Frank. Meg came along, bringing hugs and a pan of apple dumplings. The old furniture was moved to the baby's room and the new furniture was unloaded. Meg oohed and ahhed over the furniture while they carried it in until Frank snapped at her to get out of the way.

Thankfully, the only comment from Frank unrelated to the task at hand was, "Well, she came back with you. I guess everything must not've been too bad." Frank and Jack assembled the bed frame while Annie started to tell Meg about the trip. When the bed frame was in place, Jack looked at his watch. He explained to his parents their plans for the mattress and that the rest of the details would need to wait.

In town, they easily picked out a mattress set from the only furniture store in town but realized they didn't have any sheets to put on it. They thought about their limited choices of stores in town and agreed that if those stores had any, they would be hideous or of poor quality. "My mom has a bed that size. We could borrow some from her."

And so they stopped in at Cindy's asking for sheets and, in exchange for details of the trip, she gladly loaned them some. They refused supper, explaining that they had something waiting for them at home, but they agreed to come back the next night to pack up Annie's things and share a meal.

Cindy squeezed Annie's hand and said, "We'll have to do lunch soon, just the two of us." It was obvious to Jack that Cindy wanted to hear the intimate details that she had no way of knowing didn't exist. Annie was vague about when that would be, but Cindy pressed for a specific day.

Jack looked at his watch. "Wow, Annie, look at the time. We've got a lot to do tonight. We better get going. We'll see you tomorrow." He took her hand and guided her to the door, allowing her to escape without having to answer prying questions or having to set up a time in which to do so.

When they returned home, they argued a moment about whether or not to call Frank to help with the mattress and box springs. Annie insisted that she was capable of stabilizing her end of the mattress and box springs and Jack worried aloud about the safety of her doing so. Annie made Jack lift up an end of the mattress as it lay on the truck and he had to agree that it was light, so he gave in. They carried them in one by one and placed them on the frame. As they put the sheets on the mattress, Jack joked. "Boy, I get to sleep between your mom's sheets." He watched her face to see her reaction.

"Don't flatter yourself. You're just one of many," Annie replied. The tone of her response didn't match Jack's good-natured dig. He had definitely stepped over a line, but he guessed the bitterness that he heard in her voice was directed more at her mother than at him.

They heated supper and shared their meal together, appreciating the efforts of Jack's sisters. When the kitchen was cleaned, Jack announced that he would go unpack and invited Annie to come and claim her dresser drawers. When they walked into the bedroom, Annie breathed in deeply and asked, "Do you smell that?"

Jack breathed in the fragrance of cut wood and varnish from the furniture. "Yeah, I do." He wondered if he would have noticed if she hadn't been there to point it out.

It didn't take long to stow the few clean items that remained in their suitcases into the empty drawers. Not yet sure this was her home, Annie asked permission to do some laundry and, not yet sure she was truly his wife, Jack asked if she would mind if he threw his things in, too.

Jack went to check e-mail, weather, and grain prices on the computer. He heard the sound of the water rushing into the washing machine and had mixed feelings about his house echoing with noises that he hadn't created. Annie poked her head into the office to ask if she could put away a few of the shower gifts that were still stacked against a wall in the living room. "Of course," he replied, hoping that his voice didn't reveal the annoyance he felt at the question. When she walked away, he fought the urge to follow her. The computer screen didn't change for long moments at a time while he listened to the cupboard doors opening and closing. After a short while there was complete silence.

He finished at the computer and walked into the living room and stopped suddenly. Annie was laying on the couch with her shirt up and her pants down to expose her abdomen.

She quickly covered herself, blushed, and explained. "I was resting and the baby moved again and I was wondering if I could see anything."

He walked over to her and knelt beside the couch. He gently pulled her shirt back up and the waist of her pants back down. "You don't have to hide anything from me, Annie." He placed his hand on the rise that he had revealed and felt the warmth and softness of her stomach against his hand, his flesh on her flesh. He imagined moving his hand. If he dared, would he make it travel up or down?

With his eyes only, he traveled up, paused at her breasts and then reluctantly continued to her face. Their eyes held and both of them were breathing rapidly. It was Jack who moved first. He stood and immediately turned away from her so that she couldn't see the physical evidence of his thoughts. She caught his hand before he could walk away and said, "You don't have to hide anything from me, either." She released him and he went to the bedroom and sat on their new mattress.

As he sat, his heart slowed, but his words that she had repeated back to him continued to ring in his ears. "You don't have to hide anything from me." He was hiding more than she knew.

Chapter 49

Annie

With the official honeymoon over and the unofficial honeymoon postponed indefinitely, life settled into a routine. Annie rose each day while it was still dark, donned her uniform with the ever-shortening apron strings, and went to work.

Although Annie was enjoying not being sick anymore, the pregnancy and long days at the diner left her physically drained. Jack encouraged her to rest after work and, because it was a slow time of year and he was already accustomed to doing so anyway, he easily kept up with the housework so that she wouldn't have to, a fact about which she felt increasingly guilty.

Each night, they shared the beautiful oak bed, respecting the invisible line that had been drawn down the center of it. By unspoken agreement, the more delicate issues that had been shared under the quilt at the inn were not discussed and no physical contact was made while they were in their bed. Only their words crossed over to the other side, soft words that they shared about their days. This suited Annie because by the end of the day she was dead tired and ready to get to sleep as soon as possible before the alarm woke her in what seemed at this time of year to be the dead of night. And this suited Jack because any form of intimacy would have pushed him to the edge of his resolve.

Thanksgiving approached quickly. Annie had to work on Thanksgiving Day but this turned out not to be a problem because Meg would be serving supper, allowing her daughters to spend the noon meal with their in-laws.

At Meg's insistence, Annie called to invite Cindy to the Schroeder house for the holiday. She declined, informing her that she and Ray were taking an extended weekend and vacationing in the Bahamas. Annie suspected that her mother had found her next husband and was relieved. She knew from experience that her mother craved companionship and wouldn't be able to live alone for long.

On Thanksgiving Day after Annie returned home from work, they gathered the corn casserole that was Jack's designated dish for the holidays and drove down to the home place. Thanksgiving at the Schroeder household was what Annie had imagined it would be. The turkey was picture perfect, the stuffing was homemade, and pumpkin pies were joined by apple and cherry. A cornucopia spilled its plastic fruit onto the dining room table. Frank poured mixed drinks and it seemed that she was the only adult without whiskey to color her 7-up. The children ran around as usual, spurred on by their uncles and one another.

When everyone had arrived, most of them still full from earlier feasts at other houses, Meg gathered everyone for grace. The usual prayer was muttered, so unintelligible that Annie wondered if it was even in English. Then Meg started the tradition of each person sharing what they were thankful for. They went around the jagged circle and each person stated in a word or two a blessing from the past year. Even the children came up with moving responses. As her turn approached, Annie stepped back and slipped away to hide in the restroom. Jack immediately closed in the circle, helping her departure to go unnoticed, unsure of the reason for her escape.

When everyone had spoken and the wave of blessings returned to Meg, she looked around and asked, "Where'd Annie go?"

Jack gave a crooked grin, "To the bathroom, where else?" feigning irritation at dealing with a pregnant woman and her bladder.

In the bathroom, Annie could hear the sounds of the prayer ending and then of everyone beginning to help themselves to the food and knew that she needed to rejoin them. But she knew that, even more, she needed to play out in her head what had made her take refuge in here. She tried to form words for what she might have said had she stayed in the circle. But how could she ever begin to say what she was thankful for? For a husband who is patient and kind beyond words. For gaining the family that she always wished she had. For the baby growing inside her. For being here with this group of people at this moment and knowing that it was exactly where she was meant to be.

She leaned against the wall and closed her eyes. She had come to the truth that was really beyond words. In all her years of moving from house to house she had never experienced the feeling of home. And now here she was, home. The fact that she wasn't physically present in her own house didn't take away from that feeling in the least. She understood that "home" was the sense of belonging just where she was.

She opened her eyes and the first thing that she saw was a gold cross lying on the counter. The cheapness and tiny open gold ring in the hole at the top attested to the fact that it must have come loose from a necklace of one of the girls and been laid there out of harm's way. Her mind captured the image but her heart couldn't yet find a place for it.

Tina Williams

She took a breath, smiled to herself in the mirror, and stepped back out into the midst of her new family to fill herself with turkey and so much more.

Chapter 50

Jack

Three days after Thanksgiving was the first Sunday of Advent. Jack was pleased when Annie automatically got out of bed and joined him for Mass. He knew she craved sleep and that attending 9:30 Mass was a sacrifice for her, but he neither praised nor discouraged her. Jack took his usual place next to his parents and in front of Kate and her family. Annie slid in beside him. They watched as Father Bill lit the advent wreath. Jack listened closely to the homily about a time of waiting for Christ's arrival and, although he didn't turn his head, he sensed Annie's attentiveness, also. After Mass, as they drove the few miles back to their home, Annie asked, "So what's with the advent wreath?"

Jack thought a moment. "Well, it's a way to mark the time as we wait for Christmas. And it represents light in the darkness."

"I like it," Annie replied.

"Me too."

On Monday, Annie's alarm rang and Jack felt the bed adjust as she got up and went into the bathroom. He reached over to her pillow and felt the warmth that she had left behind. He imagined what it would be like if she didn't have to rush off to work. He thought about his plans for the day and frowned. He had a very lonely day ahead of him. During the day, it felt like he had never married; the house was silent and unchanged and he kept up with all the same chores that he had done before his wedding. In the evenings, Annie was tired and quiet. When she talked, it was often to tell him that he shouldn't have done some task around the house because she had been planning on doing it after work.

He got up and made coffee. He considered making Annie breakfast, but knew that his efforts would lead her to insist again that he shouldn't do so much for her.

After she had eaten a piece of toast and left, Jack went to the window as he still did each morning and prayed. Among other things, he thanked God for giving him Annie and asked for His much-needed help in making them truly man and wife.

Chapter 51

Annie

As Christmas approached, Annie and Jack did some shopping together, fighting the traffic of Findlay on a Saturday. As they crossed people off their list, Annie wondered more and more what to get Jack. She struggled with this issue for two reasons. The first was that Jack had a definite lack of appreciation for material things. The second was that she wanted her gift to be special, something worthy of someone who had given her so much.

It was on the third Sunday of Advent that Annie discovered what the perfect gift would be and the discovery was a gift in itself, given to her. In church on that Sunday, after the only pink candle on the Advent Wreath had been lit, Annie listened to the first and second readings and found them so joyful and poetic that she wanted to read them again. She committed to memory what she saw printed in the missal: the name of the books from which they were taken and the numbers that followed. She knew this was supposed to tell her where in the Bible she could find the passages, although she wasn't sure exactly how to do that.

When they stepped out onto the steps after Mass, it was clear that the weather hadn't heard the joyful news; the skies were gloomy and threatened snow. After lunch, Jack lay down for a nap on the couch which, Annie was beginning to learn, was his way of honoring Sunday as a day of rest. When she heard his breath become deep and even, she quietly picked up the worn Bible that lay on the end table by his recliner, unsure of why she felt the need for secrecy. It was a paperback version, beginning to yellow with age. She opened it, intent on finding and reading what she had listened to that morning, but was distracted by two things. First, the tissue-thin pages were falling away from the binding. Many were stuck in loose and many others were soon to lose their struggle to remain intact. This fact made a search, especially one by a novice, tricky at best. The other thing that threw her off track was that she saw that Jack had marked in the book quite profusely over the years. She found that he had highlighted many passages and written in the margins. And so she forgot about her search and carefully turned the pages, reading with interest the words that the yellow marker told her were of interest to Jack and Jack's words written beside some of these passages, scribbled words in blue and black ink which were at times comments and at times questions about what he had read.

When he began to stir, she guiltily replaced the book, feeling as though she had just been reading his diary without permission. She picked up her pregnancy book that had also been lying on the table and pretended to be reading it instead.

Now she finally knew what he needed for Christmas: a new Bible. There was no book store in town, so she drove to Findlay to a Christian book store to buy one and was amazed and confused by all of the versions available. There were Bibles labeled as "study", "annotated", "King James", and more. She had thought all Bibles were the same and she just needed to find one with a nice cover. After standing for a while she decided that she needed to ask someone. It was the next day after work that she found herself walking into the parish office.

Father was in the front talking to Caroline, the secretary. When he saw her, his face lit up and he walked over to greet her with a hearty handshake and invited her into his office without asking why she had come. She was taken aback by his delight at her presence.

Caroline stopped him using only her words, the tone of which made them more than enough. "But Father, I need your decision on this now."

He turned to Annie, "Could you wait just a second in my office?"

She nodded. She went down the hall to his office. While she waited, she stood and looked at the pictures that she hadn't taken time to examine during her previous visits with Jack. In one, she found Father's smiling face among his graduating seminary class. In another, she saw him receiving a certificate from a man wearing a beanie on his head, who Annie assumed was the bishop. While she was examining a third, a picture of him with his parents and two men that looked like they might be his brothers, he walked in. He left the door open and sank into the computer chair that was behind his desk and motioned for her to take a seat also..

"I'm so happy to see you, Annie." His countenance and tone made the words unnecessary.

Unsure of the appropriate response to his enthusiasm, she went ahead with the reason for her visit, "I had a question."

"I hope I can answer it." As always, he made it easy to feel comfortable.

"I wanted to give Jack a Bible for Christmas and I didn't know what kind." He seemed a little disappointed at the question but didn't hesitate long to answer.

He spun the chair around and reached for a Bible that lay within easy reach. It, too, had been well used, although the pages were all safely in place, and he opened it to point out to her the cross references on each page as well as helpful extras in the front and back. He stood, pulled two others from a higher shelf, and talked about the differences among the three. He also told her which translation was used in the Catholic liturgy. She listened intently and asked a few questions.

"Does that help?" he asked when he had finished.

"Yes, it does," she replied honestly.

"Is there anything else?" he asked hopefully.

"No, I don't think so," she said, but for reasons she couldn't explain she didn't move from the seat that she had taken.

"I'm happy to see you attending Mass with Jack."

"I'm happy to be there." Only after she said this did she stand, thank him, shake the hand that he offered her again, and leave.

As she drove home, the snow that they had forecast began falling. She committed to memory the tips of Bible selection that Father had told her. This done, she thought about the rest of the conversation and replayed the words she had spoken regarding church: "I'm happy to be there." She hadn't said this only to be polite. She enjoyed the music and singing along with Jack, who had a voice that was more pleasant than she would have guessed a farmer's singing voice to be. And she did enjoy the lyrical words of the Scripture, but only in the same way that she had always enjoyed literature in school. And she enjoyed watching the blessing of the bread and wine, but she didn't really understand it..

When they sat down for supper that night Jack seemed to read her mind when he asked, "Do you have my gift bought yet?"

"Have you been a good boy?" she teased.

"You know I've been extraordinarily good," he teased back.

She couldn't argue with that. "Yes, you have. So what do you want, little boy?"

"I want you to quit your job." The words instantly changed the flow of conversation, creating a serious mood.

"Oh," was her only reply.

"Well? What do you think?"

"I didn't know you didn't want me to work. I know we talked about after the baby was born but I thought I'd work until then. You never said anything."

"I'm saying something now." His words were decisive and firm, not unkind but not gentle either. "You've been so tired and I don't want you driving on the icy roads in the winter and I want you home with me." He argued his case rapidly.

She chewed and thought a moment. Her first instinct was to struggle against being told what to do. She swallowed this urge along with the food and she digested his words. He had given three reasons. The first was true, she was exhausted. The icy roads were no problem, but it was nice that he was concerned. And staying home with him? She didn't know if she wanted that or not, but she knew it was what he needed, and rightly so.

"Okay," she said. "I will. You're absolutely right."

"So you'll quit soon?" Pleasure filled his face.

She thought for a moment, "Yes. In fact, the weekend girl finishes her last semester of classes this week. I bet she would like to go full-time until she finds a better job." She continued, "But I have two conditions."

He looked at her inquiringly.

"First, I'm going in to visit with the old guys at least once a week, with or without you, on icy or clear roads. I'd miss them too much if I didn't."

"Agreed. And what's the other condition?"

"You'll have to accept two gifts for Christmas because I know what else I want to give you."

"I think I can do that." Their smile acted as a handshake, sealing the deal.

Chapter 52

Jack

As Annie predicted, the young woman who had been working weekends for the past several years was happy to have Annie's spot on the weekdays and the weekend job was quickly filled by the woman's younger sister who was still in high school. Because the woman needed the money and the semester ended just two days after Jack had made his request to Annie, Jack got his first Christmas present a full week early.

Jack knew things would change rapidly now, and they did. The fatigue that resulted from Annie's early mornings and tiring days had kept their relationship at a standstill and now this fatigue lessened. Now when they crawled into bed at the end of the day, Jack knew that she felt a pleasant tiredness but not the same exhaustion as she had before. In spite of this, Jack continued to wait but wasn't sure what he was waiting for. He wondered if he should let her make the first move or if she was waiting for him. And so they continued as before, with words being the only things exchanged each night as they lay side by side in the darkness, but they talked longer and in the darkness their friendship grew deeper.

While the change in the nighttime was subtle, the days were quite different now. Jack was more than ready to hand over many of the household chores and Annie was glad to have the time and energy to do these things for him, eager to repay him for the patience and kindness that he gave so abundantly. The fact that Jack was in and out with various jobs and errands and spent a fair amount of time working on some year-end bookwork with his father kept them from getting in each other's way while at the same time allowed a sharing of their lives that hadn't been possible before.

But the most pleasant development in that week before Christmas was that they resumed flirting with one another. They had done a small amount of teasing at the diner over the past year. If asked why, they both would have replied that it was only for the benefit of the old men who listened. But now no one was listening. This gave them the freedom to take it further than they had before and took away the excuse that it had any purpose that went beyond the two of them.

The flirting created a pleasant sexual tension that they both enjoyed. When they decorated the tree, Annie hung the ornaments where it was necessary to squeeze past him, allowing her body to brush his. When they wrapped presents, he commented about how *unwrapping* would be so much more fun and they both knew he wasn't talking about presents. When they made Christmas cookies together, he lifted a dough-covered finger to her, and she licked it off, watching the color fill his cheeks. It was obvious that things were changing between them and they both welcomed the change, gently nourishing it with their words and actions.

When they went to church on Sunday two days before Christmas, Father lit the last purple candle and talked about the time of waiting being almost over. His words had a double meaning for Jack, who had been waiting for so much for so long. Jack had always appreciated Advent and Lent and understood them as necessary to maintaining the sacredness of Christmas and Easter. Therefore, it was easy for him to understand God's purpose in asking him to wait, first for Annie herself and now for the consummation of his marriage. He looked over at Annie, who was sitting beside him in the pew, and he thanked God for the gift of waiting and, even more, for the gift of the anticipation that comes when you know the wait is almost over.

Chapter 53

Annie

Jack had explained the Christmas Eve traditions to Annie, so they arrived at Frank and Meg's at 6:00, dressed up, with a plate of elegant appetizers and large bag of gifts. Annie put the appetizers next to those created by her sisters-in-law while Jack added the gifts to the growing pile that surrounded the tree.

When supper was served, the traditional meat and potatoes were nowhere to be found and in their place was an array of unusual treats. Things like shrimp cocktail, spring rolls, and fondue, all of which would never ordinarily be served, were presented and raved over by the women, tolerated by the men, and not eaten by the children, who filled up on reindeer-shaped cookies covered in frosting.

When supper was over, Meg interrupted a discussion about the replacement of a grain bin to call Frank into the living room. Frank sat down in his chair and, without being called, the grandchildren gathered in a circle on the floor. Their usual buoyancy was replaced by solemnity appropriate for the occasion. The women quietly began clearing the kitchen while Meg lit all of the candles of a small advent wreath that had been moved from the dining table to the coffee table.

Kate, who had just finished nursing Kimberly, approached Annie and said, "Kimberly has to be in there to listen to Grandpa reading on her first Christmas." She handed the infant to Annie, more telling than asking, "Would you hold Kimberly for me? I didn't get a chance to finish my meal yet." Annie gladly but awkwardly accepted the infant and accompanying burp rag. Kimberly rested her head on Annie's shoulder, content with her full stomach. Annie took her into the living room and sat down on the floor with the children, carefully holding the baby in place as she bent to do so. Annie tilted her head to one side to rest her cheek on the baby's fuzzy head. She breathed in the unique fragrance of baby shampoo mixed with the smell of the infant's skin and wondered if she had ever smelled anything as sweet.

When everyone was in place, Frank opened the black, leather-bound Bible and read the story of the birth of Jesus to the children, who all listened without a sound except Kimberly, who let out a burp in the middle.

When he was finished reading, Frank asked the children, "So do you know why we have Christmas?" They all nodded seriously. "And do you understand that God gave us His Son and that's why we share presents with each other?" They nodded again. Frank kept his solemn tone but the twinkle in his eye gave him away as he asked, "And do you want presents?"

That question broke the spell and they called out "Yeah!" in the off-key but melodic chorus that only children can create.

"Well, I think Santa left a few things here, so after a bit we'll see who's been good this year." And with that, Frank got up and that was the kids' cue to return to their normal selves. Soon they were once again filling the house with joyful noise.

When the grown-ups finally declared the kitchen clean and had fixed themselves a glass of holiday cheer, Frank began the fun by saying, "I need all the good boys and girls in the living room to open presents!" They all came running and then he teased them by pointing and bringing up events from the past year. "I don't think a boy who hits his brother with a bat is a good boy, do you?" and "I don't know, I think I heard you sassing your mother just last week."

Meg rescued them from this by interrupting, "But Grandpa, haven't they been mostly good?"

Frank pretended to think about this and looked down on their faces that were only a little worried. "Yes, I think they have been mostly good. I guess we'll just have to see who Santa brought presents for."

And then the neatly wrapped boxes under the tree made their way across the room and, amidst camera flashes, squeals of delight, and thank-you's, became empty boxes, loose wrapping paper, and toys.

The grown-ups weren't left out. The sisters loved their pottery. Jack received a lot of socks and flannel shirts and a few tools which, Annie surmised by the comments made when he opened them, were his standard gifts each year. Annie received an oversized winter coat from Meg to replace the one that had lately been stretched to its limits when zipped up on cold days.

The sisters also each gave her a small but well-selected gift. From Sarah she received a beautiful photo frame for their wedding picture. Mary gave her a box of lotions and powder. A big gift bag from Kate contained a folded body pillow that she explained would help her rest during the last months of pregnancy. But it was Elizabeth's gift that Annie liked most of all; a beautiful journal covered in bright splashes of color, and filled with pages that were all blank except the first where she had written, "So that you can write down everything that you feel as you become a mom. Congratulations, Elizabeth".

Offerings

The next hours were devoted to the children. Batteries were pulled from Meg's well-stocked cupboard. Barbies and action figures were released from their clear plastic prisons. Directions were either read and followed or dismissed as unnecessary. Annie was recruited as a fourth player in a board game while Jack assembled a race track.

Finally, the fathers loaded the toys into their minivans and the mothers pulled pajamas from the bags that they had brought and all but the oldest, Curtis, readied for sleep. Jack disappeared upstairs and brought down out-of-date sleeping bags bearing the images of Smurfs and Strawberry Shortcake and smelling of cedar. Sarah put a holiday movie in to help the children settle down.

The grown-ups, except Mary's husband David who wasn't Catholic and who had always willingly accepted the role of Christmas Eve babysitter, donned winter coats and braved the arctic air for the short trip to Midnight Mass.

Jack had explained to Annie how attendance at Midnight Mass had always been a family tradition when he and his sisters were growing up but when they married and the babies had come along, the infants were left at home with David, having been put to bed hours earlier. When the babies grew to be toddlers, if they were still awake, they were too tired and cranky by that hour to be brought along. When they were old enough to need to hear the Christmas Story, the sisters recruited Frank to read this to them and they continued to excuse them from Christmas Mass, enjoying the once-a-year opportunity to experience Mass uninterrupted. This year, however, they were joined by Curtis, who had made his First Communion in the spring and, therefore, was obligated to participate in the full Mass.

When they walked into church, the sanctuary was nearly dark. Only the manger scene and the cut trees surrounding it were illuminated.

A small choir sang beautiful arrangements of Christmas hymns that were familiar even to Annie.

Annie noted that everyone in the crowded church was dressed in their finest. In this farming community, this meant that many of the middle-aged farmers wore suit jackets that had gone out of style a decade ago. Annie hoped that the buttons that held them closed were sewn on with good thread that could stand the stress because the fabric was stretched over beer bellies that had apparently grown over the many years since the suits were bought. Although the thought caused her mouth to briefly turn up at the corners, her amusement was mixed with fondness and respect for these farmers, some of whom she knew because she had served coffee to them at the diner.

Small white candles had been laid in the ends of the pews and Jack passed one to her. When it was midnight, Father appeared at the back of the church and from the candle that he held, other candles were lit and the light was passed from parishioner to parishioner, making the church glow. Frank touched his lit candle to the dark tip of Jack's and then Jack turned to Annie and their wicks joined until hers shone as brightly as his. The symbolism wasn't lost on Annie. She knew from Jack's answer to her question on the first Sunday of advent as well as from listening each Sunday, that this light was more than a flame to illuminate the church; it represented the light of Christ.

Wishing that faith could be passed as easily as the flame in front of her, she accepted it seriously and then reached to touch it to Curtis' dark wick. The boy's tongue peeked out past his lips and the responsibility of the flame made him focus intently. In her mind, Annie fast-forwarded to the day when their own child would fill the space beside them in the pew and she would have the opportunity to pass the flame to him or her.

After Mass, they returned to a quiet house. Sleeping children were scooped off the floor and quiet kisses of good-bye were given. Jack helped carry any remaining items for the parents whose arms were full with the limp bodies of the children who had been so full of energy a few hours ago.

And then Jack and Annie returned to their home and, yawning, readied for bed. When Annie crawled into bed, wearing the pajamas that Jack had lent her on the honeymoon, she did not respect the line that had been drawn between them in their bed. Instead, she moved her body over next to Jack's and rested her head on his shoulder. "I'm so cold. Do you mind if I use you to warm up?"

Jack wrapped his arm around her and kissed her forehead. "Not at all," he replied.

"Merry Christmas, Jack."

"Merry Christmas, Annie," he whispered back. As she drifted off to sleep she imagined that their joined bodies were one, like the flame that was created by the touching of their wicks in the darkness of the church.

Chapter 54

Jack

Jack woke up before Annie, showered, and made breakfast.

Annie stumbled out of the bedroom in her adopted pajamas, still rubbing her eyes, "It's a holiday, you know," she reminded him.

"I know. I didn't want to sleep through it," he argued cheerfully. "Want some breakfast?"

"I was planning to sleep until lunch, but since I'm up, I guess I will."

Jack dropped an egg on the hot skillet, enjoying the pleasant sizzle. He assembled a plate of bacon, eggs, and hash browns and put it in front of her, kissing her forehead as he did so.

"So when are we opening gifts?" he asked, showing all the patience of a young child.

"I feel a little underdressed. Mind if I shower first?"

"I suppose I'll let you." He feigned annoyance.

After breakfast, Jack cleaned the kitchen while Annie showered. When she emerged with her hair hanging in damp strands, Jack sat on the floor beside three lonely gifts that had been deserted the night before when the others were taken to Frank and Meg's. With some effort, Jack scooted the largest box over to her after she sat down facing him, her legs crossed in front of her. He picked up his own that Annie had disguised by putting in a larger box.

The last gift remained under the tree to be opened by Cindy the following day. Jack had secretly rejoiced when she had called the day before to tell them that she was going to spend the day with Ray and his adult children.

"You first," he stated and she obeyed.

Because of the size of the box, she lifted herself to her knees as she removed the paper and lifted the cardboard flap. Jack was as delighted as she was when she lifted out each item that he had bought at the Amish shops that morning not long ago. He watched as she revealed a small birdhouse, a set of wrought-iron candlesticks, a pine-scented candle, and small basket fashioned out of wood.

"There's one more thing," he said. She reached in and pulled away the tissue paper that lined the bottom. She pulled out what lay beneath, unfolded it, and gasped. It was a miniature version of the quilt under which they had slept at the inn. The loops at the top attested to the fact that it was meant to be hung from a rod.

"Jack, when did you get all this stuff?"

He sheepishly explained that he had shopped when he went to pick up the furniture on the Monday morning of their honeymoon. "Did I do okay?" he asked worriedly. "We looked at so much that I couldn't remember for sure what you liked the best."

"You did great." The light in her eyes confirmed her words. "But what about the quilt? I don't remember seeing one with that same pattern."

"Carol helped me out with that. I called the inn and told her what I wanted. She got a hold of the lady that made the quilt and she had this wall-hanging made and ready to sell. She bought it for me and shipped it to me. Actually, I wanted a quilt but she was the one that talked me out of it. She warned me that babies and handmade quilts aren't the best combination."

Annie crawled the short distance to where Jack sat on the floor and kissed him on the lips. The touch was soft and moist and warm, promising much but delivering little.

"Now it's your turn."

He untied the gold ribbon and tore off the paper. In a nest of brightly-colored tissue paper, he saw the gold letters printed on the black leather: HOLY BIBLE. "Annie." He looked up to meet her eyes that were worried if he liked his gift.

"I wasn't sure what kind to get, so I talked to Father about it. Do you like it? If it's not right, you can exchange it."

"I couldn't think of a more perfect gift. How'd you know I needed a new one?" he asked seriously.

"I saw it when I was cleaning and I noticed the pages were coming loose," she lied.

"It really is perfect," he repeated. "Thank you." He didn't add but thought, "…for understanding this is important for me." He stood up from where he sat and began to pick up the wrapping paper.

Following his cue, she, too, stood and then bent to bunch up the wrapping paper at her feet. When she righted herself, he caught her around the waist and pressed her to him. "Thank you," he said again, whispering. He bent his head to kiss her and, for the first time, she responded with the eagerness that he longed for. He knew that their time of waiting was complete.

Chapter 55

Annie

They dropped the wrapping paper back on the floor and moved hand in hand into the bedroom, neither one leading, both equally ready at last to share themselves physically with one another. They fell on their beautiful bed, still unmade from the night before. Jack buried his face in her loose hair, damp and fragrant from her shower. Annie rubbed her cheek against his, still smooth from his morning shave. The smell of bacon lingered in his hair. They shared another kiss, this one deeper and more urgent than before.

Jack separated from her and stood to undress. She remained on the bed, hands behind her head, and watched him with a grin of appreciation. "Your turn," he declared as the last piece of fabric fell from his body.

"Will you help me?" she asked. He grabbed the hands that she stretched out to him and pulled her off the bed. He lifted his own sweatshirt off of her body and pulled down her maternity pants until she stood before him in her bra and her flowered panties that covered less of her everyday. He took several steps back to look at her and she covered the roundness of her stomach with her hands, embarrassed by it. He fell to his knees in front of her, put a hand on each side of her abdomen and kissed her on the fullest part of it, just below the belly button.

Then he stood to finish undressing her. He fumbled nervously with the hooks that held her bra and muttered an apology. She tried to set him at ease by saying lovingly, "We have all day, Jack. I'm not in a hurry." When the bra fell away, he cupped her breasts in his hands and felt their fullness while he bent to kiss their dark tips, not knowing that both the fullness and the darkened nipples were the result of the pregnancy. Her panties then joined the bra on the floor and they again fell together onto the bed.

As they made love, Jack's gentleness made it clear that both she and her baby were safe in his hands. Her slightly protruding stomach was an unnecessary reminder of Annie's condition. Rather than being a hindrance to their lovemaking, the baby's presence helped them to communicate with one another, Jack asking and Annie telling what was comfortable and pleasurable.

Far from being disappointed by his lack of knowledge, Annie delighted in Jack's novice exploration of her body and together they began to learn the secrets of her body that no one else had ever taken the time to discover.

Afterward, they rested. Her head found its place on his shoulder as it had the night before, and his arm automatically encircled her. Their free hands grasped one another, fingers entwined. His thumb lazily ran back and forth below her thumb. Both were still naked but Jack had pulled the covers up against the chill of the room that had been more than warm enough a few moments earlier.

As Annie lie there, she tried to find a way to describe to herself the difference between what had happened with Jack and what had happened with Eric last summer, enjoying the analogies that she created in her mind. It was the difference between a watermelon sucker, hard and artificial, and a watermelon slice, bursting with flavor and texture and juice. It was the difference between looking out the window at a sunset, and sitting in the backyard in the summertime to experience the same sunset while you heard the song of the cicadas and felt the night air caressing your bare arms and the spiky green grass tickling your toes. It was difference between hearing a tune squeaked out on a soprano recorder and the same tune being performed by a full orchestra. Perhaps the most amazing part was that she could make these analogies in spite of the fact that what they had just shared hadn't been perfect at all. On the contrary, Jack had been clumsy and nervous. But she had just learned that the richness and depth of the experience had little to do with skill.

So what accounted for the difference? Her brow wrinkled as she thought back to Eric. He had asked for something and she had given it to him and that was the extent of it. This time, though, Jack had waited for her to offer herself as a gift to him and, just as importantly, he had offered himself as a gift back to her, not just taking what he wanted from her but giving back to her as much or more than she had given him. They had both seen the gift of the other as an offering of self that went beyond the flesh, but how far beyond she didn't know or understand. Thinking about it was like gazing out at the universe and knowing that there was a vastness that could be pondered but never understood.

Chapter 56

Jack

Jack, too, was lost in thought as he lay on the bed with Annie. He felt the joy of the culmination of something that had been building over time. And although he had not anticipated it, his gift of patience had been repaid when Annie showed him the same type of patience that he had shown her, never once seeming to want more than he knew how to give.

He felt God smiling down on them as they lie naked and entwined. If he had been holding any remaining doubts about whether God had truly called him to marry Annie, he let go of those doubts completely and forever. In Jack's mind, what they had shared together was a sacrament during which God had reached down to earth and made his love more tangible, something that could be touched and tasted and held on to.

But only Jack knew, that in spite of all that they had just shared, there was a part of himself he hadn't shared with her. "You should tell her." He wondered if the words that he heard in his head were his own or

God's, but he remained silent, not yet able to follow the advice, regardless of the source.

The phone rang, waking them both from the light sleep into which their thoughts had carried them. Jack rolled away from Annie and picked up the receiver from the phone on the night stand. "Hello."

"Merry Christmas," Frank's voice boomed. Jack looked over at Annie and her smile told him that she could hear, too. "Are you two bored yet?"

Jack wondered if he would ever be bored again. "No, we just got done having a cup of coffee."

Frank chuckled his dirty-old-man chuckle. "Was it hot?"

"Yes it was." Jack looked guiltily at Annie. The look on her face told Jack that she was wondering what Frank found so funny and why Jack looked so guilty for making up a white lie to avoid telling his parents that they had just had sex.

"We were wondering if you wanted to make the rounds this Christmas or stay home with your new bride. If you've already had your coffee, maybe you'd like to come along." He was referring to the annual tradition of Jack joining Meg and Frank to visit his sisters' houses so that the kids could show off the new toys that they received on Christmas morning.

"I'll talk to Annie. Let me call you right back." He hung up, rolled over to face Annie, and tried to keep his hands off of her while they discussed it. Although they needed to make plans for later, Jack knew what he wanted to do right now and knew by the light in Annie's eyes that she felt the same.

Jack explained the usual plans to her. "What time would we go?" she asked.

"Midafternoon." She looked at the clock. It was only eleven.

She inched forward so her naked body was pressed more tightly against his. "You know, it might be your last year to go. Next year, we'll have toys under our own tree. I think we should go." She kissed him. "And we still have three hours." She kissed him again. "And after we get back." Another kiss. "And tomorrow." And another. "And the next day." Their hands began exploring each other again until they were interrupted by the phone.

Annie reached across Jack to answer it. "Hello."

"Hi, Annie," came Frank's voice, loud enough for Jack to detect his annoyance. "Have you two decided yet?"

"I'm sorry. We, just, uh, got distracted." She blushed. Jack tried unsuccessfully to keep his laughter silent.

"Distracted, huh?" He listened a moment to the muffled sounds of his son's laughter. "Sounds like Jack must be getting a pretty good Christmas gift."

Jack watched as she recovered from her embarrassment and used the playful banter that she had practiced so often at the diner. "I think he likes it real well. Says it's just what he always wanted. And it fits perfectly." She changed the subject while the ball was in her court. "We'd like to go along with you."

"All right. We'll pick you two lovebirds up about two or two-thirty. Try to have some clothes on by then." He hung up abruptly. They laughed together and then continued what they had only just begun.

Chapter 57

Annie

Annie enjoyed visiting the houses of her new nieces and nephews. Although she had stopped in at Kate's house twice during the brief time they had been married, she had never been to Mary or Sarah's, so the kids showed her not only their new toys but their bedrooms and pets as well.

After they had visited the three houses, they went to Meg's for a late supper to help eat up some of the Christmas Eve leftovers. Both Jack and Annie were famished in spite of a few cookies and pieces of fudge that they had been offered along the way. Meg watched them eat and exclaimed, "My goodness, didn't you two have any lunch?" Frank started chuckling again, nearly choking on a leftover crab cake, but didn't say anything.

Just as Jack and Annie were about to leave, Elizabeth returned home. She had spent the afternoon and evening visiting with a close friend who had gone off to college in New York and was home on a rare visit. As usual, Elizabeth's presence reenergized those around her and when she suggested a game of cards, Jack and Annie were willing to postpone what waited for them at home.

Annie found out that "cards" meant euchre, a game which she had never learned. She was quickly assigned to be Jack's apprentice and they shared one hand. She soon picked up on the strategy that surrounded words like trick and trump and bower. Jack was skillful but not fiercely competitive, unlike his father who shed his jovial manner when the cards were dealt, but was careful to keep his temper in check.

It was late when they returned home and they readied for bed separately and quietly as they had on every other night of their marriage. Jack was the first to lay his head on his pillow and when Annie walked in, dressed once again in his pajamas, he said to her with a twinkle in his eye, "I want my pajamas back."

"You know, I think I'm done with them," she responded, and took them off as he watched her, her body unevenly illuminated by the lamp on the night stand. She tossed them to him and he pressed them to his nose, smelling the scent of her soap, shampoo, and body on them, before he discarded them on the floor beside the bed. Then she joined him in their bed and she wondered why she had ever felt the need to postpone this happiness.

Chapter 58

Jack

Like every other year, Jack opened his house to his sisters' kids on New Year's Eve. He had started this tradition five years ago, on the first year that he lived in his house. By that time, all of his friends had gotten married and had other plans for the night. So when Sarah complained about not being able to find a sitter that year, he gladly volunteered to help her out and it had developed from there. The problem was that the number of kids had grown over the years, so Jack was relieved to have Annie's help this year.

Between Christmas and New Year's Annie spent quite a bit of time preparing. In the past, Jack's preparations had consisted mainly of a trip to the video store and the junk food aisle and he visited those places again this year. But in addition, Annie insisted on making it more of a party. She bought noisemakers and hung streamers. She made lists of games that they could play and bought little prizes for the winners. She stuck grapes and cheese cubes on toothpicks for appetizers and made punch, borrowing Meg's punch bowl and wisely investing in plastic cups with lids. During all of this, Jack was constantly bombarded with questions about what his nieces and nephew liked to play, eat, and drink.

    When the night arrived, the kids showed up family by family, each child with a sleeping bag and an overnight bag. Annie had decided that the basement would be the center of action and sleeping bags were spread out. Jack watched as Annie orchestrated the evening. He admired the warmth that she showed the kids, the same warmth that he had seen her show time and again with the old men at the diner. When the games were done, they watched Jack's movies. At midnight, they made noise with pan lids that had been brought down to the basement. Overall, the night went smoothly with a few exceptions. There were a few tears shed by the loser of a game. One young guest wet his pants during a tickle attack by his cousins. And at midnight the noise woke baby Kimberly even though she had been sleeping soundly in her portable crib in the quiet upstairs.

    After all the "Happy New Year's" were said, Jack put in another movie and lay down with the kids on his own sleeping bag. He and Annie had decided that he would camp out with the older kids and Annie would sleep upstairs so that she could listen for Kimberly or Mary's youngest, two-year-old Michael, who had fallen asleep on his sleeping bag at about ten o'clock and been carried up and put on the couch so he wouldn't be stepped on. And so Jack spent a long night on the floor, listening to the breathing of five sets of young lungs and helping the owners of two young bladders find their way to the restroom in the middle of the night.

    Even though the kids had been up late, they woke early, ready for breakfast. Jack made and served pancakes while Annie changed a few diapers, fed Kimberly a bottle of breast milk that Kate had sent along, and helped the little ones brush their teeth. The parents arrived mid-morning, looking as tired as Jack felt. They gathered the things that were still scattered around, rolled up sleeping bags, and tracked down blankies and teddy bears. The kids were sent home with messy hair, tired eyes, and hands still sticky from syrup.

When the door was shut on the last departing child, Jack breathed a sigh of relief, happy to have hosted the party and happy to have the party over. They tidied the house and lay down on the bed together to enjoy a long nap.

Jack snuggled up to Annie and asked, "Was the bed lonely without me last night?"

"Tremendously."

Memories of the night before floated through his mind...Annie holding the baby... Annie wiping tears ...Annie gently admonishing one of the kids for teasing another one...Annie passing out drinks... Annie giving good-night kisses. He looked at her now. She was falling asleep.

"Annie?"

"Hmm."

"You'll make such a great mom."

She opened her eyes and smiled at him. "I was just thinking about what a great dad you'll be." They gave each other a peck on the lips and went to sleep, too exhausted from being temporary parents to want anything but a nap.

Chapter 59

Annie

January, like most Januaries in Ohio, was cold and snowy. After each snow, Jack would dress in his insulated coveralls and ski mask and clear the snow out of their drive and the drive of several other neighbors. Annie would wipe the steam from the window and watch her husband for a while, the snow flying out from the top of the blower that was attached to the front of the tractor. Then she would make something to warm him when he came back in. Soup if it was lunch time, cookies if it was snack time, or a pot of coffee if it was neither. Although she wasn't a good cook, she was willing to take the time to follow the recipes that she found in the cookbooks that Meg lent her, and Jack's appreciation of her efforts encouraged her to keep it up.

As she had planned, Annie insisted on going to the diner for breakfast once a week. Jack went along, teasing that he didn't trust her not to run off with one of the men there. She pointed out that most of them couldn't run anymore if they tried and they probably wouldn't be able to do anything else, either, once they had run to their destination.

But the truth was that Jack tagged along because even though they enjoyed each other's company, they both needed the company of others to help fight the coldness and loneliness of the winter.

Because her stomach was now beyond hiding and because nothing was being planted, harvested, or rained on, the baby became a popular topic of conversation when they were at the diner.

When Annie was still waitressing, the men had not said a word about the roundness behind her apron, at first thinking she might only be gaining weight and then, later, not wanting to be too personal. Teasing was one thing but talking to a woman seriously about the child she was carrying was quite another. Talking to a man about a baby, however, was not off-limits, so when Jack walked in with Annie that first time after Christmas and Annie removed her coat to reveal her rounded front, Ralph jumped at his chance.

"Dang, Jack, you don't waste any time, do ya?"

Jack grinned. "What the hell do you mean? You guys have been telling me I need to hurry up and find a woman, get married, and have kids for the last ten years. And now I do and you tell me I did it too quick. There's no pleasin' ya."

"Well yeah, but by the looks of things, you got the order wrong, Jack," Ralph wasn't going to let him off the hook too easily.

He thought a minute, knowing that denying it would be futile. "Maybe. But I got the woman right and that's the main thing." He put his arm around her shoulders and Annie was suddenly warm.

Vince, who Jack knew had a happy marriage, nodded his head, lifted his cup of coffee, and said, "I'll drink to that. Congratulations, Jack." All the men present lifted their white mugs and then sipped their coffee in sincere support of Jack's new life.

Besides the old men, Frank and Meg were another source of outside companionship as time dragged by that winter. Several times each week, Meg would call and ask if they wanted to come down and visit. Now that Annie knew how to play euchre, the visit would usually turn into a card game and they passed the dark evening hours sitting around the kitchen table, each tossing a card onto the table and the winner of the trick pulling the four cards to his or her side of the table. The focus was on the cards and only between hands would short snippets of conversation be squeezed in, resulting in a collection of random comments.

"Hear the Harper place might come up for sale."

"I made the best casserole the other night. I'll give you the recipe."

"We bought some yellow paint for the baby's room."

One night, when January was about to give way to February, and Frank was dealing another round of cards, Meg said, "They're saying there might be an ice storm tomorrow night."

"Hope it's not as bad as that one a few years back," Frank added, turning the top card of the kitty up.

They picked up their cards and studied them. "What ice storm? I don't remember." Jack said, as he sorted his cards.

Meg replied, "When the electric was out for two days, you remember. How many years ago was that Frank?"

Frank's eyes lost the sharpness that they held when he played cards and turned sad. It was the same look that Annie had seen in Jack's eyes at unexplainable moments. "It was at least ten years ago. I think it was the year you were gone, Jack."

The room was filled with silence until Frank said "Your bid, Annie."

Caught off-guard, Annie said, "Pass". She was now positive that she wasn't imagining that there was something about Jack that she didn't know. And she now had the first clue to what it was that he kept from her. But she wasn't sure yet of how to play the cards that she had been dealt.

As they drove over the snow-packed road back to their house, the crunch of the snow under the tires was the only sound. Out of the corner of her eye, Annie saw Jack steal a glance at her. 'You were gone a year? Where were you? Why didn't you tell me?' The questions in her mind never found a voice as she and Jack went inside and crawled into bed. The tension in his body that she felt as she curled up next to him told her that the secret that he kept was real and significant. She gave him a peck on the cheek, said "Good-night" and lay on her back to try to sleep.

In the darkness, she felt the baby swim inside her, a fitting reflection of her thoughts swimming around inside her mind. She listened for Jack's breathing and heard it. It was the soft, shallow breath of someone who was also awake. She wanted to talk to him, to gain answers to her questions, but the imaginary line down the middle of their bed that she had believed was gone forever seemed to have returned, and this time not even words were welcome across that boundary.

She thought about that line between them. Had it really only been six weeks ago that they had shared this bed without touching? The intimacy that had occurred between them recently had pushed those nights into the realm of distant memory. Now she pulled those memories out and examined them in the darkness. To her surprise they were good memories. Memories of kindness. Memories of patience. Memories of him letting her take the lead, waiting for her to offer herself to him. She smiled in the darkness. She knew that was what she needed to do now for him. She would wait until he was ready to tell her. She wouldn't ask; she would simply wait and trust that that moment would come. The plan comforted her and lulled her to sleep.

Chapter 60

Jack

After that night of cards with his parents, Jack knew that Annie had questions. But the days went by and she didn't ask them. At times when he was alone, he would rehearse all that he had to say, knowing that the time would come when he would need to open himself to her. But, like the world around them, the inevitable questions and answers lay dormant, waiting for spring.

In February, they prepared the baby's room, painting it a cheerful light yellow and hanging a border with pictures of blocks around the ceiling line. Mary gave them her crib, with the condition that it would be returned if she ever needed it back. In response to Jack's raised eyebrows, she added that they could definitely have it for at least nine months.

Besides the addition of the few wedding and shower gifts and, of course, the bedroom furniture, the baby's room was the first change that had been made to the house, a house that was sorely in need of updating. Jack would occasionally suggest something new but Annie held back, making excuses that she didn't want to spend his money or that she wasn't sure yet of how to decorate a given room.

Throughout this time Annie continued attending Mass with Jack and together they listened each week as a story of Jesus from Luke's Gospel was read. Annie continued to ask one question on the short drive home each week. Jack looked forward to these questions and often tried to guess ahead of time what Annie would throw at him. But after her one question and his short answer, the subject was dropped and not spoken of through the week.

One week Annie asked the inevitable question that was at the center of his faith. "So do you really believe God changes the bread and wine into the body and blood of Christ?"

"Yes, I do."

For once she pressed on. "But how? That's impossible."

"Not for God," he replied. This conversation, as usual, was held on the short drive home. When they arrived, Annie busied herself in the kitchen while Jack went to the bedroom to change clothes and ponder the question that Annie had posed.

As was often the case, Annie's question that he had answered in a word or two left him thinking long after his answer had been given and the topic had been seemingly dropped. This particular question was key and, alone in the bedroom, he reflected on the importance of it.

He wondered if his faith could exist if he didn't believe in the real presence of Christ in the Eucharist and he wondered which had come first for him, the belief in this miracle that occurred during Mass each Sunday or the belief in God's incredible power. He knew there were many people, both Catholic and non-Catholic, who had trouble believing it and Jack had himself, at times, questioned it. But he had long ago come to the conclusion that if you believed in the full power of God, you could easily believe that it is within His abilities to transform the bread and wine. And, conversely, when you come to believe in the Eucharist, then you are able to more fully know the power of God. It didn't occur to him to make this reflection out loud to Annie.

Also in February, Jack insisted that they go together to visit a lawyer to discuss the paternity of the baby. To avoid local gossip, Jack made an appointment in Findlay and they drove there and listened to a thin, balding man with big glasses describe the options that they had. He told them that because they were now married, the law assumed the child to be his unless he signed a document otherwise. He went on to describe procedures for legal adoption in the case that they would decide not to declare Jack the father on the birth certificate.

Annie was very quiet on the drive home, staring out the window at the fields, the dark earth poking out of the melting snow.

"So what do you think?" Jack asked.

"I guess it's easiest just to list you as the father." It was what Jack had wanted to hear but she said it like she was surrendering to what she didn't want.

"But..." Jack verbally nudged her, urging her to continue.

"But I always though it was unfair that I didn't know my real father. I don't want to keep any secrets."

Jack pushed aside the discomfort that he felt at the word 'secrets' and replied, "But I'll be the father, Annie. It's more true than untrue."

She continued to stare out the window. Through her coat, she rubbed her stomach gently, as she so often did these days. "You're right. If I want the baby to know the whole truth, I'll just have to explain it to her when she's old enough."

"Yes, *we'll* explain it to *him* when *he's* old enough."

She turned to him and he glanced away from the road to see her sad smile. "I love you Jack. I wish you were the father of this baby in every way."

He reached out a hand and she took hers from her stomach and met his across the bench seat of the truck. "Me too."

Chapter 61

Annie

At the end of February, Annie went with Jack to Ash Wednesday services. When ashes were being distributed, Annie was surprised when Jack leaned over and whispered, "You can receive the ashes." And so Annie followed Jack in the line to the altar that she had watched but never joined and stood while Father smeared ashes on her forehead and told her to "Turn away from sin and be faithful to the gospel." And she returned to the pew feeling like an imposter, a silly-looking imposter with a big dirt spot on her face.

When she got home, she went straight to the bathroom, turned on the warm water, and grabbed a washcloth. But before she rubbed off the offending mark, she took a moment to look at herself in the mirror, thinking that she would look ridiculous and was surprised that she didn't. She stared at the thick crisscrossed lines of charcoal and when she finally used the damp cloth, now cooled, to wipe the lines away, she heard herself saying "I'm sorry," but didn't know who she was talking to or what she was sorry for at the moment.

March brought with it the promise of things to come. The pregnancy that had been quite comfortable through the winter now began to be uncomfortable, which to Annie was a good sign that she would soon be *seeing* the baby kicking instead of *feeling* the jabs against her ribcage. The childbirth classes that she and Jack were now taking had her looking forward to the experience of labor and delivery, too.

Jack was also anticipating the spring. One evening as she was finishing the dishes, Jack disappeared. He reappeared and, with a twinkle in his eye, he grabbed her hand. "Come out here." She let herself be lead outside into the dark evening.

"Smell," he ordered.

She breathed the cool, damp air into her nostrils. "Do you smell it?" he prompted.

"I smell something," she agreed.

"It's spring. Doesn't that smell like spring?"

"I thought it was mud and worms," she teased.

"Planting season's just around the corner. I can't wait." His voice held all the excitement of a child's when Christmas was discussed.

"I guess I'm going to learn what it's like to be a farm wife, huh?" Annie asked. She wrapped her arms around his waist and his arms encircled her, providing welcome warmth against the chill of the night air.

He kissed her gently on the lips. "Well, if you believe what my mom says, you've survived the hardest part of the year: putting up with your husband underfoot all winter."

She kissed him back. "That wasn't hard at all."

It was late March when Jack announced one night at supper that he was going to the parish reconciliation service that was being held that night.

"So that's when you go to confession, right?" Annie asked.

"Mmm hmm," Jack confirmed.

"Like in the movies where there's the dark little room and you tell the priest that you murdered someone?" Annie asked.

"We don't have a dark little room. That's old-fashioned. And I didn't murder anyone," Jack replied, picturing a very real gravestone and the name written on it.

"So what are you going to confess?" Annie asked and knew that she shouldn't have.

"That's between God and me," Jack answered defensively.

"It's just that I haven't seen you do anything that you need to confess," Annie persisted, suddenly annoyed. "I don't think being too perfect is a sin, Jack."

"I'm not perfect, Annie, and you know it."

"Then quit acting like you are!" For the first time in their marriage, Annie shouted at her husband. Her questions remained buried but she now realized that a layer of resentment covered them.

"I'm leaving. I'll be back after services." He stuck his cap on his head, grabbed his coat, and left, leaving her to continue the argument on her own. When she was done yelling at the closed door, she exhumed the questions that she had buried, tried unsuccessfully to answer them, and then buried them again before he arrived home. As she finished covering them back up, she renewed her vow to continue her wait until he freely offered the answers that she needed.

Chapter 62

Jack

Because he had walked out of the house a full half-hour earlier than he had planned, Jack was the first to arrive at the church. He walked in and fell to his knees as he had so often done over the years. The heated discussion with Annie had made him belligerent and he found himself arguing, not sure whether this argument was going on within himself or between him and God. The thoughts rolled through his mind like storm clouds.

"What does she want from me anyway?"

There was no answer. The imaginary clouds were dark and full, blocking out the sun.

"Who is she to judge me?"

Still no answer. He could hear the rumble of thunder in the distance.

"She doesn't know what I think and feel!"

The silent answer came. "Maybe that's the problem." And then the rain came, pouring down in big drops. He let the words soak into him.

The next words that came to his mind weren't his own, but rather the echo of the words that Annie had asked him earlier, "So what are you going to confess?" And then he knew what he needed to confess. And he knew that after he made his confession to the priest he would go home and make another confession to Annie.

An hour and a half later, he arrived home. The house was quiet and she was reading by the soft light of a table lamp, the book resting on her stomach that was now large enough to act as a shelf. She didn't look up, apparently ignoring him. He stood before her, his coat still on.

"Annie." His words held the feeling that was necessary to break the barrier that she had erected in his absence. She looked up at him.

"Would you go on a drive with me?" he asked.

"I'll get my shoes and coat on." She didn't ask where to or why.

In the darkness of late evening, Jack drove silently toward the church and then past it as the last few reconciled parishioners left the church, homeward bound. He pulled the truck into the gravel drive of a small cemetery that sat past the last house in town. He got out and pulled the seat forward, taking out the flashlight that he kept there. Annie climbed out and walked quickly to catch up with him as he walked directly to a headstone, not waiting on her lest he lose his nerve. The flashlight hung unused in his hand. He needed only the moonlight to guide him over the familiar ground.

When he stood where he needed to be, he handed her the flashlight. She turned it on and shone it on the words carved in block letters, "Daniel Schroeder, Beloved Son and Brother". Jack let the engraved years below the name tell Annie what they could: that Daniel had died ten years earlier, just one day after Jack's summer birthday. His age at the time of his death was twenty-three years.

"Your brother?" Annie asked. Jack nodded in the darkness.

Silence. Jack was afraid to speak for fear that the levy holding in his emotions would break. He waited on Annie to ask how he had died.

When she finally spoke, she didn't ask about his death, but rather his life. "What was he like?" she asked quietly.

Jack wasn't prepared for the question. He had relived and preserved the events of his death, but had allowed the details of his life to fade over time. They came back to him now, slowly, one by one. As he spoke, he let himself be surprised and soothed by what he remembered. The way Dan wore his hair. His favorite rock group. What he liked and didn't like to eat. His favorite sport. The things they had liked to do together. The long-legged walk that was identical to Frank's. His fun-loving attitude.

Annie gently pulled him down until they both sat on the damp spring ground, the cool moisture soaking into the seats of their pants.

As Jack spoke, it was as though he was regaining, in some form, the brother that he had lost. He felt strength flowing into him, strength would soon be required in order to tell Annie the rest of what she needed to know.

When the flow of memories slowed to a trickle, Annie quietly asked the question that she instinctively knew Jack needed to answer. "How'd he die?" The words sounded harsh and rude, even though she had whispered them.

Jack let the events replay in his mind, events that he had spent almost ten years trying to forget.

When the words came, he told Annie everything.

He explained that his brother had liked to drink too much on the weekends, hanging out with friends at bars even before he was legally able to do so. He told about his own 21st birthday, when Dan had insisted on taking him drinking and how they had ended up at the bar in this same little town that night, just a mile and a half from home. It had gotten late and Dan had gotten increasingly drunk. He wanted to drive back into town to another bar to continue the fun but Jack wanted to go home. When Dan wouldn't hand over the keys, Jack said, "Fine, I'll walk home."

Not wanting to lose his brother's company, Dan had urged him to stay with the words, "Now, little brother, you wouldn't let me go alone, would you? I'm really in no condition to drive."

And then Jack had said the last words that his brother would ever hear him say, "That's not my problem."

Jack had walked the dark distance to Frank and Meg's house on that warm summer night, snuck into his bed, and was sleeping soundly from the moderate amount of alcohol that he had consumed when the police officer knocked on their door at two in the morning to tell Frank and Meg that their eldest son had been killed in a car accident.

Jack made it through the story without breaking down, determined to say everything and have it done. It was only after he was finished and Annie put her arm around him that he broke down and sobbed in the unpracticed way that men do. The tears didn't flow gently like Annie's, but burst forth from the dam that had finally broken.

"Let's go home." She whispered after a time, and led him to the truck, sitting him in the passenger seat and driving him home.

In bed a short while later Annie offered him her body and he accepted it readily. Not a cure, but temporary medicine against the pain.

Chapter 63

Annie

When Annie woke the next morning, she was surprised to find her husband still asleep next to her. The early morning sun was shining through the window and he had obviously broken his ritual of rising at dawn. She examined his features, soft with sleep, checking for signs of tension and pain the way a nurse might examine a patient. 'Resting comfortably' would be a nurse's summation. In fact, his face appeared as relaxed as she had ever seen it.

It was then that she suddenly remembered her original question and realized that it hadn't been answered. Where had he gone for a year? She studied his face some more, looking for answers.

Feeling her eyes on him, his fluttered open and the corners of his mouth lifted slightly in acknowledgement of her gaze.

"Good morning," she said.

"Good morning." He climbed out of bed too quickly and escaped to the bathroom. A moment later, she heard the shower running.

She pulled her maternity nightgown over her still-nude body and went out to the kitchen to make Jack's coffee. As she was running water to fill the coffee pot, she looked out the window. The sun was still making its ascent and the world was bathed in a soft glow. The few white houses that she could see reflected the early morning glare of the sun, making them brilliant. It was as though God had made this day extra bright as a reward for having made it through the dark night. "Yes, God, I see. It's beautiful," she said out loud, begrudgingly giving him the credit He deserved.

Lost in thought, she didn't notice Jack until he wrapped his arms around her from behind, bending slightly to encompass the baby with his large hands. She leaned back into his embrace.

"You found my special place," he whispered in her ear.

"Your special place?" she asked.

"Mmm hmm. I pray here every morning." They both looked out the window together.

"So that's what you do. I thought you were studying the weather or watching the birds or pondering the unpredictability of the grain market." He almost always planned his time at the window when he thought she was asleep or in the shower but she had caught him enough to know that it was a ritual of his. "You could have told me that's what you were doing."

"You didn't ask."

"It's hard to know the right questions, Jack." They both knew it was a reference to all that had been revealed last night.

She wiggled out of his embrace slowly, giving him a kiss on the cheek. He poured his coffee and sat down at the table, the steam drifting upward in the morning light. She sat down, too, and leaned toward him, her flowery nightgown making a tent over her belly.

"Jack." She could no longer wait for him to offer an explanation for what she had been wondering. She needed to know and knew that it was time to ask. "Where did you go?"

"When?" He was genuinely puzzled by the question.

"After the accident. Where did you go? Your dad said you were gone a year."

He inhaled deeply and grasped her hand. "Oh, Annie, that wasn't after the accident. It was before."

"Where were you?" she asked again.

"I was studying to be a priest." He said it matter-of-factly.

Her mouth dropped open. "You wanted to be a priest?"

"Yes, I did." His eyes held hers and challenged her to criticize such a vocation.

"Jack, you never told me." The pain and frustration that she felt made its way into her voice.

"You never asked."

Those words leaving his mouth for the second time that morning ignited her temper. "You knew I was wondering where you were for a year after your dad mentioned it! You could have told me then!" She was shouting and angry tears filled her eyes.

"I didn't think it was important." They both knew this was a lie and a flimsy excuse.

"You know it's important! In fact, I think it's so important that you're afraid. Afraid to talk about it. Afraid to share it with me." She knew that he prided himself on his quiet bravery and this statement was an arrow shot to the heart.

For the first time during their argument, his head dropped, indicating that she had hit the mark. "You're right." His quiet words were an admission of guilt. Annie was glad that he had admitted that she was right but the silence that followed it proved that his acknowledgement of the problem didn't change it. She was right but she didn't want to be. She wanted him to be able to talk to her.

She lifted herself off the chair, pushing her hands against the table top to help the process. She showered and dressed while creating in her mind possible scenes that might play out between her and Jack when they spoke next, which, as far as she was concerned, might be a while.

When she walked back out into the living room, he was in his chair with the Bible that she had given him open on his lap. He closed it, stood, walked to where she stood, and led her to the couch where she obediently sat. He moved a footstool in front of the couch and sat on it so that they were face to face, their four knees in a row between them, his face slightly lower than hers. He took both of her hands in his, tightly holding on to her.

"Remember when you asked me last night what I was going to confess?" he started.

It seemed a long time ago but she remembered. "Yes," she answered.

"I want to tell you what I confessed." His eyes met hers, inviting her to see into his mind and heart. She declined the invitation and moved her gaze to her stomach where the baby moved, oblivious to the outside world.

"Jack, I don't know if I can handle any more secrets."

He ignored her protests. "I confessed that I don't trust enough. I don't trust you enough and I don't trust God enough."

"Jack, you don't have to tell me this."

"I should have told you everything from the beginning but I wanted you to think I was wonderful. I didn't trust you to love me no matter what."

"But you *are* wonderful. Wonderful is different than perfect. I never thought you were perfect, Jack. Everyone makes mistakes. I can speak from personal experience."

"And that's another thing. I know you blame yourself for getting pregnant but it's my fault."

"Jack," she smiled, amused in the midst of the seriousness. "I can say with a great deal of certainty that this pregnancy is not your fault."

"No, Annie, you don't understand. I watched you pouring coffee for a year. A year! For a year my heart went crazy every time you came near me. That's never happened to me before. I knew that it was meant to be. I knew that God wanted you and me to be together but I didn't trust Him enough. I worried that you'd say no or the old men would pick on me so I just kept putting it off until it was too late. So it's all my fault."

She had never known that he had been interested in her back then or that he blamed himself for the pregnancy. "But Jack, it wasn't too late. I'm here. As long as you can love this baby, everything's fine."

"But if I would have been more trusting, more confident, it could have been my baby."

"Jack, it's your baby now. That's what you offered and that's what I accepted. If you don't trust that, we've got problems." She tried to move her hands out of his grasp, but he gripped them harder.

"I do trust it. I'm learning to trust it more." He remembered the words from the Bible: I do believe, help my unbelief.

"You better trust it." Her narrowed eyes backed up her words.

After a pause, the next words were Annie's. "So is that why you decided not to be a priest? Because you didn't trust God after he took your brother away?"

"No, it wasn't that at all." He took a breath of relief and Annie knew he was glad to move out of the realm of emotions and give her a practical explanation. "I just couldn't stand to leave Dad to handle the harvest alone that year, so I stayed home to help. I had planned to go back for the second semester but by then I just wasn't really sure I wanted to, or rather that God wanted me to. I prayed about it and decided that I would go back to the seminary when I knew that God was calling me back."

"And He never told you to go back?"

"No, He never did. The years passed by and everyday I would pray to God to tell me what to do and every day I would listen."

"So you waited ten years and God never said anything?" Annie was disgusted at the thought of God being so cruel.

Jack was quick to defend those years and the One that had given them to him. "He never told me what to do but I always felt him there with me, at the window in the morning, when I saw the corn coming up, when I crawled into bed at night. All the time, everywhere."

"But in all those years He never told you if you should go back and be a priest? He never told you what you should do?" She couldn't believe that a God that was supposed to be so loving would leave a good man like Jack waiting for so long.

At this, he gifted her with a radiant smile, "Oh, he told me what to do all right. It took a while, but he finally told me exactly what to do."

"What'd he say?"

Jack's hands let go of hers and reached up to caress her cheeks. He leaned so close to her that she could feel the warmth of his breath as he spoke. "He said, 'Follow her', and I did and that's how I ended up in the women's restroom with a pack of soda crackers in my hand."

Annie gave a soft chuckle at Jack's surprising declaration and her heart delighted in the fact that she was the happy ending to Jack's story. Jack moved to sit beside her on the couch and they held each other.

Annie didn't understand why it had taken so long for God to make things clear to Jack, but she knew that the wait had made the ending that much sweeter.

Chapter 64

Jack

The spring rains stopped long enough for the ground to dry out and Jack and Frank were able to start work in the fields the week before Easter, Holy Week. He enjoyed the change from the relaxed pace of the winter to the frenzied rush to get the seed in the ground. All his life, his body had followed this yearly pattern of the farm and it was as natural to him as the daily cycle of wakefulness and sleep.

All week he was out of bed when it was still dark and didn't return home until long after it was dark again. The only time during the day that he saw Annie was when she came with his mom to the field to bring him sandwiches. He usually took time to sit and eat with her, their legs dangling from the tailgate of the pick-up. But sometimes if there was a coming rain or if the size of the field was too big and the hours before dark too few, he would kiss her quickly, take his lunch from her, and climb back into the cab of the tractor.

The exception to this was Good Friday when he took time out to attend noon services. Although Annie was still attending mass with him each Sunday, she opted out of the extra service due to her increasing discomfort while sitting for long periods of time. When he returned home to her that afternoon, he rested with her until three, read the Bible a little and caught a much-needed nap. At three o'clock sharp he grabbed his hat and dashed out the door, eager to get a few more acres planted that day.

On Easter Sunday, Annie took longer than usual to get dressed for church. When she finally emerged, she was wearing one of only two decent shirts that still fit her and a pair of black maternity pants that she had worn every Sunday since January. Jack knew better than to point out to her that he had been right that day when they had shopped for maternity clothes.

"I should have bought a dress." she lamented.

Jack assured her that she was fine and mockingly consoled her by saying, "Look on the bright side, at least you don't have spit up and drool all over you like you will in a few weeks." When he saw that she wasn't in a joking mood, he hugged her, bending himself around her stomach to do so, and said, "You don't need a fancy dress to make you beautiful, Annie." Then he kissed her so tenderly and so deeply that, after a quick glance at the clock, they ended up in the bedroom. They quickly made up for the opportunities lost to the field work over the past week. In spite of her ever-expanding middle, both she and Jack were still enjoying sex. The humor and creativity that her stomach demanded almost made up for the natural limitations it created.

The day was unseasonably warm and sunny, a perfect planting day, but Frank and Jack stayed out of the field to be present for Meg's ham dinner and the egg hunt that followed. But, as was the case each Easter, Frank and Jack were present in body only. Their minds were still in the field. They discussed the forecast. They evaluated what they had accomplished so far. They calculated when they might take the corn planter off and put the bean drill on.

But, unlike other years, Jack's attention was divided. Even as he talked to his father in the kitchen about the performance of the corn planter, he kept an ear keened to the conversation of the women in the dining room. He knew the source of conversation among the women would be Annie's quickly-approaching due date. He hoped that his sisters would speak favorably of their experiences.

Finally his dad, aware of Jack's distraction, said, "Well, why don't we go in and interrupt the hen session."

He grabbed a handful of pastel M&M's from the dish on the table and walked into the room announcing, "You can't have it until it rains, you know" with a mouthful of candy.

"She can have it anytime. I just might not be there if the ground's fit for planting." Jack walked in behind him and joined in.

"What if I see if the doctor will deliver it in your truck bed? Would you hop out of the tractor long enough to watch?" Annie asked Jack, pretending to be miffed.

"I'll at least slow the tractor down and open the windows so I can hear," He returned. He loved joking back and forth like this with her.

"Good. I'll scream extra loud so you can hear me over the tractor engine."

"That'd be nice of you." He leaned down and kissed her quickly on the lips, a brief reminder of their morning.

The conversation lulled a moment. And then Annie took a breath and in that breath Jack sensed a warning, an apology, and a determination to do what was right and good in spite of him.

"Meg, Jack was telling me about Daniel. Do you have any photos of him that I could see?"

After just a moment to orient herself to the unexpected request, Meg was eager to comply and immediately pulled out a scrapbook that was devoted entirely to her son. She had made it in the months following the tragedy and, if one knew where to look, they could see the places where bittersweet tears had fallen on the photos before they were entombed behind the plastic sleeves of the pages. She sat down next to Annie, narrating a new chapter of her son's life with each turn of the page. Jack stood behind Annie and looked on. He saw his brother getting his first haircut, sleeping on Frank's lap in the old recliner, shooting a basket at a junior high game, standing beside his first car.

Jack had hoped that burying his brother's memories along with his body would help to ease the pain of the loss but now he realized how wrong he had been. It was as though Annie's request to his mother had resurrected, in a way, his brother on this Easter Sunday.

On the last page was a family picture taken on Easter eleven years ago under the plum tree that was in full bloom both in the photo and outside the window. They hadn't had one taken since. Jack wondered if this was a natural result of the sisters now having their own families or if no one wanted to bother with a picture of a family that would, from now on, be incomplete.

Jack looked at his sisters' faces captured in the photo. The tragic bump in the road had occurred in different points on each woman's journey toward adulthood. Sarah had been a newlywed - her husband Tim had taken the photograph that day. Mary had been about to enter her senior year of high school. Kate was going to be a sophomore. And Elizabeth, the baby of the family, had been just nine years old.

And then Jack looked at his own face smiling out from the photograph. He had been home from college where he was studying theology; the beginning of a long journey that the young man in the photo was sure would lead to priesthood.

Finally his eyes fell on his brother and his brother's laughing eyes looked back at him. There had been some joke just before the picture was snapped and Jack tried but failed to remember what it was. It was certain, though, that Dan had taken the most delight in it, just has he had taken the most delight in life. Could it be that some people weren't meant to grow old, to deal with bills and baldness, bad knees and poor eyesight?

He put his hand on Annie's shoulder and felt the reality of her. Could it be that Daniel's death was part of the greater plan for him to be here with her? He imagined for a moment that Annie was his brother's gift to him, allowing Jack to end up in the right place at the right time to fulfill God's plan for his life, a plan that was so different than what he had thought back then.

Annie reached up and covered his hand with hers. He put his questions to rest. Life and death weren't meant to be understood. Jack took a moment to recognize both as gifts that were given and that needed to be accepted graciously, with trust, thanksgiving, and hope.

Chapter 65

Annie

The weeks after Easter passed slowly as Annie's due date approached. Besides a few days when Frank and Jack were rained out, Jack spent as much time as possible in the fields. He was extra attentive to Annie when he saw her, but that wasn't much.

She strived to find things to do in his absence. She cleaned the house until it sparkled. She went to the library and spent a considerable amount of time choosing several thick books that looked like they would hold her attention and help the hours to pass more quickly. She had lunch with her mother several times while Cindy was on her lunch break from the dentist's office, lunch dates that included endless stories about Ray. On the other days, she walked to Meg's so they could take lunch to the field together and then she walked back home, enjoying the fresh air and exercise.

On some days Meg invited her to spend the afternoon, remembering well the frustrations of waiting on your own body. One afternoon, Meg pulled out the ingredients to make Jack's favorite dessert and the afternoon passed quickly while they mixed and baked and talked. Annie carried the results of their efforts back with her at suppertime and shared some with Jack when he finally came in at midnight, covered in dust but wearing the perfume of the fresh spring air.

The long evening hours were the loneliest. She made dinner for two and ate the small amount that her crowded stomach would allow. Then she piled generous portions on a plate for Jack, who came in late, starved from the hour and the workload.

Each night, after she ate her early supper and tidied the kitchen but before Jack returned, she sat. The television shows were too violent or too stupid to watch. The novels that she had gotten from the library didn't hold her interest as she had hoped. Her large body was too tired from cleaning and walking to do anything that involved physical activity.

Out of other ideas, she decided to use this time to pray, hoping that perhaps it would chase away the loneliness that invaded the house. She whispered a few words in the silent living room each night. "Please give me a healthy baby. Keep Jack safe. Help me during labor." But her words didn't ring true. It reminded her of archery in high school gym class. She had had no natural talent for the sport and she had watched with envy those that could do it well. They had a natural flow and feel for the bow and their arrows always hit the target. She, on the other hand, had gone through the exact same motions but without the same style and grace. She had watched as each of her arrows went zinging past the colored paper target, not finding its mark. That's how she felt when she prayed, awkward and unsuccessful, with no evidence that anything that she sent flying upward was hitting its target.

The boredom of those long evening hours also led her to pick up Jack's Bible and with this she experienced more success. Jack used his new Bible consistently. He had, anyway, until the fields called him away. But his old one with the loose pages was still in the drawer of the end table and this is the one that she was drawn to. Now she read the questions in the margin and understood better the man that had written them. She read the poetic Psalms out loud and enjoyed the flow and feel of the words. One night she was especially restless and, having always enjoyed school, she decided to pick the shortest Gospel and take notes. She sharpened two pencils and dug out some paper and sat at the kitchen table outlining the Gospel of Mark like she would a biology chapter.

It wasn't until Jack pulled in the drive that she realized it was midnight and she had filled three pages with notes. She was guiltily piling everything together when he walked in. "What are you doing?" he asked.

She took his plate out of the refrigerator. "Just killing time."

He pulled a sheet of paper out of the stack and glanced at what she had written, her words neat and rounded. "By outlining the Bible?" he asked incredulously.

"What else am I supposed to do?" she asked defensively.

"I just didn't know you were that interested."

Her eyes met Jack's. They showed that he was tired but intrigued by in this new development. "Well I am. But I don't want to talk about it right now." The frustration that she felt with her fledgling spiritual life together with her loneliness and her impatience to deliver the baby were making her short-tempered.

"Okay, that's fine." Jack was wise enough not to argue with a woman who was nine months pregnant. He ate the dinner that she put in front of him and thanked her for preparing it for him in an obvious effort to smooth her ruffled feathers.

In bed that night, he fought off sleep and spent some time talking to her, feeling the baby kick, and holding her in his arms. In the morning when she woke up he was already gone but on the table he had written her a note that simply said, "Dear Annie, I love you. I'll take time to come home for lunch today. Hang in there. Jack."

It was the next day that her back began to intermittently ache and the toilet paper was tinged with pink. She had read the pregnancy books thoroughly and so she knew that the day had finally arrived.

The sun was shining, so Jack was in the field. Although he had repeatedly given orders that she was to call at the first signs of anything, she didn't pick up the phone. Instead she gave herself a couple of hours, enjoying the feeling of her body beginning its work. She double-checked the bag that she had packed for the hospital and washed a few dishes that were in the sink. Then she sat down in the baby's room in the padded rocking chair that, like the crib, was a hand-me-down from Sarah. She rocked and looked at the crib, imagining the baby that would soon sleep behind the wooden bars, the baby that she would soon rock in her arms.

When the tightness began to be more pronounced, she reluctantly called Jack, half of her wishing that she could experience everything alone, just her and her body. And the baby of course. "Are you busy?" she asked him.

"Are you?" he asked warily.

"Oh, I'm not doing much. Just having the baby."

"Now?" He sounded panicked.

"Well, no, not right now, but hopefully soon. Can you come home?"

"I'm at the far end of the field. It might be a half hour before I get home. Are you okay until then?"

It had been about three hours since she sensed her labor starting and she knew there wouldn't be a sudden delivery like there was in the movies. "Yes, Jack. I'm fine," she reassured him. "You probably have time to finish the whole field if you want." She was almost sure he wouldn't take her up on that.

She hung up and went to stand at the window where she knew Jack had stood earlier that morning while she had slept. She wondered what time it had been and if he had had to look out into the darkness or if the sun had been coming up already. The ground in the nearest field that had lain empty all winter was now worked and planted and Annie could make out for the first time the green spikes of corn coming up. She saw a cloud of dust on the horizon that she had learned indicated a tractor just out of view. She gracefully pulled back the string of her bow and launched another arrow. "Thank you, God, for all your goodness and be with me today." In her mind she heard the thud as her arrow sunk into the center of the target.

Chapter 66

Jack

By the time he arrived home, Annie reported that the pains were getting stronger and closer, but not too strong or too close. He marveled at her calm. The only evidence of each contraction as they traveled to the hospital was a pause in the conversation and slight tensing of her jaw.

Jack was familiar by now with the maternity ward at the hospital, having visited it eight times as an uncle. But now he found that it was quite different entering the hospital as a father instead of an uncle and before the birth instead of after. They passed the waiting room and Jack knew that Frank and Meg would soon be sitting in the uncomfortable seats, after they stopped at the church to light a candle.

They were taken to a room where the nurse handed Annie a gown and both women disappeared behind different doors.. Jack looked around. He had never seen the labor and delivery room. Although he knew better, he had pictured Annie having the baby in the rooms where he had always gone to see his sisters, and so this room with its intimidating medical equipment caught him off guard. Annie walked out of the bathroom wearing a hospital gown and walking slower than she had just a half hour ago when she left the house. She looked at his face, which must have reflected the worry that he felt. "Women have babies everyday." Annie reminded him. He suspected that her words were intended to comfort herself as well as him.

Jack watched the nurses hook devices up to Annie's stomach to monitor the baby. He watched Annie become more and more serious as the time passed. He watched the nurses and, later, the doctor, reach inside her to check the progress of the labor. Later, he watched Annie's face become set like stone and her chest rise and fall rapidly during each contraction. Finally, he watched her lean forward to push and bring forth the miracle of a son. Their son.

Like the sound of the heartbeat so many long months ago, the sound of the baby's cry filled the room with its presence. It wasn't until Jack saw the relief flood Annie's face that he realized that she had been worried about all the things that could have gone wrong but hadn't. She took the baby in her arms and held a tiny hand and wept.

Jack stood there and tried once again to grasp the Goodness that had brought Annie and this child into his life. But he could no more wrap his mind around it than the tiny fingers of this new baby could wrap themselves around the trunk of an oak tree.

Chapter 67

Annie

Six weeks later, Jack and Annie stood in the back of the church on Sunday morning as Mass began. Annie held the sleeping baby dressed in white. Father Bill asked them what name they wished to give their son. Annie replied in a loud, clear voice, "Joseph Daniel". They were led up front and Annie sat through the first part of Mass unable to focus, knowing that it would soon be time for Joseph's baptism.

When they were called forward with Kate and John whom they had chosen to be Joseph's godparents, the baby was still sleeping. When the cold water was poured over his head he sprang to life. He flung his arms out, filled his lungs with air, and then let out a piercing cry. Annie held him close to comfort him for a moment before holding him back out to Father.

Father then anointed his forehead with oil. When Annie returned to her seat, she looked at her son, now awake but calm once again. She could see the cross gleaming on his forehead, a symbol that he was now a member of the Catholic Church. She bent her head towards his and smelled the aroma of the oil with which he had been anointed.

In her mind, she saw the same symbol, two lines crossing one another, but in blue. Her mind went back to the morning in the bathroom last summer when a blue cross had announced to her the presence of this infant inside her; this infant who now bore the same mark on his forehead.

She thought about other times during the past year when she had seen the same symbol. She remembered the crosses that were telephone poles stretching out in a row as she rode to Jack's house for the first time.

She remembered the shadow of the window pane that had made a slanted cross on the flowered wallpaper of the inn the first morning after the wedding when she had felt the baby move for the first time.

She remembered the little gold cross on the bathroom counter that she had seen when she had hidden from Jack's family on Thanksgiving, too overcome with gratitude to speak.

She pictured the white cross printed on Jack's old Bible that she now opened more and more often in spite of the demands that baby Joseph put on her time and energy.

She pictured the gold cross engraved in the leather cover of Jack's new Bible that she had so carefully chosen and he had so enthusiastically received on Christmas morning.

She remembered the cross of ashes that she had rubbed off of her own forehead on Ash Wednesday and the tears that had flooded her eyes as she had done so.

She remembered the cross carved into Daniel's gravestone and illuminated by the beam of the flashlight the night that Jack had finally shared the memories of his brother with her.

She pictured the crucifix hanging on the wall across from the bed that she and Jack shared every night. It was often the last thing she saw when she went to bed and the first thing that she saw in the morning. Even when they couldn't see it in the darkness, it was present as they talked, slept, or made love.

And now this new image was engrained in her mind, the image of this cross of holy oil on her baby's skin. She knew that it was a symbol of not only what she had just accepted on behalf of her son but also of all that God was offering to her. She knew that God had been patient, waiting for her to be ready to accept all that He offered, just as her husband had waited. And in the same way that Jack had lovingly encouraged her, even flirted with her, she knew that God was doing the same by filling her life with good things.

Jack was His greatest gift to her, showing her how to receive love and give it back again. And with Jack came the family that surrounded her. Jack's sisters would be her friends and help her raise this child in her arms. Jack's parents provided an example for Annie of a good marriage, an example that she hadn't had when she was growing up. And the community of the church that filled this holy building was family, too, a family that her son was now an official member of and one that she knew she would one day be officially adopted into also.

From her place in the front row, she watched the bread and wine being offered. She watched Father accept the gifts so that he could bless them and give them back during communion. She replayed the conversation that she had had not long ago with Jack.

So you really believe that God changes the bread and wine into His body and blood?

Yes I do.

That's impossible.

Not for God.

She looked down at the child in her arms. She thought about what she had done last summer to cause this baby and knew that this precious child was proof of God's power to take something ordinary and make it extraordinary. She thought about the recent sleepless nights and the long and frequent feedings and knew that this was proof of God's power to change suffering into glory. She thought about the three of them, Jack, herself, and this child, and she knew that their small family was proof of God's power to work miracles that were just as amazing as anything that she had read in the Bible.

Jack was squeezing past her on his way to communion. He whispered, "Annie, are you okay?"

She realized that her face was wet and that she must be crying. Again. She nodded yes and watched her husband go forward and open his hand to receive the gift that was offered. With her heart, she did the same.

About the Author:

Tina Williams lives in Ohio with her husband and three children and teaches high school Spanish. She enjoys hugging her children (even if that means standing on her tip-toes), giving grammar notes (just ask her students), and dreaming (whether she's asleep or awake). Her roles as wife, mother, and teacher give her both great joy and ample opportunity to use her favorite prayer, passed down to her from her mother: "Lord, give me the patience to endure my blessings."